Addis Ababa.
An Isaac Porter Mystery

By Steve Kasper

Addis Ababa: An Isaac Porter Mystery

Glassmoor Publishing Alhambra California

ISBN 978-0-9896025-0-1

This is a work of fiction. All names, characters, organizations, and events portrayed in this novel are either products of the author's imagination or are used fictitiously. Any resemblance to actual events or locales or persons living or dead is entirely coincidental.

To Mary with love

Dedicated to the men and women of the United States Foreign Service, especially those serving in countries most of us can't find on a map.

Chapter 1

I lost my wife on 9/11. It was a day when my known and certain world became unknown and uncertain. Certainty was one of the things I sought when I decided to go into medicine. Medicine seemed so rational. A physician gathers facts from a patient, assigns a diagnosis and treats the problem. Even more organized than the actual practice of medicine, in medical school, order was everything. Memorize facts and recall them for the test. I was good at that. Medical school was where I met her.

It was a shock to lose her that day and every time I talk to her now, it's still hard to believe. I call her disconnected number and send emails to her inactive account, but she never answers. How can something as certain and real as love be destroyed so thoroughly? Shouldn't order be more resilient?

The Lufthansa flight took off from Dulles to Frankfurt. I settled into my seat, ate dinner and tried to sleep. The Frankfurt stopover was brief, but I managed to take some pictures of my first, short trip to Germany. The flight to Addis Ababa would take me over Greece, Egypt and Sudan. After leaving the Mediterranean Sea, we flew over a bleak and bleached landscape. This was the longest airplane flight I'd been on since the time my wife and I flew to Australia.

I read my guidebook and notes about Ethiopia. It is a large country with about 90 million people. It had never been colonized by Europeans and had a culture that dated back thousands of years. As the plane descended toward the airport, I could almost feel her sweaty palm in mine. She always held my hand when we flew, especially on takeoff and landing. Out of fear or love, I never knew and didn't really care. I always assumed she needed me and losing her made me really understand how much I needed her.

As the plane banked, I could see Addis Ababa below me. The fields surrounding the city were small, seemingly random and completely unlike the fields of Kansas or California. Those American fields were symmetrical squares or circles reflecting large land holdings. The fields below me were irregular rectangles or triangles, but most with no pattern at all and few crops. A jumbled, random collection of dry yellow and light brown fields surrounding small villages seemed so disorganized. When I used to think of Africa, I'd think green like the Jungle Cruise at Disneyland. Ethiopia looked mostly brown, with an occasional green tree thrown into the mix. Brown houses, brown roads, brown cattle and dust brown fields as far as I could see. I joined the State Department to escape. Deepest Africa fit the bill - I just thought it would be green.

It was about 5:00 p.m. when the plane lowered its flaps and wheels and came in for a landing. I prepared to use my official Diplomatic Passport for the first time. It was black, the same size as the blue, so-called tourist passport, but diplomatic immunity was conferred upon me with my new passport. I was excited to use it, since it was an obvious sign of a fresh start.

The landing was smooth and I thanked the blonde flight attendant who had put up with my high school German during the flight. The familiar tone of the seatbelt sign going off and the prospect of the door opening caused some pushing in the aisle. Passengers were retrieving their carry-ons and stretching.

From the back of the plane, I could see that the mild chaos in the aisle abruptly stopped as a tall man in a dark suit came onto the plane. He spoke briefly with the flight attendant, whose name tag read Heidi. Even though it sounded unlikely, it must have been her real name. Lufthansa wouldn't let her use a phony name just because she was tall, blond and German. My wife was blond so I don't like them as much as I once did. Heidi was very attractive, like my wife, but I didn't like the way Heidi was pointing at me and nodding.

The man locked his eyes on mine and came towards me. People moved out of the way and their eyes followed him as he came down the aisle. I was taken aback and wondered what could be going on. My Diplomatic Passport was in my hand and I held it like a shield. It would give me the protection I needed. What could he want with me?

8

"Dr. Porter? I am Colonel Melenik. You need to come with me." He said it in a friendly but official tone, and looked like he would clear a path so I could walk out. There was no need. Everyone had sat back down and they were looking at anything but me. I played it cool, followed him and waited until I was off the plane before I turned to ask him what was going on. However, by that time a woman who looked to be 50, with gray hair, pale complexion and bright blue eyes appeared next to me. She was wearing navy slacks and a blazer with an American and Ethiopian double flag pin in her lapel. She was agitated but polite. "Dr. Porter? I'm Constance Powers, the Chief Political Officer from the Embassy. You are needed right away for a medical emergency."

My Diplomatic Passport was good but it couldn't protect me from my own Embassy.

Chapter 2

"Dr. Porter, please try to keep up. We have to keep moving."

Usually I don't mind taking orders. Prior to 9/11, I was even more willing to comply and revel in the lack of responsibility that occurs when you are following orders. It had been a long flight and I was tired. Running three times a week kept me in shape, but Addis Ababa is at 7,600 feet and I was feeling the altitude. I wanted more of an explanation and some time to catch my breath. "Wait a second. Just what is going on here and what kind of emergency are we talking about?"

She stopped dead in her tracks, slowly turned toward me and gave me her best diplomatic smile. It's the smile you give a wayward 4-year-old when you're trying to reason with him about not running into the street or why he can't have spaghetti for every meal. She was only about five feet tall, but she seemed to swell up and fill the area in front of me. "Dr. Porter, I know you're new to the Foreign Service and jetlagged, but we are not going to discuss sensitive information in public. Will you please just follow me?"

She began speaking in a diplomatic tone, but by the time she finished, her voice broke. I felt sorry for her, so I resumed walking and she joined me. Maybe she was playing me, but she seemed genuinely upset. Not angry, but worried. It must be a true medical emergency if she let her diplomatic posture slip.

The airport was unexpectedly large and modern. We slowed briefly at immigration control to stamp my passport and then it was out the door into the sun and a waiting Suburban. A silent, middle aged, muscular man was our driver. He looked like a law enforcement type - about 6 feet, 240 pounds with a short military haircut, aviator sunglasses, khaki pants, light brown shirt, Merrell boots and a blue blazer without a tie. The blazer had some buttons missing on the right sleeve and a small stain on the right lapel. The sunglasses didn't bend around his ear but traveled straight back from his eye to the top of his ear. He didn't say a word as he held the door for us.

Constance and I got into the back and we set off at a pretty good pace. Controlled panic is what it felt like. The windows were bordered with a thick black band. It looked almost funereal but I knew what it meant. The Suburban was armored. They had said at our one day anti-terror training course that armored vehicles could stop bullets but not rocket-propelled grenades. Did they pick everybody up in this thing?

"There has been an outbreak of some illness at the Embassy," Constance said, while looking out the window.

"More like an epidemic or germ warfare."

I hadn't noticed the man in the front passenger seat until he spoke. "We're not sure what is going on and we need you to help us figure it out. My name is Dick Lawrence and I am the DCM. This is Billy Spencer, the RSO."

RSO is the Regional Security Officer. They evaluate the risks in a region and try to mitigate them. Usually they are ex-military but can be from law enforcement.

The driver looked at me through the rearview mirror and said, "Hi, Doc."

The DCM or Deputy Chief of Mission is the number two position at the Embassy. It was unusual for a DCM to pick someone up at the airport. He spoke again. "The fact that I am here should tell you how seriously the Ambassador takes this issue."

Wanting to appear serious as well, I answered. "What exactly is going on and what steps have been taken?"

Constance continued to look through the armored glass. I almost thought no one had heard me. It seemed like a reasonable question.

The DCM turned halfway around in his seat and took off his sunglasses. His bent around his ear and looked like Ray-Bans. His suit was black, with a white shirt, blue striped tie, French cuffs with gold Department of State cufflinks and a white pocket square.

"It all began after the barbecue we had two days ago. People started to have stomach upset and diarrhea. Many became sick. Our nurse, Rhonda, thought it might be food poisoning. That sounded reasonable, but things have gotten worse.   Rhonda will fill you in when we get to the Embassy."

His voice broke and he slammed the sunglasses back onto his face. He was obviously upset and wasn't going to say anything else. Diplomats, I had learned, were very good at concealing and controlling their emotions. That is what they do best. I'd been in the country for less than 30 minutes and the first two diplomats I met had lost control of the façade of order.

The airport is located at the south end of Addis Ababa on a broad plateau. The city itself climbs up the surrounding mountains much like the urban sprawl in my hometown, Los Angeles. As we exited the airport, underneath a large concrete arch, we made a right turn through a traffic circle.

As we entered the circle, Billy swerved to avoid several large rocks. The rocks were each about two feet across and bordered a large, almost bottomless pothole. Billy was looking at me in the rearview mirror over the top of his sunglasses as he spoke. "The rocks are construction barriers. In the States we would use cones. Things are different here in Africa."

The rocks were either a really bad idea or a great adaptation to no highway funds. I wasn't sure which. We exited the traffic circle and drove up a ramp onto a four lane divided highway. The Ring Road was just a few years old and constructed with help from the Chinese. Traffic wasn't moving in any kind of a pattern that I could see, as cars, trucks and the occasional tractor weaved in and out of lanes. After about 10 minutes, the divided highway ended and we transited a traffic circle. We passed the British, Kenyan and Russian Embassies, each protected behind high stone walls topped with razor wire and cameras.

After passing Addis Ababa University, we approached the US Embassy.

The Embassy was separated from the street by a wall and a wide expanse of green lawn bordered by well kept flower beds. It was a nice touch and gave the grounds a park-like feel. It also provided more protection from truck or car bombs. The main Embassy building was pale gray granite with blue-tinted windows and nondescript enough to be part of a suburban office development in the States. The Suburban was waved through the gate and as soon as it stopped, a young Marine in battle dress, body armor and M-4 rifle opened my door. "Sir, come with me, please."

Not an order exactly, but not a request either. I followed him swiftly through the lobby of the Embassy and down a hall limed with standing people. All of them were looking at me.

The Marine held open a door for me. The waiting room to the health unit looked like any other medical waiting room. Chairs along the walls, with tables, children's books and magazines spread throughout the room. There were two sliding windows with opaque glass next to a door that must lead into the exam areas.

Every chair in the place was filled with a worried-looking person. There were lots of kids, some crying, some on the floor playing with blocks and some sitting in their parent's laps. The adults who didn't have seats stood along the walls or in the center of the room. The room smelled of vomit and unwashed clothes.

"Dr. Porter? I'm Rhonda Washington, the nurse. I am so glad to see you."

I didn't know where she came from, she just appeared at my side. She was about 6 feet tall, African-American and heavy. She looked very tired and her white coat was dingy and rumpled with brown iodine stains on her right sleeve.

"I've been dealing with this as best I can, but it has been so hard."

13

Tears gathered in her eyes as she reached out to grab my arm. There was a note of defeat and desperation in her voice. Trying to sound supportive I spoke. "I'm sure you did your best. Maybe we should talk inside."

I was thinking these people were being a little dramatic. Sure, there were a lot of sick people here, but food poisoning usually goes away on its own. What was getting these people so upset? I understood when I looked around the room and saw a young woman holding something.

She was about 25, tired, very fair and hunched over; her body protected a package in her lap. It almost looked like she was guarding her dirty laundry. The only thing I saw besides a gray blanket was a small, pale, blue foot. Her eyes knew already. She looked at me and I knew, too. An average-sized, young, brown-haired white man, with glasses and a blue blazer was standing next to her with his hand on her shoulder.

"I'm Dr. Porter," I said as knelt before her and started to pull back the blanket.

"I'm Bob Wollinsky, this is Jennifer and our little one Travis. He has been sick for a day or two like everybody else. I am sure he will be better soon." His eyes were calm. He seemed embarrassed. He was very diplomatic.

Travis was about 4 years old, dressed in faded brown pajamas, blond, very fair and very small. The blanket came away easily. He looked at me without a whimper and did not cry.

"Hello, Travis, how are you today?"

"Travis, can you answer the doctor?" Bob was trying to get Travis to talk. It worked.

"Doctor make me well?"

Even as he said it, I could see his death before me. His lips, nails and fingers were blue. His sunken eyes were so tired that he

14

could not keep them open. His hair was stuck to his forehead. There was little doubt in my mind.

"May I take him inside?" I gently lifted him from her lap. She let go and looked at me again. She knew. There were no tears and she did not protest. Mothers always know when their children are sick. Fathers are much more fallible in their judgments about their children's health. I think that mothers are just more tuned in somehow. Innate or learned, I can never tell.

He was light and cool in my arms. I walked to the door leading to the exam rooms and all eyes were on me again. Everyone parted to let me pass and Rhonda opened the door for me.

"Excuse me, Doctor, but we have been waiting for two hours to see you." She was about 55, tan and very attractive. Her dark black hair was neatly wrapped in a chignon above her head and the pantsuit she wore was dark gray, tight and very flattering. Small diamond studs were in her ears.

Bob spoke again. "I am sure Travis can wait a little while if Anita, the Ambassador's wife, needs to be seen first."

Bob must be a good diplomat. He was calm, unflappable and conveyed his message in an economy of words. He was respecting the hierarchy and giving me the information I needed in the face of overwhelming pressure. The message was clear. Rank had privileges. He didn't know what I knew. Mrs. Ambassador didn't know. Only Jennifer, Travis and I knew.

"Anita, I am sure the Doctor will get to everyone, but I think Travis should go first. He seems to be the sickest." It was another woman who spoke. She was about 5'5" with dark hair, high cheekbones, a narrow nose and brown eyes. She had on jeans, a T-shirt and a black leather jacket. Her hair was tied back but several strands had escaped and she was pushing them back off her face. As she looked at me, I saw she had been crying. She wasn't ordering me, but I could feel her willing me to take Travis inside. I walked right past her into the exam area and didn't stop until I laid him down on an exam table.

Sick children make everyone feel bad. I quickly stripped his shirt and pants off. He was covered in bruises, with cool limbs and deathly pale. I took Rhonda not so gently by the arm and led her into the hallway. "Rhonda, we need the crash cart in there and we need to get two IVs into him. Have the receptionist call Washington and we need an air ambulance ASAP."

"The air ambulance can take 24 hours."

Rhonda said it so that I would know that we were on our own for a while and moved off to the front office. I reentered the exam room and looked at the little family. Jennifer and Bob were standing on the other side of the exam table. She was crying softly and looked at me for some words of comfort.

"How long has he been sick?" The tone of my voice was as calm as I could make it. It didn't sound calm or controlled to me.

Jennifer answered. "He got sick about four or five hours after the barbecue. He just had some vomiting and a watery diarrhea, with maybe a little fever. He was feeling better last night and then the bruises starting coming a few hours ago and he got really tired."

I hadn't noticed before, but she was very pregnant. The State Department flies women out when they are 34 weeks, so she must be close to leaving.

"Do you want to sit down?" I asked.

"No, I'm fine, thank you." She replied in an exhausted voice.

"Is he going to be all right?" Bob had spoken and still didn't know. What do you say in these situations? I could get technical and explain to them that overwhelming infection was making his organs stop working and his blood fail to clot. I could get philosophical and tell them that there was a God and it all was for a reason. I could just ignore them and get Rhonda to take them out of the room.

16

"He is very sick. These bruises mean that he has a severe infection. I am going to give him fluids by vein and antibiotics and we need to get him out of Addis right away."

Rhonda was back and she started the IVs and we gave him some Ceftriaxone. We drew the labs. His blood pressure was very low. About 30 minutes later, he lost consciousness. His breathing became labored and I intubated him. We didn't have a ventilator and the bag we were using to force the air into his lungs was not much bigger than a baseball. Jennifer and Bob stayed in the room the whole time. I didn't have the heart to separate them from Travis when he had so little time left.

DCM Lawrence was outside the room and I gave him updates when I could. He was very upset, as was everybody in the unit. Most everyone left when it became clear that I would not be able to see them.

We did all we could. The fluids, antibiotics and agents to raise his blood pressure and more medicine to control the seizures when they came were all given according to protocol. The air ambulance was there in a little over four hours. We were lucky it had been in Kenya. It was on its way to Frankfurt only 40 minutes after it arrived. Jennifer and Bob were going with Travis. As they left, they thanked me. They both knew now.

"I will pray for him." I don't usually say things like that. It was a little too dramatic and unscientific. Conceding that I didn't have control over the situation. After we got back from the airport, I started working on notes and reports. I drafted a cable to Dr. Scofield, my boss, in Washington. Rhonda came into my office about two hours later. The doctor from the Air Ambulance was on the phone.

Chapter 3

The doctor from the air ambulance was professional and courteous. She informed me that Travis died over the Mediterranean Sea. The doctor said I did all I could and was sorry things had turned out the way they did. Other than Travis, everyone else recovered. Of course, other than the planes, 9/11 was a nice late summer day.

I worked for a while to treat the people who stayed to see me. The symptoms had begun a few hours after the barbecue. Diarrhea, nausea, vomiting and malaise were the typical complaints, and most people felt better by the time I arrived. Food poisoning is so common that unless someone dies or unless it affects numerous people, it is never investigated. This would be investigated. It was about 6 a.m. when the last patients left the health unit. The call from the plane about Travis had come in an hour or so earlier. I updated the DCM, who informed the Ambassador.

I sent Rhonda home and was finishing up my notes in my new office. It had been a long night and I was tired. I cleaned off one of the exam tables and took a nap.

My sleep was fractured. I kept dreaming that Travis was in my arms and I was trying to get him into an exam room. We were in a long white hallway and all the doors were locked. Trying every door again and again was futile, but I didn't know what else to do. He would wake up occasionally and ask if I was going to make him well.

I awoke, feeling groggy. I didn't notice Billy, the RSO, at the door before he spoke. "Doc, you look terrible. I knocked but nobody answered, so I just came in. The EAC will be meeting soon. Sorry this has been such a bad introduction to the Embassy."

The EAC was the Emergency Action Committee that met whenever something bad was expected or had happened at an Embassy. As the RMO, Regional Medical Officer, I would be part of the committee and they would want to know what I thought had happened. The most likely thing was food poisoning, but it was too early to say.

Billy didn't look too good himself but continued. "It's been a long and horrible night. I feel so bad about Travis."

The words just hung there and I didn't know what to say. I felt bad too, but I didn't know Travis like these people did. A small Embassy community would take his death very hard. I would have my work cut out for me in the weeks and months ahead but I thought I could handle it in a detached professional manner.

Another man came into the room. He was tall and dark haired. He wore a conservative dark suit, and carried a briefcase.

"Doc, let me introduce you to David Solomon. He's with the FBI."

"Good morning, Dr. Porter. I'm sorry we have to meet under these circumstances, but I have to ask you some questions."

"No problem. My office will be more comfortable."

We moved from the exam room. The office was in the corner of the first floor. There were four windows that looked out onto the rear of the Embassy compound. The Ambassador's residence was visible on a slight rise with a grass lawn in front. The lawn had several large trees and a small area with benches. My desk faced the door and had two chairs in front of it. There were bookshelves against two walls, mostly empty, with some old books. The newest was a review of tropical diseases dated 2001.

I sat behind the desk and they took the chairs. I looked out the window and noticed a blue haze that softened the green wooded mountains behind the Ambassador's house. Agent Solomon followed my gaze and spoke. "Most of the people in the city use wood for cooking and heating, so we get the haze in the mornings."

"Smog and mountains make me kind of homesick for LA. All we need is traffic to complete the trifecta."

They both laughed at my joke. I think they would have laughed at anything. The night had been tense and hard for everyone and it felt good to have a little relief.

"I worked out of the FBI's office in Salt Lake, so I've flown into LA a few times. Is that where you're from, Doctor?"

"Born and raised. This is my first time living overseas."

Solomon nodded his head. He was good looking, fit and about 30. He was slightly nervous. His right hand held a pen and he was tapping it rapidly on his knee. "I just have to ask a few questions. I know this is a difficult time for you."

"Not as difficult as it is for Jennifer and Bob."

I probably should have stayed quiet. It was a tragedy that a small child had died, but losing my wife had been much harder for me. Agent Solomon nodded and continued. "What do you think happened?"

"It was probably food poisoning from the barbecue. With everyone sick and the cluster of symptoms I've observed, that is the most likely explanation. The food will have to be tested and the stool cultures we started in the health unit will have to be grown, but that will take a few days."

"So you think it was an accident?"

"Millions of people get food poisoning every year in the US. It's usually just poor food handling and bad luck."

"Have there been any cases where the food poisoning was deliberate?"

"There was one case in Oregon in the 80's when a cult wanted to make people ill so they couldn't vote in an election. That's the only one I know of. You're with the FBI, you know more about that than I do."

Agent Solomon didn't say anything, but looked at a legal pad on his lap. I hadn't noticed it before, but he was taking notes. "Have you ever seen cases like this?'

"I see food poisoning all the time. I have never seen an outbreak this large before and obviously never in Africa."

He paused to look at his notes. "Doctor, do you think the Embassy has the resources to investigate this case on its own or should we call in people from the States?"

"I don't know exactly what resources the Embassy has, but back in LA this type of investigation would be handled by the County health department."

He stopped taking notes, put down his pen and sat back in his seat. Looking at me, he was deciding on something. His questions had all been reasonable and easy to answer so far, so I wasn't sure why he was hesitating. "Do you think that terrorists could be involved?"

It had never occurred to me and I answered before thinking.

"Don't they usually use suicide vests or AK-47's? Wouldn't this be a pretty unusual way to attack us?"

"You're right. This is not their usual method, and it's very unlikely that they are responsible, but they are always looking for new methods."

"It doesn't seem likely to me, but we'll have to wait and see. Most likely it was related to improper food handling at the barbecue. I'll know more in a few days. Do you think terrorists were involved?"

He seemed satisfied with my answer but did not address my question.

"Thanks, Dr. Porter. I would appreciate it if you kept our conversation to yourself."

"Can I tell Billy about it?'

We all laughed a little again, but it was a forced laugh. We got up and started walking to the EAC meeting. The thought of Travis's death and the possible link to terrorists was still present in the air like the haze from the cooking fires. It wasn't enough to alarm me, but it changed the way I looked at things.

Chapter 4

The conference room was on the third floor near the Ambassador's office. It was not big, but could hold about 20 to 30 people. A large rectangular wooden table stood in the middle of the room and a line of windows, shades up, provided a view of the mountains in the background.

The opposite wall held photographs of various American landmarks, such as the Statue of Liberty, Gateway Arch, Golden Gate Bridge and Old Faithful. Right next to Old Faithful was a photo of the World Trade Center in New York prior to 9/11. I shuddered when I looked at it.

There were 12 people around the table, six on each side, and I would make it 13. The table was neatly arranged with bottles of water at each place, a note pad and a pen. I sat down and was about to introduce myself to the people around me when everyone stood up.

Ambassador William Winston walked in and sat at the head of the table. I knew because of the name plaque. His was the only seat that had one. It is customary for everyone in the Foreign Service to stand when the Ambassador walks into a room. I was just getting out of my chair when everyone sat back down.

DCM Lawrence was on the right side of the Ambassador, Billy was on the left, with Agent Solomon a couple of chairs away from Billy. The only other person I knew was Constance, and she was next to me.

"This meeting is called to order. Let's get right down to business." As he opened the meeting, the Ambassador's head was raised, but he kept his eyes down on the papers in front of him. He was about 60 with gray hair, pale blue eyes and pale skin freckled with brown spots, probably from his years in the African sun.

"We all have been shook up by the events of recent days and we are here to try to understand those events and take appropriate action."

23

Everyone was still, but there was a tremendous amount of tension in the room. Some took notes or fidgeted in their seats. I took a drink from my water bottle and spilled some on the front of my shirt. The water made me realize I hadn't eaten since lunch on the plane yesterday.

The Ambassador continued. "We will start with a chronology of the events as we know them so far. Doctor, will you tell us what you know as of this morning?"

"Travis Wollinsky died en route…"

"I'm sorry, Dr. Porter, I meant Dr. Lessing from the CDC. She has opened a formal investigation. Dr. Lessing?"

Dr. Lessing was about 55 or 60, with dull blond hair with gray streaks surrounding a round but somewhat sunken face. Her eyes were blue and she had several vertical wrinkles on her upper lip that gave her a perpetual frown. White women seem to get those lines as they age. Was it caused by too much frowning? My wife's mother had the lines but she always seemed to be smiling. I wondered if my wife would have gotten those.

"Mr. Ambassador, I just wanted to thank Dr. Porter for his efforts. It has been a difficult and trying time for the community and I am sure he did everything he could."

Her voice was full of pity and condescension, which shocked me. We hadn't yet met and I couldn't understand why she used that tone of voice. She seemed to be letting me know that I ranked below her in the pecking order, but it seemed odd in the context of the current situation. No one else in the room said anything or reacted in any way, so I just let it go and she continued.

"The events began approximately four hours after the barbecue that was hosted by DCM Lawrence. A meal of hamburgers, hot dogs, chili, potato chips and cake was served to Embassy members and a few guests from the host government. Patients had symptoms of watery diarrhea, nausea and vomiting with some fevers. This is, of course, preliminary, and I have not interviewed everyone affected. I believe at

24

this time about 96 people have been ill. All of the symptoms have now resolved as far as I know. Mr. Ambassador, I want you to know that CDC is pleased to assist in this terrible tragedy and I am sure we will be able to come to a conclusion soon. I will lead the investigation at this end with the full resources of the CDC at my disposal."

"Do you think it was E. coli?" I said it, knowing it probably was but I really wanted to point out to everyone that she had said a lot without saying much. We already knew that people got sick after the barbecue. She looked at me like I was an annoyance and I was beginning not to like her.

"Dr. Porter is probably right. Preliminary, and I must emphasize preliminary, tests point to E. coli as the source of the infection. Usually the prime culprit would be the ground beef, but we at CDC are not making any assumptions at this point."

As she said "assumptions," she paused and looked pointedly at me before going on. "We have collected all of the remaining cooked and uncooked food and placed it in our freezers with a proper chain of evidence. One of the most common causes of E. coli infection is improperly cooked ground meat. Ground meat is particularly risky since the bacteria can be distributed through the patty. If cuts of meat like steak are contaminated, the bacteria are present on the surface and are killed with cooking. If the hamburger is not cooked thoroughly the bacteria can survive in the middle of the patty."

"Is there any reason to believe that this was a deliberate act?" The Ambassador had been quiet and respectful during her speech. He was reasserting control and getting to the point. Had he talked to Agent Solomon? Probably. Agent Solomon would report anything as important as a possible terror attack to him immediately

"We have no evidence at this time of anything other than an unfortunate incident probably caused by contaminated meat and poor cooking." She sat up straight and actually gave a slight smile. This was her preferred practice of medicine without patients, or more precisely, no patient care. Dr. Lessing could be Sherlock Holmes and solve the mystery without having to bother with sick people. I liked

25

taking care of sick people, even if they disturbed your sleep sometimes with calls or nightmares.

The Ambassador spoke again. "We can then wrap up this meeting and have everyone go back to their departments. Reassure people that it was probably food poisoning and that it is under control. I want to thank everyone for their efforts so far. I especially wanted to thank Dr. Lessing for leading this investigation. Thank you all."

I got up with the rest and prepared to leave. Some people nodded at me and I would have introduced myself, but I had noticed at the beginning of the meeting that someone close to me needed a shower. Now I knew it was me.

"Dr. Porter, could you please stay a moment?" It was the Ambassador again. He was looking at me with a diplomatic smile. He had remained seated, as had DCM Lawrence, a woman to his right, RSO Billy Spencer, and Agent Solomon.

"Would you like me to stay?" Dr. Lessing said with a slight amount of insecurity creeping into her voice.

"Madeline, I am sure you have more important things to do, but thank you for asking."

She sulked out of the room.

"Dr. Porter, let me introduce you to Felicity Gonsalves, and I believe you have met Agent Solomon. They are important members of the Embassy, and I wanted them present when we talked."

After shaking hands with Ms. Gonsalves and Agent Solomon, I sat and wondered what was going on here. Ms. Gonsalves was the dark-haired woman I had seen yesterday who helped me bypass the Ambassador's wife. The CDC doc was not warm or friendly, but Dr. Lessing was doing her job and had said everything that needed to be said. I needed a shower, some food, and some sleep, in that order.

"Dr. Porter, I am sorry we are meeting for the first time in this circumstance." The Ambassador was serious and friendly. He paused for a moment and as I was about to answer, he spoke again. "We have the utmost confidence in Dr. Lessing's skill and her ability to get to the bottom of these unfortunate events. We just think it would be wise for someone within the State Department to monitor her investigation and report directly to us. We would like you to cooperate with her, but also remain independent. We want a fair, logical and complete investigation. We expect you to assist in the investigation and to help Dr. Lessing in any way you can. I also wanted to thank you on behalf of myself and the Embassy for all you did for Travis. Do you have any questions?"

I had nothing but questions. My first question would have been was there a shower in the Embassy but I decided to ask another. "I'm sorry, I'm new. What exactly am I supposed to do?"

"We don't want the investigation to be biased in any way and think that having you keeping an eye on things will help."

"OK. I will keep you informed. Does Dr. Lessing know I will be in on the investigation?"

"I wanted to talk to you first before we let her know."

"OK. I will give it my best shot, but remember I am a family doctor and am not a trained investigator. I've met DCM Lawrence, Agent Solomon and Mr. Spencer, but who do you work for?"

I had turned toward Ms. Gonsalves. She was quite beautiful in the light from the windows and obviously had some Asian forebears that explained her facial features. It was not at all clear to me why she had been asked to stay and chat, even if she was attractive.

The Ambassador started to answer. "I am so sorry that I didn't tell you that before. Ms. Gonsalves works for…"

"I work for the…" She completed the sentence and gave the name of a government office that is found in most American Embassies.

The smile on her face seemed genuine. She was about 30, with very dark, straight brown hair that fell to her shoulders, warm, light brown skin, brown eyes and a small scar from acne or chicken pox on her left cheek. She was not wearing any makeup that I could see, but had on the standard dark blazer with a white blouse. She wore no jewelry except for a pair of small pearl earrings. I couldn't quite believe what she had just said and had to ask again.

"So the FBI and the…?"

"Yes, and please keep that under your hat. We don't want anyone getting unnecessarily alarmed," Felicity said in a calm voice with the smile still on her face.

"I am sure Dr. Porter would like to get started. May I suggest that we meet again in two or three days to review the progress so far? Dr. Porter, thank you again for helping us out." After the Ambassador finished speaking, we got up to leave. I realized that this was far more serious than I had thought.

The FBI was interested, and that was worrisome, but it had to be routine under these circumstances. That the poised and good-looking Ms. Gonsalves was interested was slightly terrifying. The office she mentioned was really only a cover name for one very special government agency. She was CIA.

Chapter 5

Descending the stairs to the health unit on the first floor, I passed the cafeteria. The clock outside the door said 2:30 p.m. The doors were closed or I would have bought some lunch. There were vending machines outside the door, so I settled for some chips and a Coke. It wasn't nutritious, but it would keep me going until I got to my house for some chili. I'd stashed several cans in my suitcase, just in case I couldn't get any food right away. As I entered the health unit, Rhonda looked at my lunch and arched an eyebrow but didn't say anything. I again realized that I needed a shower and just hoped she stayed upwind.

A cardboard box, with a crushed corner and my name on it, was on the floor in my office. Back in DC, people had told me to ship myself some household appliances and cooking utensils. Most people ship furniture, bedding, dishes, pots and pans to their new post, but that takes months to arrive in Africa. They have families and want some possessions to make them feel at home right away. There was nothing I wanted to bring, since so much of it would remind me of her.

I put down my empty briefcase and lifted the box onto the desk. Some of the Styrofoam packing material leaked out from a hole on the side of the box. I used a letter opener with a broken tip that I had found in the desk to split the packing tape and open the box. The box contained two unbreakable plastic bowls, two unbreakable plastic dishes (one of which was broken in half) and some utensils. There were also a two quart aluminum pot and a Teflon frying pan with a loose handle. In the bottom of the box I found my Swiss Army knife and some canned food. I tossed the broken plate into the trash and put the box on the floor near the door so I could take the stuff home.

I logged onto the computer to send a cable to Dr. Scofield in Washington about Travis. It took me a frustrating hour to get my account to work, but I did get to drink the Coke and polish off the chips. The cable didn't get sent, either because I was too tired or I just didn't want to face it.

I surfed the Web instead, but CNN, Amazon and TCM couldn't hold my interest. My email box contained some messages from my brother and some friends. I replied to my brother to let him know I had arrived safely and sent one to my wife. She wouldn't answer, but it made me feel better to know that I had sent it. The email just said that I was in Africa and was moving on. I wasn't sure I could move on, but it felt good to say it.

Rhonda came in and gave me my check-in sheet and said there were two people to see me. The check-in sheet is a list of people at the Embassy who I had to contact and meet. The list included the Ambassador, the DCM, RSO, Management Officer and about 25 more down to the mailroom guy. Beside each name was a line where the person could sign off. It was like being at camp and I had to get the signatures to get my merit badge. It was something that could wait until later in the week, but I should see whoever was waiting. I told Rhonda to show the visitors in.

I recognized Constance Powers, the Chief Political Officer, who had met me at the airport. The second woman was about 5'6", Asian and dressed in the requisite blue blazer and white blouse, teamed with red pants like a Shriner on the 4th of July.

Constance spoke first as she reached for my hand. "Good morning, Dr. Porter, it's good to see you again. This is Maria Katzakis, the Chief Public Affairs Officer. We just wanted to come by and see how you were doing and to thank you for all of your help yesterday."

"It is a pleasure to meet you, Ms. Katzakis, and to see you again, Ms. Powers."

I was trying to be polite, but I was tired and didn't see why we had to talk now.

"We are so sorry that your first day has been so hard. The terrible tragedy involving Travis has us all upset. Maria and I will be helping to coordinate any press releases with Washington and CDC."

"I just wanted to echo what Constance has said and to say we are ready to help with the investigation in any way we can.'

"Thanks, that is very kind of you both. Dr. Lessing from the CDC is leading the investigation. You should talk to her."

"We spoke with her earlier today, and she predicts that it will be a short but thorough investigation. Do you think it will take very long, Dr. Porter?"

"It will take as long as it takes and could be weeks."

"Dr. Lessing thought it could be wrapped up in a few days. Of course, we would never interfere with the investigation, but the sooner it is wrapped up, the better, both from a political and public relations standpoint."

It seemed that they were sending me some sort of message, but I wasn't really sure. They couldn't be suggesting that I would hold up the investigation, could they? Maybe this is what they do in their jobs. They look out for potential political or public relations problems and try to head them off. I didn't think I was a problem, but I could be wrong.

"I'll work closely with Dr. Lessing and complete the investigation as quickly as possible without compromising the integrity of the final report."

"Thank you so much, Dr. Porter. We won't take up any more of your time. If you have any questions, please let us know."

They left their cards and exited the office. I forgot to get them to sign my check-in sheet. The State Department loves forms and bureaucracy. Their universe is a certain place with known rules. Fill out the forms, do your work and get paid.

I've been dealing with a disordered world since 9/11. Like good diplomats, Constance and Maria were subtly telling me to keep chaos out of their very controlled world.

Chapter 6

The phone system seemed standard, but I wanted to make sure that it worked. I placed a call to the Ambassador's office and to Post One, where the Marine Security Guard stands duty. The phone worked, and the Marine who answered was friendly and sounded very young. I also called the motorpool and told them I would need a ride home. They asked me where I lived and I told them I didn't know. Rhonda had given me my keys earlier. The dispatcher put me on hold and came back and said that I lived in the Hansen house. Apparently housing in Addis was like living in a small rural community. Houses didn't have addresses, they had names associated with current or former residents. Living in the Hansen house made it sound like I was living in Iowa, not Ethiopia. How long would I have to live in Addis before it was the Porter house?

I locked up my office, picked up my semi-crushed box, my briefcase and told Rhonda I was leaving for the day. Back down the hall past the cafeteria and out the security doors, I left the building. Walking with some fatigue and feeling out of breath, I looked for the Toyota Landcruiser. The dispatcher at the motorpool had told me to look for a Landcruiser in front of the Embassy. Altitude is a funny thing. You can't see it, feel it or taste it but it takes away your strength like the end of a love affair. The vehicle was parked about 100 feet from the door and an Ethiopian man was behind the wheel.

"Hello, I'm Isaac Porter. Are you here to drive me home?'

"Yes, Doctor. Please get in. I am Mohammed Ali. Your bags were brought from the airport and are in the back."

Ethiopia is home to many ethnic groups and is about half Orthodox Christian and half Muslim. He was about 50 and small, but had a large stomach. His hair was close cropped and mostly gray.

"How long will it take to get to my house?"

"Your home is located in the Bole Homes section close to the airport and it will take about 20 minutes to get there."

We exited the Embassy and turned left going downhill. The road was much smoother than I would have thought it would be. People were everywhere in the street. Many were just walking, but some carried flat baskets piled with bread on their heads. Some older women were hunched over with large bundles of firewood on their backs. There were people, women or men I couldn't tell because they wore large hats, long sleeves and aprons, sweeping the streets with crude brooms. There was a guy, about 20, with dark jeans and a red T-shirt that read, "Prairie County Rodeo 2005". He was driving three donkeys down the street. Each donkey had two large burlap sacks on their backs and I just wondered how he came by a T-shirt from a rodeo in Montana.

We made our way to the Ring Road and passed several buildings under construction. They were all between 10 and 20 stories high. I had no idea that this much building activity could be found in Addis. My preconceived ideas of the city, country and continent so far had been way off the mark. It was more like LA than I realized, but I also knew that she had never been there. My main goal of losing her could still be accomplished.

We exited the divided road, turned left underneath it, and I could see a faded Ethiopian billboard advertising the new Boeing 787 coming in 2009. Passing a gravel-filled lot, where there were couches and leather chairs for sale, I was completely lost. The truck went down a paved road and over a bridge with a small stream and large fields on either side. In the unfenced fields, sheep and cattle were grazing in a haphazard fashion, with some boys standing watch. Several of the animals were very close to the road and the pedestrians, walking by, were taking it all in stride.

The road turned to gravel again and we passed several two and three story houses before we pulled up to my house. The house was surrounded by a 12 foot wall that was topped with razor wire. There was a solid black steel gate across the driveway and, when Muhammad Ali honked once, a door within the steel gate opened. A small head stuck out and an Ethiopian man smiled. The door was closed and the gates swung open. We pulled forward into the driveway and the little man closed the gate behind us. The yard was not large but was very green. There was a small asymmetrical lawn with a fountain in the middle and with flower beds on the edges.

I opened my door and the man who had opened the gate was standing next to me with my bags. The gates opened again and the Landcruiser backed into the street. After the gates were closed, the little Ethiopian man, he must not have been more than 5'5'', came up to me and smiled again. "Hello Doctor, my name is Eskander and I am your gardener. Welcome to your home."

He was thin, with a fringe of gray hair around his bald head. Dressed in khaki pants, black t-shirt and boots, he held out his hands and grasped my right hand with both of his, like a pastor does after Sunday service.

The house itself was two stories and was a mix of modern and Spanish styles. Well, really no style at all, but it did have a tile roof. There were strange angles, odd sized windows and a mix of building materials. One wall was red brick, another gray stone and another, yellow stucco. The whole thing looked like it had been put together with leftovers from a larger, better designed house. The roof overhung in the front but not on the sides. All of the windows and doors had steel bars on them like a poorly designed jail.

Eskander took my bags, opened the steel security gate in front of the entry and the large wooden double door which led into a 2-story foyer. There were stairs leading to the second floor from the marble entryway.

"Where do you want your bags, Doctor?"

"You can leave then anywhere. I'll take them upstairs later."

"I will be outside if you need anything. Here is my letter."

He handed me an envelope, gave a slight bow and closed the door as he went out. I thanked him and went inside to read his note. It was written by the former occupant of the house and explained that they had employed Eskander for two years, the standard tour of duty in

Africa, and that he had been an excellent employee. Eskander seemed nice and I could always check the database at the Community Liaison Officer (CLO) office to make sure he wasn't wanted for murder, robbery, terrorism or killing plants.

The entryway opened into a large irregularly shaped front room with off-white walls and curtains. There were matching light brown sofas and a love seat. Empty bookcases lined two walls. I walked into the dining room, which had a table with seating for 10. An empty china closet with a mirror in it reflected my face back at me. I looked very tired, pale and badly in need of a shave.

Next, I went to the kitchen, which had a gray tile floor, dark wooden cabinets, stove, refrigerator and the distiller. The water in Addis Ababa is not potable, so each house is equipped with a distiller that provides fresh drinkable water. It must be working because there was a humming noise and it was warm. I tried the tap of the distiller and water spilled out onto the floor. All of the appliances were American made and brand new. There must be some kind of federal law that requires the State Department to buy American appliances. I wondered how much it costs to ship them to Africa. The refrigerator contained some lettuce, milk in a box and butter. It was supposed to make me feel at home, but nothing is as forlorn as a half empty refrigerator.

Every new diplomat is assigned a professional and a personal sponsor. The professional sponsor looks after the business side of things, arranging for the new person to get settled into the office, makes sure they know where the bathrooms are located and when to go to lunch.

The social sponsor is supposed to make you feel at home and introduce you to people at post. They smooth the transition from being a civilian living in Washington D.C. to being a professional Foreign Service Officer living in a small post in Africa. The social sponsor also makes sure that the cupboard is not bare when you arrive. Rhonda was both my social and professional sponsor. I felt bad for her. Professionally, I would be easier to sponsor. Socially, I would be a disaster.

I moved out of the kitchen and up the marble stairs. There were three large bedrooms, each with triangular balconies on the second floor. Ceilings were high, about eight or nine feet. The master bedroom had a queen-sized bed, nightstand, dresser and a large bathroom on the other side of a walk-in closet. The same muted apartment tones as downstairs sought to soothe me. In Africa, they want you calm and happy. The bathroom was large, clean, marble and smelled like sewer gas. There was a floor drain and I poured some water down it to see if it would stop the smell. That is when I noted the singing. I couldn't tell what the language was or who was singing, but it was coming in through the window. A large horizontal casement window was eight feet off the floor and half open. I couldn't see out of it, so I went back into the bedroom and out onto the balcony.

Next door to me, behind their 12-foot wall topped not with razor wire but with broken glass fragments set in the cement, my new neighbors were having a barbecue. A tall, thin woman in a dark brown gown with a white linen wrap around her head was attending to a small fire in a small clay and brick enclosure. A goat and two toddlers stood next to her. There was no house or grass, but a 10 by 20 foot shack built of old galvanized, corrugated steel and some rotten lumber surrounded by dirt. I watched for a few minutes and wondered what she would think of the inside of my house.

As I closed the door and the security gate to the balcony, I saw the envelope on the nightstand. It was business sized and blank on the outside. I thought that Rhonda had left me a note to welcome me to Africa or maybe it was some information about when they picked up the trash. I grabbed it up and opened it.

After reading the one line message, I dialed the Marine Security Guard post on the phone by the bed.

"Post One. This is Gunnery Sergeant Cruz."

"Gunnery Sergeant Cruz. This is Dr. Porter. I need to speak with Ambassador Winston immediately."

The message in the envelope was short and to the point.

"The illness didn't need to happen."

Chapter 7

The Ambassador decided that nothing could be done about the letter that night but I was to bring it into the Embassy the next day and we would meet at 8:00 a.m. He sounded unsure about the whole thing, almost as if he didn't believe me. I wouldn't have believed me either.

My room was cool and the bed was soft, but I didn't get to sleep until an hour or two before dawn. Addis Ababa is eight hours ahead of Washington D.C. so by the time I was tired, it was time to get up.

The dream I had was new. Travis was with me in my apartment in LA and we were watching TV. The show was about a gentleman who looked like a sponge and lived underwater until Travis got hold of the remote. He flipped through the channels, found a replay of the 9/11 attacks and left the TV tuned to it. He would look at me and point. I took the remote and tried to change channels, but all of them were now playing the same images of the smoking towers.

Luckily Eskander woke me. He didn't knock on the door or call me on the phone. The noise was soft at first and became louder. At first I thought he was chopping wood but I soon realized he was digging a hole in the ground. I wasn't sure the ground needed a hole but I did need to get up. When I went into the shower, the digging stopped.

The water felt good and I wondered if I would sleep better that night. I shaved, dressed in my brown suit and gathered my State Department badge and Diplomatic Passport. After going downstairs and into the kitchen, I heated some water in my two quart pan. The instant coffee and granola bar tasted good and I felt a little better. The boxes of the granola bars had been in my suitcase next to the chili.

The horn of the Suburban outside the gate brought me back to reality. I gathered the new letter, briefcase and jacket. Dressing up at the Embassy was not required but not dressing up was frowned upon. The closer you get to the Ambassador, the more likely you would be in a suit and tie. Eskander met me at the door and already had the steel gate open so the Suburban could come inside.

"How are you, Doctor?"

"Excellent, Eskander, and how are you?"

"Very well, Doctor. Have a good day at the Embassy."

He looked at me and I could tell he was thinking about something. I opened the door to the truck and got in. The door was very heavy and armored. Billy was driving. Eskander was still smiling as he closed the gate after the Suburban moved into the street. "Billy, are you attached to the motorpool now?"

"No, Doc. Just wanted to make sure you got to work on time."

Billy's shirt buttons were straining to contain his bulk, but the sunglasses with the straight ear pieces were in place. The Ambassador had told me not to share the letter with anyone and so I didn't mention it to Billy.

We turned right out of my driveway and traveled down a gravel road past several gated houses like mine. Walls of concrete, stucco or stone interrupted by steel gates faced the street. We transitioned onto a paved road and passed the two large unfenced fields and the creek. Next to the creek several men were washing cars as the owners stood by and talked on cells. The road had speed bumps to slow us down. After making a right onto a larger paved road, I could see the airport terminal and control tower. I had heard the planes all night and didn't realize how close my house was to the runway. This larger street was lined with small shops made out of corrugated metal and they were selling bread, Cokes, sundries and cell phones.

Just before the Ring Road, a large corner shop was selling furniture with the showroom being a large gravel area in front. The couches and chairs were arranged in a random fashion, but there were customers even at that early hour. Toyota trucks carrying people or goods in the beds swirled around us. At first, the traffic flow seemed completely disordered, but it amazed me how polite everyone was when they drove. A few horns honked, but no one was upset. Certainly there were no angry gestures or words. We didn't get on the Ring Road but passed under.

"Isn't the Ring Road the fastest way to the Embassy?"

"It is, Doc, but I thought I would show you some sights on the way in." Billy smiled and pointed to a large Orthodox Church on our right. "That is Saint Michael's church there. You can hear one of the priests talking to the crowd."

Words from a loudspeaker echoed in the truck. I couldn't understand the language.

"Addis Ababa is not very old. It was founded by the Emperor Melenik II in 1886 and means 'new flower' in Amharic." He kept driving and we passed masses of people in the streets. The traffic was slow and Billy had plenty of time to point out the sights.

"The UN compound is on your right and just past that is the Hilton. The Sheraton is on the left up ahead. You can buy a day pass and use the pool on weekends."

"I think I forgot my trunks."

He laughed and continued. "No problem, Doc. As you can see there's plenty of shopping here. The people live right behind the stores and are friendly enough. It is a pretty quiet town. Not much crime except for petty theft. The University is on the left here and used to be the palace of Haile Selaisse. The Ethiopians are very proud of the fact that they were never really colonized by the Europeans."

"You aren't making any of this up are you?"

"Most of it is true."

As we approached the main gate of the Embassy, we flashed our badges at the local guards and we were waved through to the parking lot. The Suburban had become a little hot and it felt good as the door opened and the fresh air hit my face.

"Have a good one, Doc, and make sure you don't lose that letter before the meeting." Billy smiled and this time I could see his eyes crinkle behind his sunglasses. He had to know about the letter - that would be part of his job. How many others knew about it?

Obviously, the author, me and the Ambassador were in the loop but how big was the loop? The local guard waved me through the lobby door when he saw my badge and the Marine guard buzzed me into the building.

I opened the door to the hallway leading to the health unit and almost collided with DCM Lawrence. He was out of breath and seemed slightly upset, but his tie was straight and he had a white pocket square in his jacket pocket.

"I just met with the Ambassador and he told me about your discovery." He didn't say anything else but waited for me to answer under his stare. I was still tired and didn't want to play games, so I just waited for him to speak again. As a physician, I know how to make people talk. The silence was killing him.

"Well anyway, the Ambassador and I want to meet with you in 30 minutes. Can you make it?"

I wondered if he only asked to dare me to say I was busy and he could compel me to go. He was doing his job so I let him off the hook. "Of course. I will see you there."

I made my way down the hall to the health unit. The waiting room looked very large when it was empty. Rhonda and Mahedere, the receptionist, were not there so I went to my office. I looked out the window at the lawn and a lone bird circled in the sky. It was carefree and looked like it was having fun. After watching it for 30 seconds, I realized it was a vulture.

"Would you like some coffee, Isaac?' Rhonda startled me a little, and I didn't really want any more coffee, but I didn't want to say no.

"Sure, that would be great."

41

She didn't leave but stood there, not exactly leaning on the doorway but not standing straight either. I waited with a blank look on my face until she spoke. "Dr. Lessing came by, and she took all of the records for the people who have been ill. She was very rude. I don't like her."

"Not every doctor is as charming as me."

The slight smile on her face showed that she was not as amused by my humor as I had hoped. She stood still. I used my old friend silence to get her to keep talking. She held out for about 30 seconds before she started to speak, but the tears came first. "I did everything I could with very limited resources. No one could have done more and no one feels worse about Travis than I do."

"No one is blaming you, Rhonda. I went through the charts myself. These things just happen sometimes. Sometimes all the medicine in the world is not enough."

"I just don't want anyone saying it was my fault. It wasn't."

She was very upset, and the tears were now flowing steadily down her face. I hate it when women cry. It is so messy and I feel so helpless. My wife would cry sometimes when things were going badly, and I never knew what to do.

Deciding to get up and do something, I crossed the small space between us and put my right arm around her shoulder in an awkward fashion. She leaned into me and really started to weep. The sobs were deep, and I hoped cathartic. I felt like an idiot and prayed she would stop soon.

"Dr. Lessing said that she would get to the bottom of it. She is looking for someone to blame."

"I am sure she is just doing her job, and I am sure no one will blame you."

"How do you know? She is very mean. Watch out for her."

42

"I will be helping her write the report, and I will make sure that no one blames you."

This seemed to be what she wanted to hear, since the crying stopped and she leaned away from my awkward hug. I guess she just needed some support. Food poisoning this severe was not the usual thing she would see. The health units in Africa were very good at preventative care and minor stuff, but they are not equipped to deal with a very ill person. No one, in Africa or elsewhere, is prepared to deal with the death of a child. She said nothing else and, wiping her tears away with her hand, she moved out of the room. It didn't look like she was going to get my coffee which was just as well. Although Ethiopia is where coffee was originally discovered, I still didn't want any.

I sat down at my desk and unloaded some of the stuff I had brought with me in my briefcase. Most people put pictures of their loved ones on their desk. The problem is that when you've lost your loved one, and in my case it was just one, the desk looks empty without the picture. Worse than that, everybody asks why you don't have any pictures on your desk. Then I have to explain what happened. I feel sad, they feel awkward and the whole thing is really more than most of my coworkers cared to deal with.

After 9/11, I left a picture of my wife on the desk, and that worked pretty well for about a year, but then people just started telling me to move on. The Empire State Building and a Bobblehead of Manny Ramirez in his Dodger uniform were the solution and a conversation-starter. Everybody had something to say about a miniature Empire State Building and Manny. I had other Bobbleheads from promotional giveaways at Dodger Stadium but I didn't want to risk Ron Cey or Fernando in Africa. Manny was expendable. Of course I still had pictures of her and probably always would. My phone rang.

"Dr. Porter? This is Wilma, the Ambassador's assistant. The Ambassador is waiting for you for the meeting that you have scheduled."

"Oh, yes. I will be there shortly."

That was a short half hour. I just wasted thirty minutes thinking about how the desk should look without her picture. I wasted years waiting for her to come back. How stupid is that? She hadn't come back and never would.

The letter was in a Ziploc bag and I took it out of my briefcase. Before leaving the office, I grabbed a manila folder to hold the letter. On TV they always put stuff in plastic bags to preserve the evidence so I did it that morning. I would have done it the night before but I didn't think of it. What would people think if they saw the Doctor walking around with a letter in a Ziploc bag? They would think it was an Anthrax threat or that I had gone crazy. I told Rhonda that I had a meeting with the Ambassador and that I would be back in about 30 minutes.

I got to the Ambassador's office and was ushered in by Wilma, who was small, middle-aged and friendly with dyed black hair. The Ambassador, DCM Lawrence, Agent Solomon, Billy Spencer and Ms. Gonsalves were already there. There was no sign of Dr. Lessing.

"Welcome, Dr. Porter. You are having quite an introduction to the Foreign Service." The Ambassador greeted me, shook my hand warmly and smiled. He was in a navy suit with red tie and had an American/Ethiopian flag pin on his lapel. He directed me to a chair by the door. The chair was separated from the couch and chairs where the others were seated. "Do you have the letter?"

"Yes, Mr. Ambassador, it is right here."

I pulled the letter out of the manila envelope and gave it to him. He passed it on to Agent Solomon, who I hadn't noticed was wearing surgical gloves. He stood and moved to a conference table near the large windows behind the Ambassador's desk. Slowly and in somewhat dramatic fashion, he opened my Ziploc bag, removed the envelope and the note. Inspecting the outside of the envelope first, he then examined the letter. After looking at it for about 20 seconds, he turned toward me. "So you found this on your nightstand last night? Do you have any idea when it was placed there?"

"Good question. I don't know. Last night was the first time I had been in the house. It could have been there for days."

Agent Solomon looked at Billy, and they both looked skeptical. It sounded a little strange even to me. Agent Solomon continued. "Who else has access to your house? Did your wife see anything?'

"I'm single. I don't know who has access to my house."

"Housing has a key, as does Security and Post One. Do you have a housekeeper, Doc?" It was Billy Spencer.

"No, but I just got here so I haven't made much of a mess yet."

Ignoring my humor, Agent Solomon got back to business. "The envelope has no markings, and the letter looks like it was made with a computer printer."

Agent Solomon was not addressing anyone in particular. I had noticed the same things, but I thought he would have some special insight about the letter. It was disappointing to think that the FBI agent didn't have some sort of special power that would allow him to figure out what the letter meant right away.

"May I take a look, David?" Ms. Gonsalves had a pair of blue surgical gloves on and took the letter from Agent Solomon. She was wearing a tight, light gray suit with a pale blue blouse and high heels. There were no stockings on her athletic but not muscular legs. She leaned over the table just slightly and her breasts filled her blouse and made the buttons strain just enough. Everyone else was on her side of the table. While still leaning over she looked directly at me and must have known I was looking at her chest. She smiled slightly. "'The illness didn't need to happen.' What do you think it means, Doctor?"

That you know you are attractive and you use that to disarm men. "I guess someone wants us to know that the illness didn't need to happen."

Her smile broadened for just a second and then she handed the letter back to Agent Solomon. She stood up straight and took off her surgical gloves. Not with a snap like you see on TV but slowly. She was looking at me like she was waiting for me to say something.

Agent Solomon broke the silence. "Really not much to go on. I'll send this to Washington and have it analyzed for fingerprints, chemicals, etc. We'll also get the make and model of the printer, but it's probably a common one. I really don't know what to make of it. It doesn't sound like a message a terrorist would send. Do you have a computer at home?"

"I have a laptop but no printer and why would I type that letter?" I was really sounding defensive now. Fatigue can make you do stupid things. They were all looking at me like I had done something wrong.

Ms. Gonsalves came to my rescue. "No one thinks you wrote this, Dr. Porter. These are just routine questions. It has been a bad couple of days for you and all of us. Travis's father works closely with me and we all miss him. Have you had any contact with anyone outside of the Embassy since you landed? Anyone from other Embassies or locals?"

She wasn't crying but she had tears in her eyes, as I answered. "I haven't met anyone new other than all of you and other Americans."

Billy spoke now. "Except for your day guard, Doc."

"Ibrahim is a very good guy. I was in your house for a couple of months while mine was remodeled. He is kind and speaks good English." DCM Lawrence was jovial and nothing seemed wrong.

Billy spoke again. "It's a new guy, Dick. What is his name, Doc?"

"Eskander. He seems nice and friendly."

Agent Solomon and Ms. Gonsalves exchanged glances. Agent Solomon took out a pen and made a note on a piece of paper. Ms. Gonsalves spoke again but the playfulness had left her face. "Does Eskander have a key to your house?"

"I don't think so. Main gate, yes."

"Mr. Ambassador, I will have my people run a trace on Eskander and his phone and I suggest that Agent Solomon do the same."

The Ambassador nodded his head and spoke. "This is an unusual situation and I don't exactly know how to handle it, but I think we have learned all we can for now. Dr. Porter, I want to thank you for bringing the letter to our attention. Billy, Agent Solomon and Ms. Gonsalves will lead this investigation. Obviously if you get another letter, let us know."

They were all getting ready to go. Agent Solomon had brought his own baggie and had placed the letter and envelope inside it. I was still confused and thought I needed to ask a question. "Ms. Gonsalves, Bob Wollinsky is one of yours?"

She was still standing by the table but there was no smile for me this time. "Even though I trust everyone here, Dr. Porter, there are some questions I shouldn't answer in this room."

I knew there were questions you don't ask the spooks and she was reluctant to say that Wollinsky shared the same office space. Something made her want to answer though. There was something she wanted to get off her very ample chest. After a deep breath, she stood up very straight and began to speak slowly and deliberately.

"Bob is one of our case officers and recently won the Blue Nile Medal for his work here. The award goes to the best case officer in Africa. He has been an integral part of my team for 18 months."

She paused and was gathering herself. I guess I should have stayed quiet but I needed to know. "Do you think he was targeted in some way?"

It was unlikely but I wanted to hear what she thought.

"I don't know, Dr. Porter, but in the lobby of our headquarters in Langley there is a quote from the New Testament 'And ye shall

47

know the truth and the truth shall set you free.' I think a quote from the Book of Job is more appropriate sometimes. 'Even as I have seen, they that plow iniquity and sow wickedness, reap the same.' My organization and I take the protection of our people very seriously. If he or his family were targeted, there will be payback."

I believed her. Her beauty only added to the gravity of the threat.

Chapter 8

I went back downstairs to the health unit. Anita Winston, the wife of the Ambassador, was sitting in the waiting room and reading *Town & Country*. I was next to her before she looked up and smiled. She was wearing a gray pinstriped suit jacket with a tight pencil skirt, white blouse and black pumps. Anita was a very attractive woman. Tall, about 5'10'' with hair dyed dark that didn't look dyed and she had a great smile. I hadn't been able to look at her closely the first time we met when she tried use her rank and privilege to jump line on my first day.

"Dr. Porter, I just wanted to come by and apologize for my behavior the other day. I was rude and unthinking. I know you did all you could for everyone, and we all feel the loss of Travis."

She had stood up and with her heels she was about an inch taller than I was. There was not a thing out of place, from the Ethiopian/American flag pin on her lapel, to the classic pearl earrings to the way her breasts filled her tight white blouse with perfect symmetry. The charm she was giving off was the highest quality. I didn't know Ambassador Winston, but I could see how her charms could propel a Foreign Service Officer to an Ambassadorship. An Ambassadorship in Ethiopia, to be sure, but an Ambassadorship just the same.

"That's OK, I know you and everyone else were under extreme stress that day. Do you need an appointment to discuss a medical issue?" I usually like small talk, but I was tired and knew Dr. Lessing would be here any minute to talk about the case. My time was limited and I needed to get my thoughts together before another meeting. Also I felt uncomfortable with her because she was beautiful and manipulative like my wife.

"I don't have any problems now, thank you. As a peace offering, I wanted to give you a ticket to the Diplomatic Bazaar. It is a yearly gathering of all the Embassies and missions here in the city. Each nation sells country specific crafts, food or products to raise money for local charities. It really is the largest event of its kind in the region. I know it is very soon after our tragedy, but it is very fun and I think you will enjoy it."

Maybe I was on the defensive, but she was perfect. The charity angle, the peace offering and the smile were manipulating me. How many men had she charmed as she worked her way to the top, propelling her husband before her? How could I say no? "That would be great. Thank you so much."

"I think we will be great friends, Doctor. I am not the manipulative bitch you think I am." She grasped my hand and gave me a contrite smile. When she let go, the ticket was in my palm and I almost liked her. Mind reader and master manipulator, she was in a league of her own. Anita turned to leave and gave me a small smile as she moved through the door. I was still holding the ticket and frankly admiring her ability to almost change my mind about her.

Rhonda was at the window looking at the appointment book and I knew she had heard what was going on. I turned toward her and smiled. "She's good."

"Doctor, you have no idea how good she is. Be careful."

I wished someone had told me that about my wife.

"Gunnery Sergeant Cruz is in Room 1. He came in this morning very upset. Dr. Lessing from CDC said some very unkind things to him. See what you can do."

"OK, Rhonda. Do you know him very well? Does he get upset very easily?"

She laughed. "He's a typical Marine. Two tours in Iraq and he wants to go back. I don't know him that well, but I've seen him at the happy hours they have at the Marine House. He's always smiling and very outgoing. I know he was close to Travis. Travis wanted to be a Marine. I guess that won't happen now."

Her eyes had tears in them.

50

The Marine Guard is mostly ceremonial. In fact, all ceremonial until the guy with the suicide vest blows himself up in the lobby or the Anti-American mob tries to get over the perimeter wall. They man the Marine Security Guard post at most American Embassies. They are all veteran Marines and most have seen combat in Afghanistan or Iraq and take their jobs very seriously. Thoroughly trained professionals, they are the last line of defense for the Embassy and serve with distinction. It is a good and well respected duty.

I dropped my briefcase in my office and flipped through Gunnery Sergeant Cruz's chart. There was nothing unusual. He had been in for some diarrhea six months ago and a cold two months ago. No signs of anxiety or depression. I gathered myself a little before going to see him. I knocked on the door and didn't wait for a reply to enter. "Gunnery Sergeant Cruz, I spoke with you on the phone last night. What brings you in today?"

He had rolled up his shirt sleeves to his biceps and took off his Globe and Anchor insignia campaign cap as I entered the room. He stood up and shook my hand. "Good morning, Doctor. I didn't kill Travis."

His eyes were wet. What makes Marines cry? "I want my view heard, sir. That's all. I thought you would be the person I needed to talk to."

"Dr. Lessing from CDC is leading the investigation and I am sure she will want to talk to you. Why did you say you didn't kill Travis? Has someone said you did?"

"Not in so many words, sir. I just want to make sure I get a fair hearing, sir."

"Gunnery Sergeant, I am sure no conclusions have been made and no one thinks you killed Travis. It was an accident."

"Yes, sir. What happened to Travis, sir?"

"Well, it looks like he got food poisoning and then something called Hemolytic Uremic Syndrome. That's just a medical term that means his organs stopped working. Everything that could be done was done. It was a terrible tragedy."

"Sir, how did he get the food poisoning?"

He was standing, but I had sat down. His cap was rolled up into his right hand and he was trying to strangle it. His arms and hands kept tensing and relaxing. "Sit down, Gunnery Sergeant. Let's talk about it."

The chair seemed like a foreign object to him, like a meteorite had landed in the room. He awkwardly turned and almost missed the chair as he sat down. The neatness of his uniform could not camouflage his slumped shoulders and the posture of a beaten man.

"The theory so far is that he got it from the hamburgers at the barbecue. Preliminary tests show E. coli bacteria in the meat, but that is only a preliminary result."

He looked at me with his jaw set and his hands still working over the cap. He must have been around 27 or 28. Buzz cut dark brown hair and good looking, he was slim but in shape. "My best friend, Lance Corporal Miller, was hit in Iraq. IED. His leg was off but the corpsman and the Docs did a great job to save him. He's still doing well, working in a bike shop in Oceanside. Other guys in my unit were killed that day. It shook me up pretty bad, but they were Marines and knew the risks. This is much harder to take. How can it be fair that a child dies?"

Patients always ask these questions you don't want to answer. I have no idea why things happen. Sometimes I can distract them by talking about more comfortable topics like cholesterol, hypertension or herpes. Scientific, controlled and ordered is the way the world and medicine are supposed to be. Certainly medicine should be ordered and controlled. I had already looked through his chart and knew there wasn't any other subject to distract us. We would have to discuss it. "I don't know why it happens that way."

"Doc, I know it wasn't my fault. I know those burgers were cooked properly."

"No one is blaming you."

"That is not the message I got from the CDC doctor. She says that if I had followed proper procedures, Travis would still be alive."

"It was an accident. No one is to blame."

He paused before he answered and his hands relaxed round the cap. "Travis wanted to be a Marine, Doc. He and his Mom were always coming to the Marine House and hanging out with us." Gunnery Sergeant Cruz was not crying but there was a tear on his cheek.

"It was no one's fault. Dr. Lessing cannot blame you. These things just happen."

"Things don't just happen, Doc. Not this. You don't understand. My Mom was a single parent and I have four younger sisters. I started working at 18, well at least legally. My first and only real job prior to the Corps was for In-N-Out Burger."

As a Southern California native, I knew the chain well. Family owned and operated, the business had a reputation for quality.

"It's my favorite burger place, Gunnery Sergeant, but food poisoning from burgers can happen any place or to anyone."

"I've cooked thousands of burgers. I always make sure they are cooked properly. I also make sure that the cooked and uncooked meat are kept apart. Doc, I know what I'm doing. I'm even more careful here. It was not my burger that did it."

"It's not your fault. I will talk to Dr. Lessing and I am sure no one will blame you."

"Doc, I feel like I can talk to you. I've never let a fellow Marine down. Not even a Junior Devil Dog. I just wanted you to hear my side of the story. Dr. Lessing didn't listen to me."

He stood up and the tears were gone. Evaporated? Standing tall and straight like the Marine he was, the sad posture and affect were

53

gone. He was back in control and I knew he had cried for the last time about Travis.

"Gunnery Sergeant, if you want to talk anymore about this, let me know. I'll make sure that you are not blamed."

"Thanks, Doc."

A firm handshake and he was gone. The phone rang on the wall. It was Rhonda. "Dr. Porter, Dr. Lessing left a message and she wants to see you in her office as soon as you are free. She wants to finalize the report before the meeting."

"Thanks, Rhonda, I'll be right out."

Finalize the report? We had just begun.

Chapter 9

The meeting with Dr. Lessing was going to take place on her home turf, so to speak. The Centers for Disease Control, CDC, office was on the third floor in the front of the Embassy. The office door was clear glass, with the CDC logo on it, and revealed a small waiting area with a receptionist. As I entered, I noticed that the magazines on the table were neatly arranged and the chairs faced each other at a perfect angle. The receptionist was bright, young and happy.

"Hello. I'm Dr. Porter and I have an appointment with Dr. Lessing."

"Good morning, Dr. Porter. Dr. Lessing is expecting you. She asked me to give you this report and her card."

The report should only be preliminary at this point and it looked to be about 100 pages long, bound and heavy. PEPFAR, an anti-malaria program and the clean water initiative logos were neatly arranged across the front of her card like ads on the hood of a stock car at Daytona. What kind of doctor advertises on a card? I sat down in the nearest chair, which was not very comfortable. I scanned the title page of the report:

"The report on the recent outbreak of E. coli food poisoning in the US Embassy in Addis Ababa, Ethiopia: Evidence of poor food handling as the primary cause with recommendations for avoidance at this and other Embassies in Africa and the Near East."

Madeline Lessing M.D., Ph.D., Deputy Head of CDC for Sub-Saharan Africa

Sounded like a real page turner. I turned to the conclusion page. The blame was placed on improper food handling by a Marine who was cooking at the barbecue. Gunnery Sergeant Cruz wasn't named, but it sounded like it was completely his fault. The report advised that all cooks and cafeteria personnel be given a six hour proper food handling course, overseen by the CDC, within 6 months. Wallet cards were to be issued to prove they could cook without killing.

55

Those words were in the report. Cook without killing? Cruz was right, she was laying the blame unfairly on him.

There were some interesting points in the report. E. coli was found in the cooked burgers. That was consistent with undercooked meat as the source. The raw tomatoes and lettuce could also be the source, but they tested negative. Only condiments that had come in contact with the meat were positive. But it was too early to say for sure and Cruz should not be blamed for an accident.

"Dr. Porter, Dr. Lessing will see you now."

As I got up, I noticed that I had been waiting for 25 minutes. I took the report down the hall to her corner office and entered. It was a large office, larger than mine, with a desk, bookcases full of books and journals, and a separate seating area. Sitting behind the large desk that held four neat piles of journals, papers, mail and boxes, she rose and extended her hand across the desk. "Good to see you again, Dr. Porter." There was no move to come out from behind the desk.

"Good morning, please call me Isaac."

"I see you have the report. Did you get a chance to read it?" As she sat down, I noticed the neatly arranged pictures behind her on the wall. Diplomas from Harvard and Johns Hopkins were next to some photos and plaques. The best picture was of her and the President as he was handing her an envelope. Placed over her right side, it looked like the President was sitting on her shoulder. "I think the report speaks for itself, Dr. Porter. What do you think?"

The whole "call me Doctor or my first name" debate isn't a big deal for me. I think it helps patients to call me Doctor when they are sick, but I never insist upon it. It builds confidence in my abilities and comforts them. But let's be realistic. If a 75 year old wants to call you Isaac, just go with it. They are older and don't mean anything by it, it is not an insult. But when a fellow doctor doesn't call you by your first name, especially when invited to do so, it's just power at play. She was trying to get me to call her Doctor. "Madeline, it looks good so far, but I'll need more time to read it thoroughly."

Her mouth scrunched up just slightly as if she had eaten something that didn't agree with her. "The evidence is pretty clear. Undercooked meat was the cause of the outbreak and, with proper education, we can stop this from happening again."

She took the tone professors take with wayward students. She would be a formidable professor and could have intimidated me when I was in school and 25. Unfortunately, I was 40 and no longer easily intimidated. It felt like exerting control over me was more important to her than doing a good job on the report. "I think you are being too hard on Gunnery Sergeant Cruz. If the meat was the source, it was an accident."

"Who is that?"

"He was the cook. You blame him in the report."

"Oh. Well, proper cooking would have stopped the E. coli. I think it is important to assess the source of the illness. It is not blame that I mean to place, but only to use the experience as a way to stop this from happening again."

Her phone rang before I could answer her statement and she picked it up. She listened silently for about 30 seconds, but her expression did not change. Finally she reached across the desk and handed me the phone without a word. As I took the phone, I accidentally knocked over her stack of journals. "Hello."

"Dr. Porter? This is DCM Lawrence. I think I know how the meat got spoiled. Can you and Dr. Lessing meet me in the commissary?"

"Sure. How about in 30 minutes?" She nodded as I looked at her for approval.

"Sure. It looks like a routine case of negligence to me."

"I don't think we can blame Gunnery Sergeant Cruz."

"It wasn't Cruz who was negligent. Let's talk more at the commissary, goodbye."

"It sounds like the DCM doesn't blame Cruz, either."

He voice raised a little as she answered. "As I said before, Dr. Porter, I am not here to assign blame but to investigate. I have years of experience in these situations. I am not saying you cannot contribute, but I will be lead author on the report."

I was no longer surprised by her tone and attitude. She was mostly interested in the credit from the report, not the outcome. That was fine with me. "I don't care who gets credit, Madeline. I just want an accurate and complete report."

"Good, then we agree. I have to make a phone call before we meet the DCM. Will you excuse me?"

I stood up to leave and she straightened the stack of journals on her desk.

Feeling hungry, I went down to the cafeteria for an early lunch of spaghetti and meat sauce. The cafeteria was clean and looked new. There were very few people there since it was only about 11:30. The spaghetti was hot and not that good, but I figured there was less chance of food poisoning now than last week. After lunch I headed outside.

The commissary was behind the Embassy in a small round building that had a rectangular wing attached to one side. The round portion was about 30 feet wide and the wing extended for about 50 feet. The white plaster walls contrasted with the green window trim and it actually had a thatched roof. There was a door in the round portion that was open and a closed door in the rectangular area. It looked very African, like a movie set looks African. I was standing just outside one of the windows, near the closed door, looking at the thatched roof and heard something. The voices were plain, loud and angry. I recognized one of them, but couldn't remember from where. Open windows are very poor secret keepers.

"Don't give me that bullshit, Dick! This has nothing to do with my work performance. This has everything to do with your hatred of me, and you know it."

58

"I am not going over that again. There is evidence here of negligence and if it contributed in any way to recent events, you will be held accountable."

"You can't threaten me, Dick. Don't try to attack my professional competence. There has been no negligence."

"I've told you what you need to know and we have nothing further to discuss, Frederick."

I moved quickly to the door since it seemed like there was a break in the action. It was unlocked. The commissary is a small store operated by an employee association so that the Americans can get American food. They are located in Embassies that are far from America and that don't have access to familiar food. Most of the Embassies in Africa have one since it's hard to find your favorite brand of canned chili in the local stores.

The inside of the commissary looked like the small grocery store that it was with rows of tightly spaced shelves that held American brand canned and packaged foods. There was a local employee behind a small desk, and DCM Lawrence and another American were standing close to the desk but apart from each other. The floor creaked in the room away from the door and it was clear someone else was in the room, probably shopping. The voice I recognized belonged to the DCM. The other man was brown haired with a deep tan, younger, taller and in better shape. He wore a white shirt with sleeves rolled up above his elbows, khaki pants and Merrell shoes, one of which was untied. I knew his face from the EAC meeting.

"Hello." I said it loud so they were sure to hear me since I didn't want to hear any more of their argument right now.

"Hello, Dr. Porter. Let me introduce you to Frederick Stevenson, our Management Officer. He oversees the commissary."

"How do you do, Doctor?"

"Pleasure to meet you."

They were still mad. The DCM had it under control, but Stevenson was unsure which side I would take and was a little hostile. Dr. Lessing came in behind me and walked up to the DCM. "Dick, I am very busy with the report so if you have something let me see it."

She didn't even acknowledge me, which took some concentration since she was only two feet away.

"I've had some complaints about the products sold from the commissary recently. Frederick has tried to address some of them, but some of them are beyond his control." It was an interesting start to the conversation. Just before I got inside it sounded like they were coming to blows and now the DCM was defending Stevenson. "People have been complaining about some of the food sold here as being past its sell-by date."

Madeline spoke. "That could be a problem, but what has it got to do with my investigation?"

"That has nothing to do with it. If a bag of Fritos is stale, it will not harm anyone. That is not Frederick's fault. The items are sent from a warehouse in Germany by ship, offloaded in Djibouti and then trucked overland to Addis. It can take months, and some food inevitably arrives here past its code date. I do not blame anyone for that."

The DCM was very good, very diplomatic and very controlled. It sounded like the two men were the best of friends and had not had an argument in years. "There is something else. On previous overt and covert inspections, there were some vermin in the storeroom. I sent some formal and informal notes to Mr. Stevenson to correct the matter and I thought he had done so."

"There are no rats in this building, Dick." Stevenson was not as good as the DCM in controlling his emotions. He was angry and yet confident.

"How do you explain this then?"

The DCM moved into an adjacent room that had four large freezers along a wall as well as pallets of flour, canned goods and pet food. One of the bags had opened and some flour was on the floor. He walked up to one of the freezers and opened the door. The stench of rotting meat filled the small room and I almost gagged. The DCM took a small flashlight from his pocket and used it to illuminate the back of the freezer. A dead rat with a frayed electrical cord in its mouth stared back at us. The DCM spoke again. "Dr. Lessing, couldn't improper freezing or storage of meat contribute to food poisoning?"

"Yes, it could."

"That freezer has been working fine, and I have the logs here to prove it." Stevenson didn't sound as angry or as sure of himself now. He was fumbling with a clipboard that must have held the logs he mentioned.

"I am sure that Frederick meant no harm, but by not adequately controlling the rat population, it could have lead to the rats chewing through the wire and the freezer malfunctioning." The DCM was coming in for the kill. He had started off supporting Stevenson and then had, reluctantly, found that Stevenson was at fault. If I hadn't heard them quarreling, I would have bought the whole thing.

Madeline looked at the freezer and spoke. "Thank you, Dick. Was this the freezer that contained the ground meat?"

"Unfortunately, it was."

"I think you have helped us a great deal. I don't know about negligence, but it seems like this could have been handled better."

Stevenson was staring at the rat and didn't know what to say. He had been outmaneuvered by the DCM. "I don't know how this could have happened. We keep a clean and rodent-free storeroom."

"There is evidence to the contrary and, as DCM, I will have to inform the Ambassador and it will also be included in Dr. Lessing's report."

Dr. Lessing finally looked at me after the DCM spoke and had a gleam in her eye like I was going to be reported to the Ambassador as well.

There were footsteps behind me and Felicity Gonsalves came up munching on a bag of barbecue flavored chips and spoke. "What do you think about the rat chewing on the freezer cord theory, Dr. Porter?"

I could see the scar on her face more clearly under the halogen light in the storeroom. It wasn't acne but could be chicken pox or more likely a burn. Had hot water fallen on her as a child? The scar really just set off the attractiveness of her face. Wouldn't a great painting look actually better in a bad frame? The beauty of the picture would be accentuated by the blemish. I spoke so she wouldn't notice me looking at her scar. I realized I wasn't cut out to be a diplomat. "I worked with lab and feral rats in college. It is true they will chew on just about anything, but no self-respecting rat is going to eat an electric cord when there is a pallet of flour nearby."

The DCM and Dr. Lessing did not hear or did not want to hear. "I will include this in my report, Dick, and can you let the Ambassador know we discussed this?'

"I will do that. By the way, we are having a conference call with Washington in about an hour. Can you and Dr. Porter be there?"

"Yes, we will be there."

Even though I was in the same room, she was answering for me and completely ignoring my statement. The DCM didn't say anything else and walked out of the room with Dr. Lessing. Stevenson gave me a nod and followed.

"Do you enjoy upsetting her?'

"No, it just happens."

"Just happens? Chip? They're a little stale but still taste good." Felicity smiled as I took one of her chips, then she turned and walked out of the room.

A busted freezer could help explain the poisoning but if the meat was cooked as Cruz insisted it was, it shouldn't matter. The cooking would kill the bacteria.

Chapter 10

I went back to the health unit, where Rhonda was talking with a young woman about 25 dressed in a blue skirt and white blouse. She was about 5'4" with blonde hair and dark horn-rimmed square glasses.

"Oh, here he is. Ms. Susan Bell would like to see you, Doctor, here is her chart."

"Certainly, hello Ms. Bell. Rhonda, could you put her in a room, and I will be right in."

I went into my office for just a minute to sit down and think. Rats eating wires, busted freezers, beautiful CIA officers, death, a guilt ridden Marine and a bitch of a CDC doc made for an interesting mix. How did this happen? I looked through the chart. Susan had been seen six times in the last year for various ailments, including colds, diarrhea, insomnia and headaches. That was a lot for a 25 year old. I wondered what was causing her so many problems. After exiting my office I went to Exam Room 1 and knocked before I entered. "Ms. Bell, I'm Dr. Porter. What brings you in today?"

I sat down on the stool and looked into her eyes.

She was sitting on the exam table, but was nervous and looked down at her hands before she replied. "I had sex with someone last night and I am afraid that I might get an STD."

"Who did you have sex with and why do you think you have a sexually transmitted disease?"

"I would rather not say who it was, but after talking to a friend here at the Embassy, she said I should get checked."

"Did you use a condom?"

"How do you know it was a man, Doctor?"

"Good point. Was it a woman?"

"No, Doctor, I was just being juvenile. It was a man here at the Embassy and we didn't use a condom. We've all been upset about Travis. I had been on a couple of dates with him before and last night I was feeling insecure and scared. I went to his place and we had some wine. I didn't think it was a bad idea at the time, but on reflection this morning…"

"Did you know Travis well?"

"No, Doctor, I just think it's so sad that a little boy can die like that."

"It is very sad and feeling that way only makes you human."

There was a pause and I waited for her to speak again.

"I don't think I have anything, I just want to be sure."

"Of course. Looking through your chart I see you have been into the health unit several times in the last year. I know it can be difficult to live here and sometimes people who are under stress get ill more often. Are you feeling a lot of stress?"

She stared at me for a moment and shook her head no just as the first tears rolled down her cheek. I reached for the tissue box, handed it to her and just waited. "It has been hard for me. About three months after I got here, my boyfriend from college broke up with me. This is my first overseas posting. It was hard enough before that and when he said it wasn't working, things just kind of fell apart. I was just getting it back together when Travis died."

It must be hard to be so far away from people you love. Just as I was about to answer her, the phone rang.

"Dr. Porter? This is Wilma, the Ambassador's assistant. You were scheduled to be here for a meeting 10 minutes ago. Can I tell the Ambassador that you are on your way?"

I was late for the meeting. That shouldn't be such a big deal, should it?

"Please come right away. We are expecting the Secretary and the Director on a conference call from Washington."

"The Secretary and the Director of what?'

"The Secretary of State and the Director of the FBI. Are you on your way?"

"Yes, I'll be right there."

"Ms. Bell, I'm sorry, I have a meeting with the Ambassador that I have to attend. Rhonda can check you for the STDs or you can come back later to have me do it. Although it is possible you have an STD, I think it is unlikely. I want you to come back tomorrow or the next day so we can talk more."

"Thank you, Doctor, it will be fine for Rhonda to check me. I don't think there is anything going on. I just feel unsettled."

"I understand, I'll let Rhonda know."

I got up, went to the door and I turned toward her. "If you want me to go kick your ex-boyfriend's ass, just let me know."

She laughed and got up to shake my hand. "That's OK, Doctor, I'm better off without him. Thanks for the offer, though."

I found my way back to the conference room on the third floor. There were printed name tags placed in front of each seat. Seven people were around the table with Ambassador Winston at the head of table with DCM Lawrence to his right. Dr. Lessing was on the Ambassador's left with Agent Solomon from the FBI next to her. Ms. Gonsalves was opposite Agent Solomon and gave me a small smile as I tried to find my seat. Billy Spencer was next to Gonsalves and Frederick Stevenson was opposite him. My seat was next to Stevenson and my name tag was the only one that was handwritten like I had showed up to the party with a last minute invitation.

The Ambassador pulled the sleeve of his coat back and extended his left wrist to look at his watch in an exaggerated fashion.

"Our video call will begin in 20 seconds, Doctor." His voice was flat and controlled but showed disapproval at my tardiness.

"Perfect timing, I guess."

Dr. Lessing scowled at me like I was late for class. The Ambassador was not really listening. DCM Lawrence smiled slightly and Agent Solomon was staring at me in a neutral way. Ms. Gonsalves' smile did not show any reprimand, and I would have sworn her eyes twinkled. Do CIA people have a sense of humor?

In the center of the table was a triangular microphone. On the wall opposite the Ambassador was a flat-screen monitor and above it was a little camera on a swivel that looked like a small cannon. A disembodied voice came from the triangular microphone. "Please stand by for Washington."

The monitor came on and displayed the seal of the State Department. The screen then split and two faces appeared. Both were recognizable. On the left, the newly appointed Director of the FBI, Hamilton Harrison, 55 years old, African-American and dressed in a dark suit, with glasses and a red tie. The right side of the screen showed the Secretary of State. She was wearing a light-colored jacket and held a pen in her left hand. Both of them had the American flag behind them.

The Ambassador spoke. "Good morning, Madame Secretary and Mr. Director."

They both exchanged greetings with the Ambassador, and he continued. "Let me introduce the people around the table. This is my DCM Dick Lawrence, our RSO Mr. Spencer, Dr. Lessing from CDC, Mr. Solomon from FBI, Ms. Gonsalves, our CIA Deputy Chief of Station, the Chief of Station is on R and R, and Frederick Stevenson, our Management Officer."

The Ambassador had stopped and was waiting to hear from the screen. Had he skipped me on purpose or was it an oversight? I didn't know what to do. What is the protocol in this situation? Ms. Hayes, my Protocol instructor at the Foreign Service Institute, had been so kind and I would have paid more attention to her if I had known this situation would arise. I was waiting for someone to say something. In a video call it's hard to tell, but it felt like the Director and the Secretary were staring at me. Someone kicked me under the table. I almost jumped and based on the geometry it had to be Ms. Gonsalves. She was looking at me and inclined her head toward the screen just enough for me to see it. "I am Isaac Porter, the Regional Medical Officer, Mr. Director and Madame Secretary."

"I am so sorry, Doctor. I should have introduced you as well." The Ambassador looked apologetic after he spoke, but I still wasn't sure why he had neglected to introduce me in the first place. Ms. Gonsalves was looking out for me, and it felt good. Or, she could have just been stretching.

The Secretary continued. "It is a pleasure to see you all and I wish it was under better circumstances. The Director and I had a small discussion before we joined you and we would like to hear your thoughts so far. Dr. Lessing, I believe you are heading this investigation. What have you found?"

"Madame Secretary and Mr. Director, I want to thank you for taking the time to meet with us today. CDC and I stand ready to lead this investigation and devote whatever resources are necessary to getting to the bottom of this tragedy. The death of a small boy is a loss felt by all of those around him."

"I know I speak for the Director when I say that we are grateful to CDC and you for volunteering to lead the investigation. We will offer whatever support you need."

Dr. Lessing sounded like a commercial for the CDC and the Secretary was buying it. It was controlled diplomatic talk at its finest and I didn't care for it.

"I hope, Mr. Director and Madame Secretary, you realize in these tough budgetary times that CDC is doing more with less and supporting our nation in over 180 countries."

Was she kidding? Were we there to discuss Travis' death or to increase her budget?

"Thank you again, Dr. Lessing. What have you found so far? The Director was saying that you thought it was bacteria."

"Our preliminary results point to undercooked hamburger meat as the probable source of the E. coli bacteria that caused the death. It was found on over 75% of the patties we tested. As you know, it is a common source of food poisoning in the US and can usually be prevented by proper food handling techniques. We of course tested the lettuce, tomatoes, cheese and onions that were consumed. Some of the lettuce, onions and tomatoes also contained E. coli. None of the cheese did and the only condiments that tested positive were on the hamburgers themselves. This proves that the source of infection was the beef. DCM Lawrence has pointed out to me a possible freezer malfunction that could have contributed to the illness as well. DNA testing will be done in Atlanta to confirm if one phenotype of E. coli. was responsible but that will take a few days."

"Thank you, Dr. Lessing. So it is your opinion that this was a tragic accident?"

"Madame Secretary, it was improper food handling by the person who cooked the meat. That is not an accident. All food preparers should be instructed on how to cook hamburger to avoid this very outcome. CDC has some effective training programs that we will be implementing here to avoid this happening again. I have already talked to the Marine who was the cook at the barbecue. I am sure he has learned his lesson, even if it was too late for poor Terrence."

"His name was Travis."

The voice was cold and angry. I was shocked that it had come from me since I usually try to avoid confrontation.   Something else was bothering me about what she said. Actually a lot was bothering me about what she said. She couldn't remember Travis's name, but she could make a pitch for increased funding. She was ready to blame a

Marine, who was volunteering to be 9,000 miles away from home, for, if anything, a mistake. There was something else though. What was it?

"I am sorry I misspoke the name, Dr. Porter. I am sure that your emotional reaction is quite normal and I want to assure you that no one is faulting your care in this case."

Fuck you, lady. Maybe it was jet lag or the lack of sleep, but it took great control not to hurl my handwritten name tag at her. She should have remembered his name.

The Secretary spoke. "Thank you, Dr. Lessing. It is your conclusion then that this was not an intentional act? I just want to make sure that the Director and I understand what you are saying."

Something was not right with Dr. Lessing's logic. She was leaving something out. There was a flaw there and I could almost grasp it.

"Madame Secretary, this was not intentional and it could have been easily avoided. Unfortunately, as in so many cases, simple negligence led to the death and illness we saw at this post. I am as sure as I can be that there was no intent to harm."

"Although this has been a terrible incident, the Director and I are relieved that no more sinister force is at work. As you may know, this incident has attracted widespread coverage here with much speculation as to the cause."

"I have seen some of these reports and I along with my CDC colleagues in Atlanta have drafted a press release blaming the illnesses on improperly cooked hamburger. We, of course, did not name the individual responsible."

"Very good, Dr. Lessing. The press release should be reviewed by State people before it is given to the media. Unless anyone else has any more to add, I think we can conclude for today."

"Dr. Lessing?'

It was my voice again but it was not angry or passionate. It was bad enough to forget Travis's name but her blaming Cruz had stuck in my craw. I didn't know what I was going to say before I started. I just knew I had to speak.

"Hamburger is often the culprit in these cases because it is not thoroughly cooked?"

"Yes, Dr. Porter, that is correct. The meat is usually contaminated at the slaughterhouse, and without proper cooking the E. coli can cause serious illness as in this case."

"Hamburger is especially bad because the meat is ground and the bacteria can be in the interior of the patty. Steak isn't as bad because the contamination is on the surface and the E. coli is killed more easily with cooking."

"Yes, Dr. Porter that is correct. I assume you concur with my conclusion." She was smiling a smile of triumph and no doubt counting the new budget money that would roll into her accounts.

"How do you explain the lettuce, tomato and onion?"

"Dr. Porter, it was cross contamination from the hamburger."

"Why was it only on the cooked burgers? Wouldn't the bacteria on the surface have been killed by the cooking? How could it contaminate the lettuce, tomato and onion?"

She paused for a moment and fired back. "The bacteria leaked from the interior of the burger where the meat was undercooked."

That sounded reasonable and I felt like she did have all the answers. Maybe it was a simple as she said. I wish I could say it was well thought out but the question simply popped into my head.

"Did the uncooked meat show E. coli?"

"The results were inconclusive."

"Inconclusive means... no?"

"The results on the uncooked meat did not show E. coli but the cooked meat did. Since no other source has been found, the E. coli had to be there before cooking."

"Unless it was added after cooking."

No one spoke. Dr. Lessing was scowling at me again. She had jumped to a conclusion and didn't like me pointing that out to everyone in the room.

"Never let the facts get in the way of a good theory." I almost regretted saying it. Almost. The Director spoke for the first time.

"I guess we need to keep our minds open until we get more information. In light of Dr. Porter's statements and the letter he found, I need to tell you all about some intel we have received. This information should not be communicated to anyone outside this room. A credible source has given us a statement from Al-Qaeda in East Africa or AQEA. The statement reads in part: 'Even your food and your children are not safe from our retribution'."

No one spoke. Everyone stopped moving and it seemed like we had all stopped breathing, it was so quiet.

"I think that is all we have for now. We will be expecting an update tomorrow. Thank you, everyone."

After the Ambassador thanked the Director and the Secretary, the call ended. Al-Qaeda could be involved. That was more than I had bargained for when I signed up to start over. The Ambassador looked at me with some anger in his eyes. No one said anything and I think everyone was a little stunned.

"Mr. Ambassador, may I suggest we all get back to work and try to make sense out of this situation. Felicity, David and Billy can look into the terrorism angle and Fred and I will try to see if anything else happened with the commissary. Dr. Lessing and Dr. Porter can put their heads together as well." The DCM was stepping in to fill the breach as the Ambassador seemed overwhelmed. It sounded like a reasonable plan, but I wasn't sure I could work with Dr. Lessing. We

72

all agreed that we would do as he said and got up to go. I lingered behind to look out of the window at the mountains. Things were getting out of control.

Chapter 11

After the call to Washington, I was tired and decided it was time to go home for the day. I gathered up my briefcase and cell phone (the simplest and cheapest Nokia the State Department could get), and went to the front of the Embassy to wait for my ride home. Rhonda had given me the cell when I returned to the health unit. As the Suburban pulled up, I was thinking about Travis and how sick he was when he left here. Could a terrorist have penetrated the Embassy and poisoned the beef? And if so, why? Was he targeted because his father was CIA? Al Qaeda would love to hit the Agency, but it would be much more effective and accurate to kill with an AK-47 or a bomb. Food poisoning is difficult to pull off and if Travis hadn't died, it would never have been investigated.

The honk from the driver brought me back to Africa. Billy Spencer was at the wheel again. I opened the armored door, got in and carefully shut it, making sure it did not slam on my leg. It weighed several hundred pounds. "Hey Doc, I thought I'd give you a ride home and get to know you a little better. How are you doing?"

"I'm tired and hungry. That can of chili is going to taste like T-bone steak tonight."

He laughed and adjusted his sunglasses. His white shirt had become untucked on his right side, and his belly was protruding over his belt. "It's been quite a welcome to the Foreign Service for you. For what it's worth, I think you've done an excellent job under very difficult circumstances."

I didn't feel the same way, so I just kept silent. We had exited the Embassy grounds and were heading south on Entoto Road driving past several open storefronts selling meat that was suspended on a white wooden rack. From the size of the carcass it must have been goat or lamb. Our pace was leisurely as we were not in a hurry and that way we wouldn't run over any pedestrians or donkeys. I changed the subject. "Where are you from, Billy?"

"Little town in Wyoming, called Cody. My Dad was an auto mechanic at the local garage, Mom worked at the Safeway. I did OK in high school and went to a JC for a year but didn't know what to do with myself. So I joined the Army."

"How did you end up here?"

"The Army sent me to Germany. Started in infantry and moved into intelligence. I put in my 22 years and looked for another job. I knew a guy in Austria, when I was there, who was in security for State. When I got out, I gave him a call. He got me an interview and I have been doing this for eight years now. First in Armenia, then Georgia, and now I'm here."

"Sounds like you've been around. Do you like it?"

"I've had worse jobs and it keeps me out of the house. My wife, Laurie, would kill me or I her if I was home all of the time." He laughed. I liked him. He wasn't pretentious and was willing to talk about something besides Travis. "You married, Doc?"

"I was. Lost her on 9/11."

As soon as I said it, I regretted it. It was my standard response to questions about her over the years and it would stop people in their tracks. It used to get me a lot of sympathy and that was good, but really I used it as a way to avoid speaking about her. After a pause Billy began again. "Sorry, Doc. I didn't mean to…"

"It's OK, Billy. You didn't know."

After an awkward pause, I continued. "What do you think about the terrorist angle?"

"Doc, like Agent Solomon said, this would be a highly unusual way for Al-Qaeda or anybody else to attack us. They like bombs strapped to their chests or packed in their cars, not uncooked meat. Plus, it's a pretty low kill rate. A car bomb at a market can kill a hundred people and would be a lot easier to pull off. That being said, it is a unique way to get us and they are devious, inventive bastards."

He was silent again. We had turned onto the Ring Road and through a traffic circle with a large grassy area in the center where a large, very shaggy ram was grazing. Further down, we passed the Russian, British and Kenyan Embassies. "I like you, Doc. You're a straight shooter. You kept Dr. Lessing in line today. I also like the way you stood up for Gunnery Sergeant Cruz and Travis."

"Thanks, Billy, but I was just doing my job."

"Doc, sometimes just doing a job is the hardest thing in the world."

We slowed a few times for people crossing from one side to the other. It was a limited access highway for cars, but pedestrians seemed to be able to access it just fine. Billy took us through a roundabout and drove under the Ring Road. The area under the highway was used as a nursery and plants of various shapes and sizes were for sale. It was like the land under high power lines in LA that was used by nurseries to grow their plants. The pothole Billy and I had passed the other day came upon us. The large rocks were there, but the hole was much deeper and surrounded by a large pile of gravel. It must be a water or sewer main break to make a hole that large. The neighborhood was getting more familiar and I recognized a few of the stores and houses along the way to my house. After a few more turns, we pulled up to my house and he honked. Eskander stuck his head out for a second, flashed a smile, and disappeared again. The gates opened up and we drove in.

As we came to a stop, Billy took off his sunglasses and turned toward me, "Well, Doc, here you are. Sorry about your wife. I really do appreciate everything you've done. Travis was a special kid. Cruz is a Marine, so it's not like he's Army, but I don't like anyone getting buffaloed."

"No problem, Billy. Thanks for the lift. I'll see you tomorrow."

I opened the door and got out. I shut the door and waved as he backed the Suburban out of the gate. Eskander closed the gate and came over to me. "Hello, sir. How was your day today?"

"It was very good, Eskander. How was yours?"

"It was a beautiful day. The men who came could not spoil it."

"The men who came?"

"Yes, two men. Mr. Billy, your chauffeur, and another man from the BFI."

The FBI? It must have been Solomon.

"What did they want?"

"They asked me questions about you and the letter you found. I hope I did nothing wrong."

"I don't think you did anything wrong."

"Thank you, sir. I told them that you are kind and that you are honest. They were just asking questions and did not accuse me of anything." I am honest about some things, not so honest about others.

"Eskander, do you work seven days a week?"

"No, sir, I do not work on Sunday and only half day on Saturday."

The letter must have been placed in the house on Sunday when I was at the office or before I even arrived.

"You don't have a key to the house, do you?"

"No sir, only to the front gate, guardroom and the bathroom I use here in the yard. The guardroom is that small building over there." He pointed to a concrete block building about 10 by 10 feet on the other side of the fountain and seating area. Next to it was the green steel generator enclosure.

"I think they were just being complete. A little boy died and we are trying to figure out why."

"Yes. It is so sad. He is with God now but it is still hard."

I didn't know what to say about that. Was he with God? How do we explain to anyone the death of a child? It shouldn't happen in a perfect world but the world wasn't perfect. I moved to the door and got out my key.

Eskander was not done. "Dr. Porter, I have a question to ask you."

"Sure, Eskander. Shoot."

"Shoot?"

"Go ahead and ask your question."

I realized I should watch my slang more.

"Is your wife coming out to cook for you?"

"I'm single, Eskander."

"Oh well, then you need someone to cook for you. My niece is looking for a job, and she is a very good cook. She would be able to clean, too, and make your house a home."

My wife never cooked and we had a housekeeper; a very pleasant woman named Maria. Maria was very concerned about me and told me to move on about a year after I lost my wife. I fired her on the spot, but she was right. It was just that her advice had come too soon. Eskander's concern for me and his niece touched me.

"Why don't you have her come around this week and we can give it a try. How much am I paying you, Eskander?"

"1200 Birr per month, 600 every two weeks."

At 16 birr to the dollar, that was less than $100 a month.

"Let's make it 1600 a month. You seem to be working hard."

"Thank you, sir. I will tell my niece to be here tomorrow."

"OK, Eskander."

I turned to the door and unlocked it. After setting down my briefcase, I went inside to the kitchen and got the chili can out of the box. It was enough to keep me alive and healthy until I could order more or get some locally. The chili had a pull top on it so I could get dinner ready in no time. As the chili heated, I kept thinking about the burgers. It didn't make a lot of sense to me, and the only sure fact was that Travis was still dead and we didn't know how it had happened.

I dumped the chili from the pot into a bowl and grabbed some crackers out of the supply box. I opened the package and some of the crackers fell onto the counter. I scooped them up and dropped them into the chili bowl. How clean was the counter? The chili was in a can so it was sterile, but I could be introducing bacteria from the counter. Had the meat been inadvertently contaminated or was it deliberate? If deliberate, who would or could do it?

Chapter 12

The alarm woke me from a troubled sleep. I used to dream about my wife a lot, but in the last few years it was usually only when I was stressed. The dream I had was hard to describe and I didn't actually see her. We were still together and I was looking for her in our house. Her clothes were in the closet, her purse was on the coffee table and her car was in the driveway, but I couldn't find her anywhere. I would call her name but she would not answer. I kept hearing voices coming from whatever room I wasn't in. Finally in the study, I found that the TV was on and the twin towers were falling again.

I showered, ate my granola bar and had my cup of coffee. The horn honked and I heard the gate open and the Suburban drive into the yard. I unlocked the front door and the security grill that covered it.

Eskander was smiling and greeted me. "Good morning, Doctor. How are you today?"

"Very good, Eskander. How are you?"

"Very good, sir. My niece will be coming by later to see you, if that is OK."

"That would be fine, Eskander, but I am not sure when I'll be back."

"Do not worry sir, she will wait."

"OK, Eskander, see you later."

Billy Spencer was behind the wheel. His blue blazer was stained on the right lapel and his tie was crooked. "Morning, Doc. How did you sleep? You look terrible."

Whenever I dream about her, people tell me I look terrible, but I always look the same to me. My brother told me once the twinkle in my eye was gone. "Oh I slept OK, just some things on my mind."

"I know what you mean. I have been going over cables and reports trying to assess the terror threat. It just doesn't make sense to me, Doc, but I could be wrong. We were all wrong about 9/11, weren't we. I mean we never saw that coming."

"You can say that again. I never saw it coming."

"Oh shit. I'm sorry Doc, I forgot." The ride in was silent after that. I wanted to say something to make him feel better but didn't really know what to say. It wasn't his fault.

We flashed our badges at the guard at the gate and we were waved through to the parking area. Billy parked the Suburban, and he turned to me as I motioned to open the door. "Doc, there is one thing I'd like to talk over with you."

"Sure, Billy."

"I know you are a great Doc and that you have a lot of experience but the State Department is very different from the real world." He smiled and reached out with his right hand to touch my shoulder. "Order and hierarchy mean a lot to people. I like you, Doc, just be careful who you piss off."

"Thanks for the heads up, Billy. Anyone in particular you are talking about?"

"You're a smart guy, Doc. You don't need me to tell you who might not like you. I will tell you that I like you."

"Thanks Billy, I'll watch my back."

"I think one of the CIA people likes you, too, and she is better looking than me."

He smiled again and we got out of the Suburban. It was good of him to warn me. I grabbed my briefcase and headed into the Embassy. The local guard smiled and waved me through the door. After the walk down the hall, past the cafeteria, I entered the health unit and said hello to Rhonda. She looked well and more rested. "Morning Dr. Porter, how are you?"

"Good morning, Rhonda. Please call me Isaac, you look better today."

"I finally slept last night, and how about you? I have some mint tea that could work wonders for you."

"I look bad?"

"You look overwhelmed and tired. Are you OK?"

"Yeah, just a little tired and overwhelmed."

She laughed and went back to looking at the day's schedule. I looked over her shoulder at the list and it was empty. "Everybody must be healthy."

"Or they're afraid of you, Isaac. Good luck." She motioned her head toward my office. I walked over to my office and was surprised to see Dr. Lessing sitting in front of my desk. She was reading some papers and making some corrections. She had pushed aside the Empire State Building and Manny to make room. Manny had fallen over and the Empire State Building was leaning precariously against my computer monitor. "Good morning Madeline, make yourself at home."

Sure it was sarcastic, but did she have to knock over Manny?

"Good morning, Dr. Porter. I came by to give you my final report and to let you know that I have found no evidence of food tampering. This is a simple case. All the pieces fit together. You don't need to agree, but my report will close the matter."

"How can you close the matter when we don't know what happened yet?"

"Dr. Porter, I have 25 years of experience in cases just like this. The facts are not in doubt. I've come across doctors like you in the past. You want to ignore the facts, the procedures and the methods that allow us to make scientific conclusions. You accuse me of ignoring the facts to stick to my theory. At least I have a theory."

"I am not going to sign that report until I am satisfied that we can explain all of the facts."

"I realize that you are new and that this has been a difficult week for you. I came here to offer the olive branch and give you a chance to recover."

"I think you came here to make me sign." She was gathering her stuff and standing up. She turned toward me and smiled.

"Dr. Porter, I spoke with the Secretary this morning and told her that you were under a lot of stress. I explained to her that my theory fit all of the facts and that you had no facts to back you up. She agreed with me that it was important to end this investigation and stop needless speculation about terrorism." The glow on her face was one of triumph.

"The report will be released today by CDC and State at 8:00 a.m. Washington time. That will be in eight hours. It does not need your signature." She walked past me and turned for a parting shot. "Your desk is a mess."

She was right on two counts. The desk was a mess and I didn't have any real evidence of anything but a tragic accident. The bureaucracy was moving to seal the leak, and I wouldn't be able to convince anyone to keep the investigation open without more evidence. Dr. Lessing was in her element, and she was outmaneuvering me easily. I was an amateur, and as Billy said, I was new and had pissed her off. There was really only one thing to do. I picked up the phone and dialed the Marine Security Guard.

"Post One this is Gunnery Sergeant Cruz."

I thought that was a good omen. "Cruz, this is Dr. Porter. What time does your shift end?"

"Morning, Doc. I'm off duty at 0800. In five minutes. Why?"

"I need your help. Do you know where they are keeping the food from the barbecue?"

"Yeah, Doc, it's in freezers in the basement. I helped Dr. Lessing put it there. Why?"

"We need to help Travis one more time. Bring the keys and meet me when you get off duty."

He paused and I could tell he was wondering if it was a good idea to help me. I was about to lie, and tell him the Ambassador wanted me to do this, when he spoke again.

"I'll be there at 08:01"

Chapter 13

The storage area was in the basement and down a clean, well-lit corridor. Cruz led the way and I followed. He had not said anything since we left the health unit. I hadn't warned him of the consequences of our actions because I wasn't really sure what the consequences would be. The Ambassador had asked me to investigate and that was what I was doing. Dr. Lessing was in charge, and maybe I should have just asked her to see the food, but she had not been acting very collaboratively. She was definitely mad at me, but she was not out to get me. We just didn't agree about her conclusions. Besides if she had really talked to the Secretary of State, she had the influence to send in any report she wanted and the Ambassador could not stop her. That didn't matter as long as I could find something that could refute her theory. Cruz spoke. "Thanks for letting me come along, Doc."

"I'll tell anyone who asks that I ordered you to come."

"Why do you say that, Doc?"

"I'm not sure Dr. Lessing will be happy when she finds out."

"I don't like that …"

He used a noun that is not uttered in most American Embassies, even by Marines. It was a word that has not lost its ability to shock and it rhymes with punt. I was starting to like Cruz. We stopped in front of an unmarked door and he took a couple of keys from his pocket. The steel door opened into a large square room that had overhead fluorescent lights and several large freezers. There were no shelves or furniture except a small desk by the door with an aluminum chair. Opposite the door was a sink area with an eyewash station. The freezers were all sealed with a sticker on the door. The sticker said that the freezers were not to be opened unless Dr. Lessing was present. I walked over to the freezer nearest the door and opened it, after breaking the seal.

"You're in deep now, Doc." Cruz laughed and stood behind me. "What are we looking for?"

"I don't know exactly." I reached into the freezer and immediately wished I had brought some gloves. The freezer was packed with several dozen small plastic bags and had the mild scent of onions. Each one was labeled with a number and a description of what was in the bag. Each shelf was well organized with the bags neatly placed in rows. The labels seemed more like a shopping list than clues to an investigation that could involve terrorists. Lettuce, onions, cheese, hamburger patties, buns, chips, paper plates and cups were all present. Everything would be tested, if it hadn't been already, for the E. coli. "We need to find the inventory list, otherwise this will take too long."

"How much time do we have, Doc?'

"Probably not much. All of this stuff will be going back to the States soon, probably today, maybe this morning."

We both looked at the desk by the door. There were blank labels, empty plastic bags and markers on the top of the desk. There was a drawer in the center of the desk. It contained several pens, a few pencils and some tape. I spoke. "The inventory must be on a computer, probably in Dr. Lessing's office in CDC. Without her password we couldn't get to it."

"Doc, maybe we should just take the time and go through each piece until we find what we're looking for."

"That might take too long."

"What other choice do we have unless you can hack her computer?" Cruz smiled and seemed very relaxed. Doing something to help Travis was relieving his anger and stress. Doing anything was better than doing nothing. Cruz reached into the drawer and moved the stuff around looking for something. "Doc, this government pen has just leaked all over my hand."

He moved over to the sink and started to clean up. I stood looking at the six freezers and tried to figure out what to do next. The answer was here. We just needed to find it. Six freezers holding hundreds of bits of food were the obstacle we needed to overcome. I moved to the freezer we had opened and eased the door back.

"Doc!" Cruz was carrying a wastebasket over to me. I thought he must have dropped his wallet in there.

"What is it?" I was a little annoyed, not at him, but at me for not having a better plan.

"Check this out." He was holding up a handful of papers that had been torn in half and stained with what looked like coffee. Well, coffee or blood. They were hard to tell apart when dried on paper. "I was just washing up. Turns out the ink won't come out. I threw my towel at the trash but missed. I picked it up and when I slam dunked it, I saw these."

He held the papers out to me. The title said it all. "Inventory List for the E. coli Investigation at the US Embassy Addis Ababa Ethiopia compiled by Dr. Madeline Lessing. List and contents of shipment property of the US Government."

"Good work Marine. I'm glad you're not better at basketball."

"Travis used to come out with his Mom and watch us play. One time I was shooting a foul shot and he called my name. I missed the shot. Maybe he's watching now, Doc."

"Maybe."

I believe in being haunted, but not in ghosts. The loss of my wife had haunted me for years but she never visited me as an apparition. The inventory list was in bad shape.

"What do we need to find, Doc?"

"The cooked meat and condiments placed on the burgers were positive for E. coli. The uncooked meat and condiments that had not come in contact with the cooked meat were negative for E. coli."

"That doesn't make sense, Doc. If the meat was the source, the E. coli should be in the uncooked meat."

"You're right, unless it was only some of the meat that was contaminated and by coincidence that was the only meat that was cooked."

"That is about as likely as finding bird shit under a cuckoo clock."

"Freezer three holds the meat, condiments, buns and plates that were not used."

We looked around and found the freezer next to the sink. I broke the seal and looked inside. Again, dozens of plastic bags confronted us. They had been placed in a haphazard fashion with no seeming order or reason. There was something else that confronted us. The freezer did not smell like onions. "Do you smell that, Cruz?" He leaned in and took a deep breath through his nose.

"Smells like shit, Doc."

"E. coli gives feces its characteristic odor."

He was not impressed by my scientific observation and just looked at me like that was a piece of information he didn't need to know. One of the bags on the top shelf had a jagged tear in the plastic that must have torn as it was placed on the shelf. Some of the plastic bag material was hanging from a loose screw in the ceiling of the freezer. The outer bag, placed by Dr. Lessing, was torn but the inner bag put on at the bakery seemed intact.

I asked Cruz. "Where did the buns come from?"

"They were flown in special, fresh from Frankfurt." I held the bag up. There was knocking at the door. I turned to look at Cruz. He just smiled and held up the two keys. "We got a little while yet, Doc. These are the only two keys to this room in the Embassy."

The knocking got louder and more insistent. They must have heard us talking. Time was not something we had in abundance. As I held the bag up, I could definitely smell the foul sewer aroma of the bacteria. That would make sense. Dr. Lessing wouldn't have checked

88

for E. coli on fresh buns. Baking would have killed any bacteria. How did they get contaminated?

"Dr. Porter, are you in there?" It was Dr. Lessing. I don't know how she knew we were down there, but I didn't think she would be pleased about us disrupting her chain of evidence. We had a little while, since, as Cruz said, we had the only keys. Besides, I was just doing what I had been asked to do by the Ambassador.

"Gunnery Sergeant Cruz, are you in there? This is Agent Solomon. I want you to open this door."

Agent Solomon? Why would he be down there with Dr. Lessing? She must have been telling him things were wrapped up and that I was delaying the successful conclusion of the investigation. Cruz leaned into me and whispered. "I can't hear a thing, Doc, can you?" I shook my head and wondered how long it would be before they got the Defense Attaché.

"Gunnery Sergeant Cruz, this is Colonel Chan. I am issuing you a direct order to open this door. I know you can hear me."

Cruz looked at me and wanted to know what to do. They could only fire me but they could court-martial and dismiss him. It would have been better if he had waited outside, but then I would have never stumbled across the inventory list. Grabbing the bag of buns, I headed for the sink and spoke to Cruz. "Open the door."

"Are you sure, Doc?"

At the sink, I ripped open the outer bun bag, taking care taking care to keep the inner bag intact. The bag held eight buns. Cruz walked to the door and opened it with his keys. I could hear it swing open and several people come into the room. I couldn't see anything wrong with the bag, but the sewer smell was stronger once the outer bag was removed. The mouth of the bag had a blue twist tie that was easy to undo. Dumping the frozen buns into the sink made them clatter like stones. I put the open bag under the faucet and turned on the tap to fill the bag. As soon as it was full, I turned around to face the door.

"What are you doing? You are destroying valuable data and tampering with a closed investigation." It was Dr. Lessing..

I could see DCM Lawrence, Agent Solomon, Colonel Chan and Billy Spencer in the room as well. Cruz looked subdued, and everyone else everyone else looked mad or confused. The top of the bun bag, full of water, was in my left hand and I twisted the bottom with my right. Four small holes on both sides of the bag sprayed small jets of water. The bags had been tampered with, and E. coli had been injected into the buns. It explained why cooking had not killed the bacteria and why the uncooked meat did not contain the E. coli. I couldn't resist saying it.

"Your theory has some holes in it, Madeline."

Chapter 14

After showing Dr. Lessing and a skeptical Agent Solomon the holes, Billy and I examined the rest of the bun bags. We found three more with holes. Dr. Lessing kept those. The buns in the sink were frozen, but one had split into its familiar upper and lower halves and in the middle of the bun was a small pinpoint area of dark brown. Even in the semi-thawed bun, it smelled like feces. Everyone in the room came over to the sink to look at the bags and smell the buns. Cruz was back on duty outside the door to keep anyone else from the Embassy coming into the room.

The march up to the Ambassador's office was kind of fun. DCM Lawrence led the way and I was second and the rest trudged up behind us. Cruz and I were elated, but for different reasons. He was glad we were doing something for Travis and I was happy because I had proved Dr. Lessing wrong. I know it was petty, but showing her that she had rushed to judgment made me feel good. Her orderly universe had been turned on its head, and she could live in my world for a little while.

I explained to the Ambassador what Cruz and I had found in the basement. Dr. Lessing explained that the altered bags would be shipped to the FBI and CDC for further investigation. The buns in the bags would be tested here for E. coli., but even Dr. Lessing conceded that based on the preliminary evidence they would be positive. As my initial elation wore off, I realized that this didn't tell us how the bacteria had been introduced into the buns, by whom, or where it had happened. The Ambassador spoke. "So I think I understand what you are saying, Dr. Porter. The buns were tampered with and were the source of the infection?"

"That is what the evidence shows, Mr. Ambassador."

"Was this a deliberate act or could this have happened by accident during the manufacturing process or in transit?"

It was a good question.

"An accident seems unlikely to me, since the holes were very symmetrical. I don't see how the buns could have come in contact with the bacteria at the bakery. I would assume the buns did not come into contact with any meat during shipping, and even if they did it is hard to explain the holes."

The Ambassador was sitting at his desk. I was standing in front of him with one of the offending bags lying between us. Dr. Lessing was to my right. Even though I had shown that her initial theory was flawed, she was not upset, at least not on the surface. She held the pen in her left hand so tightly that her knuckles were as white as the inside of the buns. The DCM, Agent Solomon and Billy were behind us. DAT Chan and Cruz had been thanked and dismissed by the Ambassador when we reached his office. The Ambassador's face was red and the gray hair on his head was getting messed up as he continually ran his fingers through it. With an expression of acute dyspepsia, he looked directly at me and spoke. "I don't suppose you have any idea who did this."

"I wish I did."

"Dr. Lessing, do you agree with Dr. Porter?"

"We will need to culture and DNA sequence the bacteria to make sure it was the same strain as the one that caused the illness. I think Dr. Porter has done an excellent job for someone who is not trained in epidemiology. His unorthodox methods will win him no prizes, but he has helped me see a new and unexpected way to understand this terrible incident."

She was much better than I had imagined. The recovery she made was amazing. In the basement freezer room, she had been on the verge of assaulting me. The self-control she possessed was far above anything I could ever hope to have. It was no wonder she had a picture of the President on her wall and could get the Secretary of State on the phone. In my irrational and uncertain world, control was only an illusion.

"Mr. Ambassador, I need to call the Director and let him know that this was not an accident and that we could be facing a wider threat."

"I agree, Agent Solomon, I will brief the Secretary. Dr. Lessing, I know you have work to do on the report and getting the evidence packed up. Dr. Porter, could you brief Ms. Gonsalves on the developments?"

It would be nice to see her again. The DCM touched my elbow and said. "I will show you up to her office."

The Ambassador stood up and buttoned his coat before he addressed us again. "Well, I think we all have some work to do. I want to be kept up to speed on any new developments. Dr. Porter, if you plan on any other unusual missions to the bowels of the Embassy or anywhere else, let me or the DCM know about it first." The Ambassador ended the meeting and we filed out of his office and headed in various directions.

DCM Lawrence stayed next to me as we walked. "Good work, Dr. Porter. I thought this was all taken care of and wrapped up. Now I see that things are darker than I could have ever imagined. What do you think made the holes in the bag?'

"It could have been a syringe or a pipette or maybe a needle."

"Interesting. Shall we go downstairs? Have you been to the CIA station before?"

"I know it seems longer, but I've only been here a couple of days and I've been busy."

"Of course, that was a stupid thing to ask."

We walked out the door of the reception area outside the Ambassador's office and into the hallway. Passing the elevator, we went to a stairwell down the hallway. The DCM swiped his badge across a pad next to the stairwell door and the electric lock clicked open. He opened the door and held it for me. The DCM made sure the door was shut and followed me. At our floor, the DCM swiped his badge again to unlock the door. We entered a new room that was about eight feet square with industrial carpet and another door opposite the one we had come through. The white walls had no adornment, and without the camera or the doorbell, I would have thought we were in the wrong place. "Dr. Porter, do you know how to get into any CIA station anywhere in the world?" His eyes were almost mirthful when he asked the question because I had no idea. The course at the FSI had mentioned the CIA but basically said don't bother them. They had never told us how to get into their space at the Embassy. He moved to the button next to the door and pushed it. A chime sounded and then a buzz to let us know the door was unlocked. "You just have to ring the doorbell. If they don't want you to enter, they just won't answer. She knows you are coming and can show you back so you won't get lost."

He gave me a friendly smile, opened the door for me and patted me on the back. I felt like my Dad was sending me off to school. I walked through the door and was greeted by a young woman in her twenties. She was short, brunette, with a pageboy cut and wearing a purple flower print dress with low heels.

"Dr. Porter, I'm Emily. The DCOS will see you in just a minute. Can I get you some coffee?"

DCOS was Deputy Chief of Station, the number two person of the CIA in Addis. The room was rectangular with a couch and a small coffee table opposite Emily's desk. There were pictures of the American West on the walls and a current *Time* and two day old *Wall Street Journals* on the table.

"That would be great. Thank you." I sat down on the couch, suddenly very tired. It was very comfortable, soft and used. It was warm, too. It had been cold in the freezer room and going through all the bags had given me a chill. Plus, I was coming down off the high of finding the bags. What had I really proven? I had no idea where to go next. Emily seemed to be taking awhile with the coffee. I just put my head back and rested my eyes.

The laughter woke me. It was Ms. Gonsalves. "Well, you must be tired. I could hear you snoring all the way from my office."

I didn't know what to say and didn't really remember where I was. She was standing next to the couch and wearing a white blouse and dark skirt with her arms across her chest. Her dark eyes were narrow but friendly. I wondered if she was single. "Sorry about that. I haven't been getting much sleep."

"That's OK, Doc. Come into my office."

"Call me Zack."

"Ok, Zack, if you call me Felicity." With a smile, she turned around and led the way through a doorway and into a hall. Her skirt was tight, but not too tight, and she looked very good going down the hallway. Moving with confidence while looking over her shoulder and smiling, her body was smooth and athletic. It was the movement of ease and sexuality. "Here we are. Have a seat."

I sat in one of two chairs in front of her desk while she sat behind the desk. The room was not large, but was well arranged. Her UC Berkeley diploma hung behind her desk on the wall and next to it was a slightly crooked certificate from a cooking school. The desk held a picture of an attractive Asian woman and a tall bearded Italian, or Spanish, looking man with Felicity in a cap and gown. The same group was in another picture taken in Yosemite and a third showed them near the Golden Gate Bridge. It must be her parents. Another picture showed two two dark-haired men, who looked like her brothers, standing in front of the famous Las Vegas strip sign. A Moscow guidebook and a Russian phrasebook were next to the pictures on her desk. The bookcase was filled but the books were slightly tilted and not arranged in any special order. "So, Zack, I guess you had a breakthrough this morning."

"Better a breakthrough than a breakdown."

She smiled politely. It was lame. Should I be flirting? Was that against CIA rules and was I really ready for that?

"The DCM gave me a call soon after they found you. Well, actually he called me before that. He wanted to know where you were. Why do you think he would call me?" She was flirting now. Or was this the way they taught her to get the information she needed?

"Well, you spies know everything, right?" I smiled in spite of myself. There was a sense of the unreal. How often do you get to be interviewed by a beautiful woman who works for the CIA?

"The CIA doesn't employ spies. They employ Intelligence Officers." She had turned serious and I thought I had already made a fumble. But then she winked and let me off the hook.

"Keep my employer under your hat. Not everybody knows."

"All of your secrets are safe with me." It was my turn to wink. She was sitting with her elbows on the desk and her hands clasped in front of her chin. Somehow her tight blouse had come slightly open and I could see a crucifix on her chest. If the chain broke Christ might fall into the valley of her breasts. She must be Catholic. It always seemed strange to me that a good Catholic girl would wear a crucifix and a low-cut blouse to accentuate her breasts. Isn't that a mixed message?

She caught me looking. There wasn't recrimination in her eyes as I looked back at the scar on her face. She lowered her hands from her chin and rested them on the table as she leaned forward slightly. It was almost imperceptible but it made her breasts even fuller. I was either being seduced or being interrogated. It felt good either way. "So, Zack, how did you know those buns were contaminated by a person or persons unknown?"

"I didn't. I just knew that the story Dr. Lessing was pitching wasn't the whole truth." She kept silent to see if I would go on. Her smile and a slight nod of the head were all the encouragement I needed.

"The meat was the key. Cooked meat showed the bacteria, but the uncooked didn't. Only the lettuce, tomatoes and onions that were on the cooked burgers were positive for E. coli. The rest of the vegetables that had not come in contact with the cooked meat were

96

fine. The bacteria could have come from the meat or the vegetables, but it should be present in the uncooked source. We had no uncooked source."

Silence came down again in the room. Her face was placid and she was looking at me with her dark brown eyes. Not staring with a fixed gaze, but slowly moving her focus from one part of my face to another. I felt naked and was just about to break the silence when she broke the tension. "So is a tomato a fruit or a vegetable?"

"So you are beautiful, intelligent and have a sense of humor?" There was no point in denying her beauty. She knew she was attractive and had been using that to get information. A trained CIA officer should be able to outmaneuver a lowly family doc. We could admit it and move on to more important topics. I couldn't think of any more important topics though.

"Zack, do you always flatter women you hardly know?"

Putting the focus back on me was a good move.

"Once you get to know me, you'll know I never flatter anyone."

She smiled what seemed to be a very genuine smile and flushed. Could she be embarrassed? It was probably some kind of super-secret CIA training. Maybe she could control her autonomic nervous system and cause herself to flush when she wanted to appear embarrassed. "So what's the next step in your investigation?"

"I don't have a next step. FBI and CDC or maybe you will determine the next step."

"Me. I'm just a lowly CIA officer." The professional was playing with me again but in a pleasant fashion. I wondered if mice ever enjoyed it when the cat played with them before they were eaten. Probably not, but I was enjoying this and didn't want the questioning to end. It was clear, I was being interrogated. She might have been gathering data for the investigation, but I hoped she was interested in me as well. "I don't have any more questions. Is there anything you wanted to ask me?"

"That was a very pleasant interrogation. How long have you been doing this?"

"About eight years. I got recruited out of Berkeley because of my language skills. I majored in International Relations. I always wanted to go overseas and work, so this sounded like the perfect job."

"What languages do you speak?"

"Mandarin and Portuguese. My Mom was a language instructor at the Army language institute in Monterey. She was from China and was raised speaking Mandarin. My Dad's parents were from Portugal, and my grandmother taught me when I was growing up. I think she was afraid the Mandarin would overwhelm my Portuguese blood."

"You would be a hit in Macao. How did you wind up here?"

"Just working my way up. I've been stationed in Singapore, Bangkok and here. I've never been to Macao. Officially, that is. This is the first time I've been Deputy Chief of Station." She seemed to be opening up to me, but who could tell? "How about you, Zack, how did you wind up here?"

"I needed a change. I had been in practice about 11 years in Los Angeles and just wanted to do something different."

"How does your wife feel about it?"

"I lost my wife on 9/11." Just like with Billy, as soon as I said it, I knew it was a terrible mistake. I could just say I'm single -that would be the truth. Felicity was a stranger, but I was ashamed and felt like leaving. It had made me sound guilty about something, but what was there to be guilty about?

"I'm sorry to hear that. Was that part of the reason you came out here?"

"I guess. I needed to get away from LA Places I would always associate with her and with us are no longer mine because they can longer be ours. I saw an advertisement in the *Family Medicine Journal* for a State Department Regional Medical Officer. The job would take me overseas.   Service to the nation, a chance to live abroad and to travel were the reasons I gave my partner and my patients for the new career. All of those things were good reasons to change the direction of my life, but they weren't the real reason. I needed to go far away to lose myself, and us, so that I could move on."

"It's been almost 10 years. Are you seeing someone else?"

"I'm taking it one step at a time and moving to Africa has been a pretty big step."

She just sat there and her eyes were still studying me. The look she had on her face was not pity, sadness, remorse or embarrassment. I had seen all of those over the years and knew what they looked like. There was curiosity on her face. That was bad. Curiosity brought inquiry and rehashing of the details. I was starting to panic like I had committed a crime. Africa was going to be my sanctuary and fresh start, but all I had found so far were death and questions. "Broken hearts take time to heal."

"You know from experience?" There was a slight edge to my voice. I don't think it was anger but it could have been. I was feeling cornered.

"Now who is the interrogator?" She smiled and again the tension in the room was broken. I think she was being genuine but it could all be an act. "Well, Emily will take you back down to the health unit."

She stood up and it was clear the interview was over. After crossing over to my side of the desk, she gave me an overly firm handshake. I was just turning to leave when she spoke again. "A man who will mourn the loss of a woman for ten years is a fool or a romantic. I'll find out which you are, Zack."

The smile was back on her face and it seemed friendly, but I was still disoriented. She had timed her statement perfectly because just as she finished, Emily walked into the room and I didn't have time to answer. I didn't have an answer anyway. I had been looking for one for ten years.

Chapter 15

Emily was kind enough to take me back to the health unit. We didn't say much. I was still feeling probed by Felicity. Rhonda was eating her lunch with her door closed, and Mahedere, the receptionist, was talking on the phone with her husband. I decided to go to the cafeteria to grab something to eat. It's always an adventure for a physician to eat in a cafeteria or a restaurant where they may run into patients. People are hungry for medical advice and will reveal their most intimate details in the most public of places. When I first became a physician it used to really bother me, but not anymore.

It was toward the end of the lunch hour and the tables were about half full. The cafeteria was not large and had about 20 tables with four seats each in an L shaped area with the kitchen opposite the entry door. I walked to the counter and picked up a tray, silverware and a paper napkin. As I turned to head for the food line, I ran into someone and my silverware fell noisily to the floor. Everyone was a little on edge due to the recent events, so they all turned to look at me. As soon as they saw that it was just an accident and not the start of a terrorist attack, they looked away again.

Ms. Gonsalves was next to me and had been the cause of the disruption. "I'm sorry, Zack, I didn't mean to make you drop your silverware." She bent down to pick up my silverware and I bent down to stop her. It felt weird having her pick up my mess. Our hands grasped my wayward fork at the same time, and we both held on longer than I thought socially appropriate. She smiled and let go.

"That's quite all right, it was all my fault. Can I buy you lunch?"

"Just finished."

"You must eat fast. I just left your office."

"Lots to do today. Take care." She stood looking at me, studying me for a while longer, then smiled and turned to go.

I replaced my silverware and, keeping a close eye out for rogue CIA agents, moved to the food line. They had spaghetti on the menu as well as local food. I ordered the spaghetti and was told by the very pleasant woman behind the counter that they were out of spaghetti. I next ordered the local food with the bread that rolls up like gauze. Unfortunately they were out of that as well. Apparently the only things they did have were hamburgers, which the woman told me were usually big sellers, but this week no one was buying. She assured me that the meat had been tested by Dr. Lessing of the CDC and was perfectly safe. I didn't fight it and went for the burger. After getting my coke and paying my 50 birr, about three dollars, I went to an empty table and sat down.

The hard part about getting a good burger overseas is that the buns are never right. They're always the wrong shape or size or texture. That's why they had flown the buns in for the barbecue. Ground meat is ground meat, but no one makes hamburger buns like an American bakery. The bun on my burger was chewy and so wide that it took me two bites to reach the meat.

"Hello, Doctor, do you mind if I join you?"

"No, not at all."

I lied. It was Frederick Stevenson, the management officer. He was wearing a tight white shirt, narrow tie and black flat front trousers with highly polished black shoes. He sat down with a plate of spaghetti and a bottle of Ambo, the local mineral water. I'm not sure how he got spaghetti but maybe they held some back for the management officer. He would oversee the cafeteria and would be the boss.

"It's been a tough week for you, hasn't it, Isaac?"

"Well, it has been a tough week for everyone."

"Dick Lawrence, the DCM, told me about your discovery this morning. That was quite a bit of detective work. How did you do it?"

"Lucky guess?"

102

I didn't want to go through the whole story again after having just been grilled by Felicity. Felicity was a strange name for a CIA officer and I wondered how she got it. Everyone at the CIA should have a mysterious name like Natasha or Katarina. After lunch, I would Google her and find out what I could. Eating faster so that my mouth would be full and I couldn't answer his questions, I hoped he would go away.

"It does seem strange that someone would go to the trouble of tampering with the buns. I wonder where it happened."

I kept chewing and shoveling fries into my mouth. The burger wasn't bad and had a smoky barbecue flavor but the bun was too much bread. I shrugged my shoulders in ignorance, but he was undeterred.

"Dick was very surprised. He and I don't always see things eye to eye, but he's a good DCM. We're lucky he's here because the Ambassador is not up to this challenge. I served with Dick and his wife Marisol when we were all in Ankara together. You haven't met her – she's in the states on R&R. I'm so glad he pointed out the problem with the freezer yesterday and I've already taken corrective action. He could have made a much bigger deal about it."

I kept chewing and my burger was almost gone. He kept talking and didn't seem to notice that I was eating quickly and not answering his questions.

"I guess this means the freezer wasn't the cause of the problem with Travis. Is that what your report will say, Isaac?"

I understood now. Although he and Dick were now buddies, he was worried that he could still be implicated in the final report. I just kept chewing. Why were he and Lawrence arguing inside the commissary when I overheard them? The silence was hard for him to take, so he started talking again.

"I know it's early and this morning will change things, but it would be good to know that my department wasn't responsible for the illness."

I had no more burger to eat, so feeling a little naked, I decided to answer his question.

"I won't write the final report. Dr. Lessing will do that."

"I know, Isaac, but with your, how shall I say, novel methods, I was wondering if you expected any further breakthroughs?"

Novel methods? I wondered if he had been talking to Dr. Lessing as well or if the DCM had used that phrase. My method was not according to protocol but it did get results.

"As far as I know, the investigation will be led by the FBI and CDC. I haven't been officially dismissed, but I think my investigation is at an end."

"I'm glad to know you are around and thank you for seeing Susan. She was quite upset this morning, so I told her to see you. She has been having a hard time at post and I've been trying to help her out."

"The health unit is open for everyone." I was being noncommittal since I shouldn't even acknowledge she was there unless she gave me permission.

"Did everything check out OK?"

I smiled and shook my head. "You know everything is confidential."

"Sorry, Isaac, I just was concerned about her. I know she couldn't have gotten anything. I get a thorough check every six months."

He kept eating his spaghetti. The look on his face was friendly contentment. It seemed strange that he had brought up Ms. Bell, but I think he was gloating. He wanted me to be impressed with the fact that he had slept with a vulnerable 25-year-old junior officer. Dr. Scofield, my boss in D.C., had told me before I left that the Embassies, especially in Africa, were full of liaisons between members of the Foreign Service. The communities were small, often isolated and with

104

limited recreational activities. People sought solace in the company of others. I got up and gathered my tray. He was chewing and about to wish me a good day when I let him have it.

"What were you and the DCM arguing about in the commissary before I got there?"

He choked and turned red. He reached for his Ambo and took a few big swallows. The charm was gone from his eyes and he wasn't smiling. "We weren't arguing. I don't know what you mean."

"The window was open. I heard the whole thing." I hadn't really, of course, but a little bluffing couldn't hurt and I wanted to know.

"It was nothing, Isaac. You'll have to ask Marisol or Dick. It's all over now."

"Ok, well it was good talking to you."

He just nodded his head and put down his fork. I've been in practice a long time. I've seen a lot of things. When a man has an argument that almost comes to blows with another man, money or a woman are involved. He didn't mention money.

Chapter 16

Leaving the cafeteria, I headed back to the health unit and checked in with Rhonda. There was nothing going on, and I made an executive decision to go home and get some rest before the Diplomatic Bazaar. The motor pool dispatcher said it would take about 20 minutes for my ride to be ready, so I got my briefcase and told Rhonda my plan. She looked at her watch to emphasize to me that it was not quitting time yet. I knew that and it felt good cutting out early, kind of like playing hooky at school. The few hours off would give me some time to rest, but I really just needed to get away. Africa was turning out to be far more stressful than I had anticipated and far more complicated.

I waved to the Marine guard as I left. He smiled and waved back. It wasn't Cruz, but he seemed like he knew who I was. The day was beautiful. The Embassy is on the north end of the city near a national park. The mountains are very close and covered with pines, eucalyptus and what looked like juniper or cedar. There were no clouds and the sun was very strong even with the low humidity. In school they always tell you that the sun's rays are more powerful near the Equator, but frankly I never believed it. I could feel the difference now; the sun was brighter and warmer than in LA. The horn of the Suburban gave me a start and I quickly moved to the passenger door and opened it.

"Hey, Doc, sneaking out a little early?" It was Billy Spencer. I thought I must have the wrong car.

"I gave myself a Doctor's note to take the rest of the afternoon off."

He laughed. "Damn, I wish I had gone to medical school."

"Billy, I called a car from motor pool, so I think you're here for someone else."

"I cancelled the car from motor pool. The Ambassador asked me to keep an eye on you. He's afraid you're going to go off on a, how did he put it, an 'unauthorized and unorganized investigation.'"

It was my turn to laugh. "I thought I was authorized to investigate?"

"You are, Doc, it is just that everybody likes Dr. Lessing's organized methods better than yours. You tend to stir up the pot."

"Well, you can tell the Ambassador that I'm off the investigation and that I'm going home for a siesta."

"Well, get in then. I can definitely drive you home as long as you promise to stay there until I come get you tonight for the Bazaar."

"Sounds like a plan." I climbed up into the Suburban and closed the heavy armored door, being careful not to smash my leg in the process. When I took my evasive driving and anti-terrorism course they kept stressing the weight of doors on the armored vehicles. It made me paranoid about getting my foot or leg caught in one. He waited until I was buckled in and we headed for the gate. The local guards saluted us as we left. Billy let some oncoming traffic pass and pulled out. Just as we were making our turn, a battered blue and white Toyota minivan that looked about 20 years old pulled from the curb and came within a few feet of hitting us. Billy braked and turned hard at the wheel, but armored Suburbans don't handle like Aston-Martins. We avoided a collision through a last second change of direction by the minivan.

Only after we started going again down the road toward my house did Billy speak. Actually he let out a long low whistle like a boiler letting off steam. "That was a dreaded Blue Donkey that almost hit us back there. That would be bad because I would have to fill out a bunch of paperwork. The driving around here is the worst I've ever seen. There's no order or rules. Lane lines are treated like mere suggestions and you can't depend on a rational act by the other drivers. The pedestrians are the worst, though. They'll walk right into the street and not look first. They almost dare you to hit them. Of course, if you do hit them, it is your fault even if you were obeying all the rules."

"It reminds me of coming out of Dodger Stadium after Opening Day."

He laughed and looked at me with his sunglass covered face. His collar was tight and his tie was loosened. After a few minutes of silently driving down Entoto road past Addis Ababa University, he relaxed in his seat and took one hand off the wheel. "You did a good job today, Doc, even if your methods were a bit wild. When Cruz opened that door, I was afraid I was going to have to arrest you."

"If I need arresting, Billy, I hope you're there."

"Dr. Lessing looked like she was going to have a stroke. I have never seen her so upset."

"I never meant to upset the cart."

"Sure you did, Doc. What did Felicity Gonsalves and you discuss this morning?"

"It wasn't a conversation so much as an interrogation. She used every technique short of waterboarding."

"I bet she just turned on the charm. I think she likes you, Doc."

"She just uses charm as an interrogation technique."

I said it to cover up the fact that I hoped she did like me as much as I was getting to like her. It wasn't for Billy's benefit I said it. I could tell by the look he gave me that he didn't believe me. After a few more minutes of silence, he spoke again.

"How have you been liking your house?"

"It seems very nice, but it's too big for one person."

"I know what you mean about the size. My wife and I are in a three bedroom and our boys are off to college. It's one of the perks of living in Africa. You get a big house and domestic servants. American and other expat community members are an important source of income for the local populace. Another reason for the staff at the houses is that it cements the social hierarchy. The Ambassador will have the most staff since he entertains the most. Depending on the post, 10-15 would be considered about right for the Ambassador. Even

108

the most junior consular officer on his or her first assignment would have a maid and a cook. The Foreign Service loves order and protocol. The calming effect of organization even prevails when they are home for the weekend. Have you gotten a maid yet?"

"My gardener is bringing his niece over today to interview. I will probably hire her."

"Don't pay too much. About 1200 to 1400 birr a month for 50 hours a week should be plenty. If you pay too much, it drives up the cost for everyone else. Make sure she can speak English and teach her about hygiene. Some people here never wash their hands."

1400 birr was about $88. 50 hours a week was 200 hours per month and equaled less than 50 cents an hour. Could that be right? I could see how easy it would be even for a nice guy like Billy to fall into the colonial mindset. Although $100 a month was a lot of money here, I wasn't sure I would feel comfortable paying her so little. Not wanting to upset him, I changed the subject. "What is the Diplomatic Bazaar like?'

"It's just like Anita said, the social event of the season." He was smiling again. "Anita told me she gave you a ticket as a peace offering. Bring a bag. The French, Swiss and Italians sell cheese, which isn't always easy to get here. The Norwegians sell smoked salmon which is really good, but I like the Russian booth the best."

"Why is that?"

"Great vodka."

He winked as we pulled up to my gate and he honked the horn. Eskander peered out from the door in the gate and smiled. He went back inside the gate and the large halves opened one at a time.

Billy pulled into the driveway and stopped the Suburban. "I'll pick you up at 7. We want to get there early before everybody runs out of the good stuff."

"That would be great, Billy. I also wanted to ask you about my address. The Motorpool asked me where I lived the other day and I didn't know."

"Addis has about three to four million residents but it is really just a big village, or really a set of villages thrown together. There are no addresses. You live in Bole Homes in the Hansen house. Hansen was a CDC person who left. Just tell the driver or anybody else you live in the Hansen house. That will get them here."

"That's what the dispatcher told me the other day. It seems strange for such a big place not to have any addresses."

"Maybe someday, Doc, they will get around to it. You did a really good thing today, Doc. I'm glad to see that you ignored my advice about staying out of trouble. Watch out, though. State is not infinitely patient, even if you do get results. Remember the hierarchy."

"Thanks, Billy, see you at 7."

I got out of the Suburban and Billy backed out into the street. Eskander closed the gate. I got my keys out of my pocket and Eskander came up to my side. He smiled. "Doctor, my niece is here and would like to speak with you if it would be convenient."

"Sure Eskander, no problem."

She had been standing around the corner of the house. A small woman about 5 feet tall with an ankle-length dark brown skirt and a white top with her haired tied up with a dark brown scarf came toward me. She looked to be about 20 and was very pretty, with fine features and a high forehead. She bowed slightly and took my outstretched hand. Her grasp was very soft, but her eyes and smile were firm and friendly. I decided right then to hire her. "It is a pleasure to meet you, Dr. Porter." Her English was not accented and I was shocked. OK, maybe paranoid.

"What is your name?" I let go of her hand and she continued to smile.

110

"Kokeb. My uncle was very kind to talk to you about me. I would very much appreciate the chance to work for you. I have not done this type of work before, but I am eager to get the job."

"Where did you learn your English? It is excellent."

"I moved to New York City when I was three years old and went to school there through 2 years at the CUNY. I was to be married about three months ago and spent all of my savings to get here. Unfortunately, I found my fiancé with another woman about a week before we were to be wed." I stood there, shocked and sorry for her and very embarrassed. Why was she sharing so much? I would have given her the job any way. Eskander came over and said something in Amharic. I couldn't understand him but he must have said what I was thinking or she wouldn't have reacted as she did. She remained calm and waited for him to finish. Her weight slightly shifted onto her right leg and then she crossed her arms. "I will never be ashamed to tell the truth, Uncle. My uncle thinks I have told you too much, Dr. Porter, but I wanted you to know why I was looking for a job here."

I wish I could be so fearless about the truth.

"I think that is an admirable sentiment. Are you planning to stay here?"

"No, I think I will go back to New York and resume school. I just need enough money for the plane ticket and then I will be able to get by."

"What are you studying?"

"Believe it or not, I want to be a physician."

"How much salary do you want?"

"My uncle tells me that 1500 birr per month would be a good salary here."

"I will pay you $10 per hour for 40 hours a week, but don't tell anyone in the American community. They will be upset that I am causing inflation."

111

"Dr. Porter, that is too much. I couldn't possibly accept."

"Take it or leave it." I shrugged my shoulders and gave her a blank look. There was no way I could take advantage of her, of a potential colleague. Or maybe I liked her because she could take a loss and keep going on with her life. Or maybe it was her smile. I may be lonely and emotionally screwed up, but I have lots of money, so there was no reason to make her work for local wages.

"I will accept, Dr. Porter, but when I get back to the states I will pay you back."

"Nonsense, I'm a doctor, I can afford it. Can you start tomorrow?"

"Yes, thank you so much. My uncle said you were kind and generous."

She grasped my hand with both of hers and the tears came down her cheeks in an unembarrassed stream. Many people have told me it is cathartic, but crying never made me feel better.

Chapter 17

After putting down my briefcase, I walked up the stairs and decided that a nap would be a good idea. I went past the two empty bedrooms and into the larger one that was mine. Checking the night stand for any notes, I slipped off my shoes and fell backward onto the bed. There was a cobweb in the corner by the door, but otherwise it was just a blank ceiling. I got out my iPhone and set the alarm for an hour.

The dream must have started right after I fell asleep. It was very vivid and involved her. We were in a hotel room overlooking Central Park in New York. It could have been the Essex House or The Plaza. We were looking north and it was a beautiful day. Breakfast was set out on a table. Bacon, eggs, hash browns, toast, coffee and OJ were all arranged in a formal way. There was a yellow rose in a bud vase in the middle of the table. Is it possible to smell during a dream? I couldn't smell breakfast but the rose was fresh.

She came into the room wearing one of my shirts unbuttoned halfway down her chest. Her blonde hair fell to her shoulders, and she looked great. Exercising two or three times a week with a trainer kept her in shape but not too muscular. Her breasts moved freely under my shirt and I could see the delicious curve of her bottom just peeking out from under the white cotton. The kiss she gave me was warm and wet. She turned on the TV and sat down to eat. I was just staring at her.

The veil of reality was beginning to slip and I knew it was a dream. A feeling of loss was coming over me. She was still there next to me and she was eating but that image was only a dim reflection of memory, not reality. A piece of scrambled egg, the only kind of eggs she would eat, had fallen onto her breast. In a moment of passion I was bending over to close my mouth around the wayward egg when she stood up and dropped her plate onto the floor. Eggs, bacon and toast splattered all over the carpet and the plate was shattered. The TV showed the South Tower collapsing.

"I have to go." She turned and was going out of the room.

As always happens in a dream, when you need to move fast, you can't. By the time I could get up, she was out of the room and gone. I kept repeating in a calm reasonable voice that she shouldn't go. Any louder and I would wake up. The entire room began to shake and I awoke to see Eskander and Kokeb standing near the bed with very concerned looks on their faces.

Eskander spoke while he reached out to touch my arm. "Are you all right Dr. Porter?"

"Yes, Eskander. I was just having a bad dream."

"You were calling out and we thought you needed help. That is why we came. Otherwise we would never disturb you."

"I'm glad you came. How did you get in? I thought you didn't have a key."

"The door was unlocked. We were very worried."

Kokeb looked at me with some understanding. Her arms were crossed and she stood at the foot of the bed. She looked small and young, yet motherly as her gaze stayed on me. I wondered if she had been able to understand what I had said. "Why did she go?" Kokeb was still looking at me but was not waiting for an answer. After a minute or two they left the room and I got up and showered. How many dreams had I had about her in 10 years? There were thousands, no doubt.

Billy was a good as his word, and was there exactly at 7. The shower had revived me more than my refreshing siesta. Eskander smiled and waved as he shut the gate behind us, but he seemed a little concerned. He wasn't the only one. Two dreams about her in the last two days. It must be the stress and the jetlag. Sleep would be better that night since I couldn't sleep any worse. "Did you get some rest, Doc?"

"Yes. I had a good rest." I didn't want to go into the screaming dream.

"You're lucky, Doc. You live very close to the hall so we'll be there in a minute. We won't miss a thing."

"Damn, I forgot my bag."

"No problem, Doc. I brought you two extra."

There were two large plastic bags on the backseat and Billy motioned with his head over his shoulder so I would notice them. I didn't really want to buy anything, but I guess the bags would make me look less like a tourist. As we turned in the parking lot of the hall, I could hear the bags slide off the back seat. The guards stopped us and looked under the car with long-handled mirrors. It was three guys in light blue camouflage uniforms. Two were looking under the car while the third held his AK-47 in his left hand with casual indifference. They waved us through, and Billy found a parking spot between a battered white Toyota Landcruiser and a battered blue and white compact car.

"That is a pretty beat-up Fiat."

He looked over at the car and smiled. "Doc, that's a Lada. It looks like a Fiat because the Soviets bought an old Fiat plant, moved it to Russia and rebranded them as Ladas."

"What's it doing here?"

"The Ethiopians were in the Soviet sphere from 1974 until the end of the Cold War. They had a revolution in 1991 and threw out the commies and have had a socialist government since then."

"They just haven't gotten rid of the Fiats."

"You got it, Doc. Of course, it is ironic that that Lada is next to a Toyota from the Russian Embassy. Don't forget the bags or your ticket."

"How do you know the Toyota is from the Russian Embassy?"

"See the plate has the CD, then 10. The initials mean Corps Diplomatique French for Diplomatic Corps. That lets the police or

115

anyone else know that the car is registered to an Embassy. The code is 10, for the Russians. Our code is 04 for the American Embassy."

"Why do they label the cars at all? Isn't that a security risk?"

"Yes, in a way. But let's face it, Doc. Neither one of us is going to be mistaken for a local. It keeps the police from harassing us. That isn't a big problem here but in some countries it can be."

He handed me the plastic bags and I got out my small paper ticket with the logo and name of the Bazaar on it. We walked toward the entrance to the hall. There was a low building that contained several turnstiles. Several eager and friendly young people from European embassies were collecting the tickets. The metal detectors were just inside the turnstiles, and we made it through without a problem.

There were several hundred people in the large plaza just outside the exhibition hall. Large lights on poles about 70 or 80 feet high illuminated the entire area as the sun had gone down about 30 minutes before. The air was fragrant with cooking meat and spices. Several booths were arranged around the open plaza and flags were draped on the fronts as identifying markers. South Africa, Namibia, Turkey and others were selling various national dishes, and people were mingling in front of the stands to get the food. "Doc, I have to go over to the American booth and serve some hot dogs. Do you want to come along?"

"I'll meet you over there in a little bit. I'm going to walk around."

"Doc, do me a favor. Stay out of trouble. The Ambassador will send me to Outer Mongolia if anything happens to you or if you pull another freezer stunt."

I held up my plastic bags and gave him a wink. "Billy, I am just a shopper tonight. Not an investigator or even a doctor."

He held his hands up in surrender. "OK, Doc. Have fun and when you get over to the American booth, I'll give you a good old-fashioned American hot dog."

He turned toward the American booth, which was opposite the entrance of the hall. I turned left into the hall. It looked like any building you would see in the States at an industrial site. It was about 30 feet high and faced with corrugated steel siding in pale brown and orange. Each side measured about 500 feet, about the size of a small warehouse or a large Wal-Mart. It had a large open space with a concrete floor and high roof with exposed steel beams.

Booths were lined up in several neat rows and there were hundreds of people walking around with shopping bags and eating various foods. It had the atmosphere of a county fair. The Norwegians were selling smoked salmon with a scrambled egg on toast for 25 Birr, and I decided to splurge on two helpings. The French were playing American hip-hop, something about boots with fur, while they were selling cheese, and all of them were wearing shirts that said "I love to speak French" in English. Several were wearing berets. The Italian booth was dominated by two large middle aged women who were selling cheese, wine and pasta. Anyone one came close was pulled into their orbit and no one left without a purchase. The Italian women were forces of nature like black holes, and I could not escape their gravitational pull. I bought some wine and pasta before I could reach escape velocity. It felt good to be pulled in and I smiled as I left.

The Belgians were selling waffles and chocolate while playing more American hip-hop, this time Fred Flintstone was going to make my bed rock, and the Mexicans next to them were selling enchiladas with rice and beans. The booth across was Kenya and it had a large selection of carved wooden figures. Elephants, rhinos, giraffes and various human figures of different sizes and wood colors were placed neatly on a large Persian carpet. I bought a small elephant that was carved from black wood for 150 Birr.

Wandering up and down the aisles, I relaxed for the first time since I had arrived in Addis. The UK booth was just ahead of me. Several people were looking through a stack of magazines and books

117

while others were looking at bottles of Scotch whiskey. That reminded me, I had purchased some Scotch on the plane, duty free, but I had neglected to get it from under the seat in front of me. I wondered who had it now. After my purchase of some Scotch, I walked away from the UK booth and kept moving. The booths of Iran and Cuba were across from each other and the people in them were very friendly. I spoke to them only for a little while. Without official diplomatic relations between our countries, I wasn't sure if I should interact at all. Billy would be quite upset if I caused an International Incident.

The Russians had a large booth, and many of them were dressed in traditional and colorful folk outfits. The men and women were wearing white peasant blouses with embroidery and bright red or blue trim. There were several refrigerators in their booth much like you would see at the LA County Fair. The machines were about five feet tall but only about two feet wide. Looking like they would be appropriate for a mobile home or a college dorm room, the refrigerators would not impress the average American. As I approached the booth, a man about 50 with unruly gray hair, a large red nose on a rugged face and a peasant shirt came toward me. "Good evening. American? My name is Alexander. What would you like to buy? It all goes to charity." His smile and demeanor were disarming. He was taller than I was and seemed to be in great shape. He wasn't drunk, either, so my stereotype of Russian men was being shattered.

"Hello, my name is Isaac Porter, and I work at the American Embassy."

"Excellent, what do you do at the Embassy, Isaac?"

His English was perfect and had only a slight accent. The State Department has strict rules about interacting with Russians, but it was harmless enough. "I am the Doctor. How about you, Alexander?"

His eyes widened and he looked somewhat shocked. He dropped his voice before he answered. "I am so sorry to hear of the death of the young boy. It is a tragedy. Is it true it was food poisoning?"

"It is unclear what the cause was, but it seems to be linked to the barbecue."

"I am sorry that your start in Addis has been so hard. It is hard to lose a patient that young. I am the doctor at the Russian Embassy, so we are colleagues"

I was going to ask him how he knew about my start in Addis and the death, but before I could speak an attractive woman of about 45 came up to us and threw her arm around Alexander. Her blonde hair was in braids and her peasant blouse matched Alexander's. Both of them were wearing wedding rings on the ring finger of their right hands as is the custom in Russia. She whispered in his ear and he turned to her and then to me. "Isaac, my wife says that I should introduce you to her because you are so good looking. She has an eye for handsome men! Irina, let me introduce you to Isaac Porter, the new American Embassy doctor. Isaac, my wife Irina."

She had very deep blue eyes and a friendly round face that took on a look of pity after Alexander had said I was the doctor. Her hands reached out to mine and her voice was low when she spoke. "It is so hard to believe little Travis is gone. We met him, Bob and Jennifer when they came over to our house with Felicity. It was only two weeks ago. Now he is gone to God."

I knew that Bob and Felicity worked for CIA but what they were doing with the Russians I could not guess. Were Alexander and Irina working with them? How did it all fit together? "I just arrived a few days ago. Did you know Bob and Jennifer well?"

Irina paused before she spoke and she did not look at Alexander but it felt like she wanted to try. "Not well, we had met a few times at various functions. They are such a nice couple and Travis was so cute. How did it happen?"

"Irina, give Isaac some time to shop. He cannot know what happened yet. It is too soon. Isaac, if you need anything from us, let me know."

119

"You can be of help right away. I need to get some Vodka for a friend"

Alexander smiled and turned toward the table next to us. There were about 30 bottles of Stolichnaya and Standart Vodka in two somewhat uneven rows. "You have come to the right country! Take these bottles as a gift from me and Irina." He held up two of the Standart bottles in his hands. I didn't know quite what to do. There was probably a rule against accepting gifts from Russians, but I did not want to seem rude and he was a colleague.

"Thank you, Alexander, but I would like to pay. It all goes to charity after all."

"Nonsense, Isaac, consider this my welcome gift to you. Irina will be insulted if you do not take it. Please do not embarrass me in front of her."

On cue, Irina looked at me with mild scolding. I was beaten and put the vodka in the bag. Alexander gave me his card and I promised to stay in touch. The card read: Alexander Lebed, Medical Officer Russian Embassy Addis Ababa Ethiopia in English with Cyrillic underneath that must have said the same thing. The crowd around the booths was getting larger and as I walked away from the Russians, I spotted Felicity looking at me from across the aisle. I started to move in her direction, but a group of Chinese diplomats crossed between us and I lost sight of her. When I got to the spot where she had been standing, she was gone.

Chapter 18

I decided to exit the hall and work my way over to the American booth and see if I could ask her about the Russians. That would be a delicate conversation and I was not sure what she would say if anything. There was a large crowd around the booth and I could see several Americans selling hot dogs, Doritos and peanut butter. There was a large barbecue off to the side and 50 people were in a neat line waiting for their grilled dogs.

I didn't see Felicity come up behind me. "Well, let me see what you bought, Zack." She was wearing tight black jeans, white running shoes with a pink swoosh and a tight white V-neck sweater. The sexuality she gave off was a mixture of exotic and home town. I handed over my bag without a word and waited for her verdict. "Two bottles of Scotch, two bottles of Vodka, a half a pound of cheese, some pasta and a hand carved elephant? You really are a bachelor."

It was a true statement and for the first time in a long time I was feeling like a normal single man.

"Just the essentials for survival here in Addis."

"I will have to take you out to dinner tomorrow; otherwise you might starve to death or die of cirrhosis." The smile on her face was both happy and concerned. It would be great to go to dinner with her but I knew it would be just more interrogation. Anita walked up next to me and Felicity handed my bag to her. I wanted to ask Felicity about the Russians but wasn't sure I should in front of Anita. "Look what our Doctor bought for himself, Anita. Not exactly health food."

Anita took my bag and peered inside. She laughed and handed it back to me. "Looks like the makings of a good party for 2."

Like the cavalry in the movie *Stagecoach*, Billy arrived to save the day. "Here's your hot dog, Doc. How have you been doing with the Bazaar?"

"It reminds me of the LA County Fair. All we need is a Ferris wheel and a Country band."

121

They laughed. Billy's was a genuine laugh that included his eyes and his belly. Anita laughed with a strict politeness and never let her face betray her true feelings about Country bands. Felicity laughed discretely and was looking intently at my face, trying to read it for information she needed. She had seen me talking to the Russians. She was relaxed, but I felt like the questioning she had given me in the office was about to start again. It had happened quickly, but I was beginning to want to spend more time with her under any circumstances.

"You know, that's not a bad idea about a Ferris wheel. I will get the Ambassador to look into it for next year." Anita must never stop being the diplomat's wife. That must be hard, never being able to express your true opinion. To always be aware of what you were saying and to never get out of line.

"So what did you buy, Doc? Did you find the Russians?"

"Yes, Billy, I did and they were very friendly. I met Alexander Lebed and his wife Irina. He is the doctor at the Russian Embassy. They said they knew you, Felicity."

I was trying to catch her off guard but she just gave me a small smile and brushed the hair off her face with her left hand. The scar was barely visible in the dim light next to the booth. "You would be surprised at how many people I know, Zack."

There was no awkwardness in her reply and I couldn't tell if she was upset, amused or indifferent. The only reaction I didn't want was indifference. Billy took my bag and opened it. "Doc, you're going to do very well in the Foreign Service. Where did you get the Scotch?"

"From a Scotsman at the UK booth."

"Billy, you are not actually encouraging his behavior? He should be setting a better example. Anita and I were just chastising him." Felicity was acting upset, but the wink she gave me made me feel like I had already taken a hit on the Scotch. There was a warm sensation from my groin to my chest and neck. I hoped I wasn't blushing.

"You're right, Felicity. I should take these evil spirits off your hands, Doc. I wouldn't want Felicity and Anita to be mad at me."

"Oh, no, you don't, Mr. Spencer. The good doctor may need these if I ever come over for a drink."

It was Felicity again. If she ever came over for a drink? Dinner and drinks? Billy was right. She was interested in me. I hoped it was for me and not for any information I could give her about what happened to Travis. Falling in love with someone trained in interrogation and deceit would be hard. How would you know when you were being played for intelligence?

She took the bag from Billy's hands and gave it back to me. As she handed it off, she grasped my hand with both of hers and gave me a slight but seductive squeeze. She was very good. I would already tell her anything she wanted to know.

Billy spoke. "Doc, you've got to go out back behind the hall. There are several local vendors and you might find some stuff you need for your house. They've got all kinds of pots, pans, jugs, brooms, you name it."

Felicity kept her eyes on me when she answered. "That's the first sensible thing you have said Billy. Don't you think, Anita?'

"There are many very useful things back there. The prices are very reasonable as well."

"Would any of you like to come along?" The only one I wanted to answer yes was Felicity, but I didn't want to be rude.

Billy winked at me and answered. "Doc, Anita and I have to finish cooking some dogs, isn't that right, Anita? But I bet Ms. Gonsalves would love to go with you."

It was like having your big brother talk the homecoming queen into going with you to the prom.

"You want me to go out behind the hall with this handsome doctor, who conveniently has several bottles of alcohol? Mr. Spencer, I

123

am shocked! Unfortunately, I have to meet with the Ambassador and sell some comic books. Will you be all right by yourself, Dr. Porter?"

The flirtation between us was refreshing and frightening. She was so sexual and available. It felt dangerous, but I had nothing to lose really. "I think I should be OK, but if anything happens, I will send up a flare."

They all said goodbye and Billy pointed me in the right direction. I passed back though the hall and thought about buying some Scotch for Billy but decided I would get it just before I left. That way I wouldn't have to lug it around. At least one hand should be free in case there was something useful behind the hall to buy. Things that were useful were often heavy.

The crowds were even thicker and a local school group was singing Edelweiss from *The Sound of Music* on a stage in the middle of the hall. They sounded very good and I stopped to listen for a minute. As I continued through the hall, I didn't see any other Americans but felt like I was being watched. Perhaps Felicity was following me after all. She would be trained to do that sort of thing.

The area behind the hall was not as well lit, but was very busy with the smaller, more irregular stalls of local merchants. There were pots, pans, blankets, local vegetables and bootleg DVDs on sale. The Ethiopians were doing brisk business with the large crowd of expatriates and it was loud. The atmosphere was busy, pleasant and more exotic than the interior of the hall. I walked down the rows of the marketplace and found some clay pots. Hanging from irregular wooden poles, the same kind used in the scaffolding on the buildings in town, the pots were red and came in various sizes. The pot stall was at the end of the row and very close to the street. Some small pots would be great to start some tomato plants.

A car on the street backfired with a loud crack, and the pot near my head exploded. Some of the shards of the pot hit my face and I could tell that I had been cut. I turned toward the street and realized that everyone around me was on the ground. The only thing I could think was that they must have fainted. The second backfire from the street was associated with the demise of a very large pot near my right leg. Again I could feel some of the shards hit me but I didn't think I was cut this time. My jeans felt intact. This was very strange. There were rapid footsteps coming up behind me and I knew someone was running toward me. I felt myself running before I realized I had started. Something primitive in my brain had told me to run and my consciousness was just now catching up.

There was also a slow realization coming into my head that I had been shot at twice and now someone was chasing me. Actually they were gaining rapidly, the altitude of Addis was making me very out of breath even though I had run only a short distance. It was not so much the fact that they were going to catch me, but the fact that they were going to catch me from behind that upset me. The thought of being taken down like a Zebra was annoying. When I stopped, turning away from the street and toward my pursuer, a third shot went by my head. It is true you can hear a bullet pass if it is close enough. It made a strange buzzing sound like a hummingbird or large bee. I couldn't see who was lunging at me. It was dark and I was confused, and they hit with such force that I was knocked backward onto the ground. The only thing I heard before I lost consciousness was the breaking of glass.

Chapter 19

Darkness. Movement. Being lifted and being put down. Voices before I was completely conscious. Some were in Amharic, some were in English, but all of them were unintelligible. I could tell I was on my back on the ground, but I wasn't sure where I was or why I was there. Someone was holding the back of my head and somebody else was on my right arm. Was that an accident or was I being held down?

"We need to get him to a hospital." It was a voice in English and close to my head. It might have been female, it was hard to tell.

"No hospital." That voice was very close and very familiar. It was male, but sounded groggy and confused.

"Doc, are you OK?' That was Cruz. My eyes opened and I saw him kneeling close to my right side. Two uniformed Ethiopian police were at my feet next to Billy. Felicity was kneeling above me and holding my head. I could feel some of my blood in her hands and my shirt was soaked in Scotch.

"Cruz?'

"Yeah, Doc, it's me."

"Get off my arm."

"He sounds better already." Felicity smiled at me as she spoke and her face was beautiful even upside down. The scar stood out with the flashlight that someone was holding. Cruz shifted his leg off my arm and I took that as a sign to sit up. I almost hit Felicity on the way and when I got there my head really started to ache. My vision was OK, and I reached around to the back of my head. There was an irregular laceration about three inches long and the sticky feel of coagulating blood. Luckily there was no skull fracture that I could feel. There were several people around, including the Ambassador, Anita and Agent Solomon. It was starting to come back to me and I remembered that someone had been shooting at me.

"Why were you chasing me, Cruz?"

He looked at Billy and then at me. Cruz didn't look happy. "Doc, when you are getting shot at, you shouldn't just stand there like a statue. I was chasing you to knock you down before you got your head blown off. You're the only doctor we have, even if you are kind of a dumbass." He was smiling now and it was a compliment, sort of.

"Sorry, Cruz, this is my first experience in this area. So you were chasing me, but who was doing the shooting?"

Billy moved forward and bent over to look me in the eye. "The shots came from a construction site across the street. We found some 7.62 mm shell casings and a recently fired AK-47 there. No shooter, though."

They must have moved pretty fast to get over there while I was knocked out. "How long was I out for?"

Felicity spoke with a concerned look. "You were out for about five minutes and then you've been babbling for the last ten to fifteen minutes. You kept telling us to get away from the TV." I had been out longer than I thought. I must have been thinking about 9/11 and didn't want to see those damn buildings fall down again. The hospital was an option, but there was really no point. If there was something seriously wrong with my head, they couldn't fix it anyway. We were several thousand miles from the nearest competent neurosurgeon. "You also told Travis you were sorry."

It was Felicity again. Everyone was frowning and looked very concerned. I couldn't blame them. It sounded like I had scrambled my brain and who wants to think their doctor needs a doctor. I must have sounded like a lunatic. "I'm glad I slept through it. Just one question?"

"OK, Zack, what is it?" She was still close and over the scent of the Scotch I could smell her and she smelled good. It was a fresh outdoor scent with some floral component.

"Any of the booze survive?'

They all gave a laugh of relief. Their doctor looked like he would survive the night. Rhonda was there, holding the flashlight. She had a large orange medical bag with a blue cross on the side next to her. I spoke. "Rhonda, it's good to see you. Could you sew my head back together?"

"We should take you back to the Embassy."

I didn't want to go back to the Embassy and I wanted to look tough in front of Felicity. If I went to the Embassy, I couldn't hear what everyone was saying about me and Felicity couldn't touch me. She still had her hand on my neck even though I was sitting up. I hoped getting shot at was a onetime thing, and I wanted to know what everyone else thought about it. "No need for that. Let's do it right over there on the bench. Billy, give me a hand."

Billy came over and he and Cruz helped me onto my feet. Felicity let go of my neck, but her hand slid down to my back. The bench was only 10 feet away but it felt a lot further. My head was starting to pound and I felt slightly nauseous. I prayed. Please, God, don't let me throw up in front of her. I turned to Billy. "So do we talk to the police or what? What the hell happened?"

"The police are here, but we need to discuss things before we speak to them."

"We can talk while Rhonda sews up my head. Then we can tell them I have a concussion and can't talk. I could faint if they are skeptical."

"Do you think you are going to faint?"

"Not yet, but I will try to give you warning."

We made it to the bench and they lowered me down. The front of my shirt was stained brown and there were some shards of glass. They sparkled in the light and looked whimsical. That's when I knew I must have a concussion. When you start admiring broken glass on your shirt, you are either in love, or post-concussive or both. Rhonda and her flashlight moved around to examine the back of my head. She took

128

a sharp inward breath and started to touch the wound. That made it hurt like hell. "Does that hurt, Isaac?"

"Not at all, Rhonda, how does it look?"

"You have a complex laceration about six centimeters long on your occiput. The skull looks intact. We should get you to the hospital for a CT scan and get this sewn up."

"I feel fine. Just irrigate it and sew it up with loose interrupted sutures."

"Are you sure, Zack?" It was Felicity. She was still behind me and was looking at the wound. I hoped she thought I was being tough. Wouldn't a CIA agent want a tough guy for a lover? "Don't be so macho. You don't need to impress anyone."

"Billy and I need to talk anyway, and after this I just want to go to bed." That seemed to settle the argument. Rhonda got the suture and saline out of her bag. She transferred the flashlight to Felicity and Billy sat down next to me on the bench. The local police had cleared out the area, and the Bazaar had been closed down. Billy looked at me and seemed very concerned.

"What happened, Doc?"

"Somebody shot at me."

"Did you see anything?"

"I came out to the back of the Bazaar and was looking at some pots when the shooting started. I didn't realize what was going on. I figured it out after the second shot and then thought running was a good idea, so I took off. I then heard someone chasing me and turned around to face them. They hit me and the lights went out. What happened after that?"

"All hell broke loose. I heard the shots and realized that it was an AK-47. I figured that couldn't be good. When I got there, Cruz had you down on the ground and the shooting had stopped. I took off across the street with Solomon and a couple of local police. That's when we found the casings and the gun."

"I never thought I would be the target of terrorists."

"It is a little strange, Doc."

"I agree with you." I winced a little as Rhonda irrigated the wound with saline. Felicity was holding some gauze on my neck so that the fluid wouldn't run down my back. It was nice to feel her hand, even if it was gloved. Billy looked concerned and Agent Solomon, standing behind him, kept peering around like he was expecting someone to start shooting again. "Billy, this doesn't make any sense. Don't terrorists just put the rifle on full auto and stay and spray?'

"Spray and pray, Doc, spray and pray. That would be their usual practice."

"So why were they so careful this time? They shot at me three times." I felt the needle bite into my skin as Rhonda started to close the jagged wound in my scalp. No wincing this time, Felicity was rubbing my neck. Very slowly and very discreetly but I could feel it.

"It doesn't make sense, Dr. Porter, unless they were specifically targeting you." Solomon spoke as he moved in closer to the rest of us. He had stopped looking around and was staring at me.

"Can you think of any reason why you would be targeted?'

Rhonda stopped for a second and pulled hard on the suture so that my head was forced backward. I turned slightly toward her and she just smiled. Targeted? That made no sense. This had to be random act. "I'm sure I wasn't the target or more precisely, I wasn't the premeditated target. They just decided to shoot after they saw me. It couldn't be preplanned."

My words just hung in the air, not convincing anyone. The shooter fired only three shots from a rifle that empty a 30 round clip in six seconds and kill anyone who gets hit. That didn't make sense even to me. Rhonda cut some suture, and I could feel her dabbing my wound.

"All done, Isaac. Does it hurt much?"

"Not at all, you did a great job." My head was killing me and my vision was blurred. I considered throwing up but I didn't think Felicity would find it attractive and I didn't want to see the Norwegian salmon twice in one night. I stayed seated, hoping someone would suggest that I was not the specific target, but no one was willing to give that opinion.

Solomon leaned in and spoke again. "I don't think we will get this all sorted out tonight. We can meet tomorrow to get to the bottom of it all."

DCM Lawrence stepped forward. I hadn't noticed him before. He was dressed in khaki slacks with a white French cuff shirt and a blue blazer. He absentmindedly pulled at his cuffs and realized that one of his cuff links was missing. His right hand went into his pocket and came out with the missing cuff link. He was replacing it when he began to speak. I wondered if he was going to give me a lecture about not getting shot at in the future. "I think Agent Solomon is right. Dr. Porter needs to get some rest. If there is anything I can do for you, Doctor, just let me know. Billy, will you make sure he gets home OK."

Billy nodded as Agent Solomon and the DCM moved over to talk to the police. Rhonda was packing up her stuff. Felicity and Cruz were standing next to me. She spoke the words I wanted to hear. "Zack, let me give you a ride home. Do you think he'll be OK, Rhonda or should I review my CPR training?"

"He should be fine. He has a hard head." Rhonda smiled and looked at me like I was a wayward child. She was a good nurse, and I did have a hard head. Cruz stepped forward and put his right hand on my shoulder.

"Doc, take care of yourself and next time you hear gunfire, hit the deck, OK?"

131

"Next time? I may stay on the deck permanently just in case."

He smiled and helped me to my feet. It was good he was next to me because I almost fell over and my head moved into a whole new realm of pain. The hall was spinning, but I felt steadier after a few seconds. Felicity moved to my left side. "Cruz, can you walk with us to my car to make sure he doesn't fall over? I don't want to have to carry him."

"Roger that, ma'am."

"I'm fine, I don't need your help to walk, Felicity." I took a step and almost fell onto my face.

"Rhonda, do doctors always make such poor patients?" Felicity had grabbed my left arm just under the armpit and was holding me up. Her grip was firm and steady, much stronger than I thought it would be. She was holding on harder than Cruz was on my right arm.

"Doctors are the worst patients. They cannot follow orders. Isaac, if you fall again, I am not going to sew you up."

"I just thought stitches on my face would balance out the ones on the back of my head." No one laughed but me.

We started to walk out of the hall. I did pretty well and tripped just a couple of times. Felicity and Cruz were on either side of me, with Rhonda taking up the rear. It took us 15 minutes to make the five minute walk to Felicity's Jeep. After I got in, Cruz and Rhonda said goodbye. Felicity climbed behind the wheel and I passed out, but would have told her, if she asked, that I fell asleep. The road was uneven and several times my head bumped against the headrest and woke me. She honked the horn and the steel gates opened. The Jeep stopped and she came around to my door. She opened it and I opened my eyes. A two-story white house with a garden, lawn and two symmetric wings coming off the main building didn't look like the house I had left earlier.

"Felicity, this isn't my house."

132

She smiled and took my right hand. "Rhonda said someone had to keep an eye on you. Tonight, you're staying with me."

Chapter 20

I stepped out of the Jeep and staggered a little. Felicity had come around to my side and the night security guard frowned and shook his head. He said something and Felicity replied in Amharic. The only part of the conversation I understood was "Dr. Porter." The guard looked at me closely and then spoke some more. Felicity answered and they both laughed. I was sure they were laughing about me. "Mekonnen, the guard, thinks you should go to the hospital. He says you look very bad."

"I'm sure I do look bad, but I feel better. Did you tell him that I am a doctor?"

"Yes."

"What did he say to that?"

"He said he hopes you take better care of your patients than you take care of yourself."

We made our way to the front door and I realized that her house must be twice as big as mine. Probably better to hold her husband and three kids. I had never thought she could be married before that. There was no wedding ring on her hand but that didn't mean anything. This could be a very awkward moment indeed. I was thinking I would be better off at home when she opened the door. A high pitched electronic tone sounded and she left me leaning against the door frame to go shut off the alarm.

"Husband not home?"

"He's out with a black ops team hunting Bin Laden." My heart skipped a beat until I realized she was kidding. "Just you and me tonight, Zack. Do you want something to drink?"

"Do you have any beer?"

134

She gave me a disapproving look. "I was thinking more along the lines of water."

"Water would be good for a start, but I may want some beer later."

We walked through the entry hall with a highly polished wood parquet floor. The living room was large and rectangular. There was a sofa, some chairs, and the walls were lined with bookcases. The book shelves had books, small baskets and pottery items. All were arranged in a tasteful and not mechanical fashion. There was a square white area rug in front of the couch with a glass coffee table. A Jackson Pollack art book shared space with a copy of Turgenev's *Fathers and Sons*. A paperback of *Gorky Park* was on the sofa. She guided me to the couch like a salvage tug guiding in a crippled freighter. I sat down while she remained standing. "Are you going to be OK while I go into the kitchen?"

"I promise I won't bleed on the rug."

She smiled at me, turned around and headed for the kitchen. The walls of the living room had several prints in thin black frames. One was a Jackson Pollack, but I didn't recognize the others. The bookcase opposite me held more pictures of her parents, and the men who must be her brothers. I felt around to the bandage on my head and it seemed intact. The pain was lessening and the blurry vision had almost resolved. There was the sound of a bottle of wine being opened and she came back into the room. In her hand was a tray with cheese, crackers, the bottle of wine and 2 glasses. "Sorry, didn't have any beer. I don't keep it around since I got rid of my boyfriend."

Felicity sat next to me.

"I am sorry you don't have beer, but not sorry you don't have a boyfriend."

She handed me a glass of red wine and sat back on the sofa. Her left knee came to rest against my right thigh. Neither one of us attempted to move. "So, Zack, why did you get shot at tonight?"

"Isn't that more of your area?"

"It doesn't make any sense. You should be dead." She wasn't looking at me, but was looking at the wall opposite and sipping her wine.

"Sorry to disappoint you."

"You haven't disappointed me yet, but there may more tests to come tonight." Turning on the couch to face me more directly, she put her left hand on my arm and raised her chin a little to reveal her neck. The white V-neck she was wearing dropped slightly and I could see the same kind of scar that was on her left cheek was on her chest as well. The skin was mottled and wrinkled. It looked like a burn. "But back to the subject at hand. Why do you think you were shot at tonight?"

I took a sip of wine. It was a good Merlot, and I tried to put my thoughts together. Was this seduction just part of the interrogation process? "A random attack is still the most likely scenario. I don't know anyone in Addis and those I have met don't want to kill me. Not yet, anyway."

"There are several people at the Embassy who may want to kill you. You've upset quite a few people with your stunt. Do you always rock the boat?"

"Only if it needs to be rocked."

I had finished my glass of wine and she poured me another. As she leaned close to me I could smell citrus. I took some cheese and crackers from the tray. It was Swiss cheese and would have gone well with my chili. She was looking at me.

"What aren't you telling me, Zack?"

"I've told you everything I know, I'm not holding back."

She squeezed my arm and took a sip of wine. I could feel her moving closer and she spoke again. "Do you still love her, even though she has been gone ten years?"

"Yes, I do, but I need to start a new life without her." She had leaned into me with her left hand still on my arm. This form of interrogation was much more effective than waterboarding. "Can I ask you a question?"

It took her a few seconds to answer. She must have been thinking about something and just nodded slightly as a sign to go ahead.

"Could I borrow your shower?"

Looking slightly disappointed she answered. "Sure. Do you think you can make it there on your own? It is just upstairs and on the left."

I stood up and wobbled for a second, but she left me alone. Moving across the room wasn't easy, but I didn't fall or break anything. She didn't follow, but I could tell she was looking at me. The stairs were directly opposite the door and I grabbed the banister and ascended like an old man. It was one step at a time, bringing both feet up to the step before going on to the next. Just as my head was going to be obscured by the second floor, I looked back to see what she was doing. She was sitting back on the couch, not looking at me but at the bookcase across the room. It was the one that had the pictures of her family in it. There were tears on her face.

The bathroom had soft Egyptian cotton towels on a rack by the shower, some photos of Paris on the walls and a hair dryer on the counter. A pleasant citrus scent, the same as what I had noticed near her earlier, filled the room. I took off my clothes, left them on the counter and pulled off the bandage on my head. The wound was dry, crusted with blood and swollen. I found some Ibuprofen in medicine cabinet and took four. The shower was very clean and I stepped inside. Warm water washed over my head and shoulders. It felt very good to feel the dried blood coming off my head. I scrubbed my head and body thoroughly with the citrus soap. The shower was so warm and comforting that I did not hear her before she spoke. "Are you all right?"

I was startled and the water felt so good that I didn't answer right away. She wouldn't be bold enough to come all the way into the room. She must be at the door or in the hall. The shower door slid open and she was standing there in a white robe with a glass of wine in her hand. "You have been in there for 25 minutes. Do you think you'll be coming out tonight?"

I looked at her eyes which were fixed on mine. "Is water rationing in effect?"

"No, I just thought you may have drowned." She was smiling now and took a long deliberate look at me from head to toe. It was like I was a stripper at a Gentleman's Club. All I needed was the pole.

"You have me at a disadvantage, Felicity."

"How is that, Doctor?"

She brought her eyes back up to mine and took a sip from the wine glass. The scar on her face was clearly visible in the bright light of the bathroom.

"You have a robe."

Her eyes never left mine until she turned and moved toward the door. "Hurry up, Zack, I want to show you where you're going to sleep tonight."

I shut off the shower and dried myself. The next decision was whether to get dressed first or to try and catch her before I put on my clothes. It was an easy decision, my clothes were missing. I opted for the robe hanging by the door. It matched hers.

There was music playing down the hall as I exited the bathroom. All the lights were off in the house except for the room where the music was coming from. I moved in that direction. The wood floor was cool on my feet. The door to the lighted room was partially open and *Scheherazade* by Rimsky-Korsakov was playing. As I entered the room she was sitting on the bed, robe still on, and looking at a magazine. She looked up from the magazine as she stood. Putting down the glass of wine she faced me and slowly untied her robe. The whiteness of the robe contrasted with her warm brown skin as it slowly fell to the floor. Her breasts were large but asymmetric, with the left being larger. The irregular scar of mottled skin was jagged, skirted her left breast and ran almost to her navel. It looked like it had been poured out of a bottle and on to her body. Her nipples were a deep brown, large and made the scar seem very harsh. A large Koi fish had its tail under her right armpit and ran down her side with its head just above her hip. She obviously had never received the memo outlawing pubic hair, for she had a large unruly bush between her legs. Her eyes had never left mine.

139

"I think you have me at a disadvantage, Doctor."

I fumbled with my robe and was unable to get the knot undone before she crossed the room. With her eyes still on mine, she untied my robe and pulled me to her. My hands were on her head and in her long dark hair. As I kissed her, I could think of nothing but being inside her.

We found our way to the bed and she laid me on my back. My head did not hurt at all and my vision was clear. She was fully on top of me. Her heart beating against my chest, I could feel the hard nipples of her breasts. Still kissing my head and neck she straddled me. I could feel myself hardening as I grasped her waist. When she guided me inside her, she smiled. Leaning backward slightly she began to moan, grabbed my shoulders and with an increasing rhythm thrust me deep inside her. She never took her eyes off mine. The intensity of her gaze was almost frightening as she climaxed. I followed shortly after and realized that my head was bleeding. Extending her legs, she lay next to me and brought her head down to my chest. We made love another time or two. Afterward or maybe during, I fell into a deep and dreamless sleep.

Chapter 21

I woke some hours later, while it was still night, with her staring at me. She was on her right side with her left arm over her head and her body next to mine. There was a light in the yard that dimly illuminated the bedroom.

"Where did you get your blue eyes and black hair, Zack?"

"Both of my parents had dark hair and brown eyes. My grandmother had blue eyes so you can blame her. Where did you get the Koi?"

"From an artist at a place in LA If you ever want a tat, I can give you her name."

"No tattoos for me, I'm afraid of needles."

Her smile widened and the sparkle in her eyes increased. Could a person have teeth that white if they weren't whitened? I just looked at her in amazement. The surrender she had made me give was unconditional, total and frightening. A thing like this can lead to so much pain.

"I was always my parents' favorite."

Her tone was serious, even more serious than when she spoke about Travis and her commitment to retribution. I didn't understand why she was telling me anything. I was trying to enjoy the moment and didn't really want her to explain herself to me. Especially if she was going to tell me that making love to me was all a mistake. It had not felt like sex but like love. Finding out it was different for her was not something I was looking forward to hearing.

"My parents and two older brothers are very protective. I always obeyed my parents, did well in school and stayed away from trouble. You may not believe this but when I went to college I was so shocked by the behavior of my fellow students. Being a good Catholic high school girl, I was a prude! School was easy for me, but worrying about not doing well was hard. I worried about disappointing my family, especially my Dad. Gymnastics, in high school, was my first love, and I didn't know it at the time but now, looking back, it was so fun to be in control of my body. The mental discipline helped me cope with the need to please and gave me a way to burn off stress. My body became too voluptuous and I got too tall to continue competitively so I quit. I mostly run now, but still do some floor exercises."

She brought her arm down from her head to touch my chest. Was she looking for approval from me? That would be ridiculous.

"It has been almost 10 years since I got the burn you keep looking at." She paused to see what I would say. The words seemed to fail me but I wanted to reassure her.

"It may sound like a cliché but it makes you even more beautiful. It makes you more human. We all have scars."

"You are so smooth sometimes and yet so clumsy other times."

I was wondering which I was mostly, smooth or clumsy, when she spoke again.

"Another student was very interested in me when I was a senior in college. I was just being friendly but he thought we should be together. He wouldn't leave me alone and things got out of hand. I didn't know about all the evil in the world then. Three days before 9/11, there was knocking on my apartment door and when I answered he threw a container of gasoline on me followed by a match. My oldest brother, Pete, just happened to be visiting. After putting out the fire, Pete chased the guy and just as he was going to catch him, the guy killed himself with a handgun."

I brought her close to me and she resisted for an instant before she allowed herself to be held. I knew just how she felt. Getting close to anyone is hard when you have been wounded. I just stayed quiet. Sometimes you're just supposed to listen.

"After that, I graduated, and met the people whom I work for now at a recruitment fair. It sounded interesting and challenging. My language skills made me an ideal candidate. Did you know I get a bonus if I maintain my languages?"

"Bonus, are you sure you're worth it?"

She reached up and pulled the hair on the back of my head in a playful fashion. "I am worth it, Doctor."

I believed her and I didn't want her to open my wound by more pulling.

"I joined up and went to the Farm, in Virginia, for training. It was fun, challenging and a good release from the burn incident. My family was so proud of me. I learned what we like to call tradecraft there and met him. He was another case officer in training like me."

It felt like a confession. I kept listening.

"Christopher was ex-military, tall, blond, handsome and very fit. He had been a gymnast at college. He was at the top of our class and heavily recruited by several divisions."

I hoped that the sheets were hiding my thin runner's body. What chance would I have against Superman?

"We dated for a year and moved in together. I was going to Bangkok and he was going to be assigned to Singapore. We felt like we should get married. The wedding was to be held on a beach near Monterey. Several hundred people were invited. We were so ideal that it almost made you sick. Young, good looking, well educated and embarking on careers that few people can even dream about.

"The morning of the wedding I knew I was making a mistake. I was in love with him but more in love with the idea of him. My father and I have always been very close and I thought I could discuss anything with him, but my words failed me that day. I couldn't disappoint him and all those people. When I woke up that morning I told my maid of honor, 'Let's get this shit over with.' That wasn't a good sign and I should have stopped the wedding then. As the obedient daughter, I went through with it. There were no problems with

Christopher; he was not like that man who burned me in college. I was simply not ready to be married.

"It was wrong almost from the beginning. Even on the honeymoon, things were not as they should have been. I started working very long hours just to stay away from him. Less than a year later, I decided I needed to end it. The hardest thing I ever had to do was tell him and my parents that I wanted a divorce. My brothers tried to talk me out of it. They were married and said everyone goes through difficult times but, I knew this wouldn't change. I couldn't stay in the marriage just to fulfill everyone else's wish that I be the perfect daughter and wife."

She paused again and I could feel her tears on my chest.

"We went through the divorce. Everyone took his side and I can't blame them for that. He had done nothing wrong. That was all about six years ago. Recently, the Africa division needed a DCOS and I had done some good things in Bangkok, so I got the job. He's in Moscow now. I've done things all through my life to please others and to make them proud. Getting the divorce was the first thing I did in my life strictly for me. My parents and brothers have gotten over it and we are doing fine now. I wanted a symbol of my new freedom. I wanted a concrete example of my new path in life. That is why I got the tattoo. I am ready to swim alone now."

I didn't have anything to say so I just kissed her on the forehead and held on to her. The tears did not stop until she fell asleep.

The sun was coming up, it was about 6:30, when I awoke again. Since Addis Ababa is very near the equator, the days are almost of equal length throughout the year. She was gone and I couldn't hear the shower. I sat up in bed and waited for the pain in my head to ease before I stood. The blurry vision was back and some nausea. Standing was probably a mistake, but there was so much I had to do today and I had to get started. The room didn't spin as much as it seemed to be tilted and if I wasn't careful I could roll out the door. Fully dressed in a dark gray business suit, she entered the room carrying a tray. "I

144

brought you some breakfast and, I must tell you, even in the opinion of a nonprofessional medical person, you look terrible."

"Thanks. I feel good." The smell of the food was making me even more nauseous.

"I made you an omelet, toast and coffee. I want you to stay here today. The maid knows you're here and will look after you. It will be very busy at the Embassy, and I will be working late. I expect you to be here when I get back."

She put the tray down on the bed and I picked up the coffee to see if that could help. It tasted good. I realized again I was naked but she didn't seem to care so why should I? My robe was across the room, neatly folded on a chair by a large walk-in closet. How did she get dressed without me hearing her? Probably silent dressing was one of the courses she took at the Farm.

"Zack, do you need anything else before I go?"

"I think you've satisfied most of my needs for now. I just had one question. Why were you and the Wollinskys at Alexander Lebed's house two weeks ago?"

She stood very still and her smile faded from her face. The change was only momentary and then her face became warm again. It was like watching a cloud pass in front of the moon. "So that's what he told you last night. Did you make wild passionate love to me just to get information out of me, Zack?"

"I think it was you who seduced me. I'm the one with the concussion, remember?"

She inclined her head backward and laughed. Her eyes never left me as she moved in close to me; the citrus scent was mild but alluring. It was like being in love with an orange grove. With her arms around my neck she kissed me with a slow deliberate passion. I felt myself stirring and she felt it, too. She looked down and back at me with a slight smile. "No time now, but rest up for tonight."

She let go of me and turned for the door. Just as she entered the doorway, she stopped and turned to me with her left hand on the door frame.

"I hope you don't bleed every time we make love." I didn't know what she meant until she motioned to my pillow on the bed. The white Egyptian cotton had a large brown stain of my blood on it. She winked at me. "Don't worry, Zack, pillow cases are easy to replace."

Without looking at me again, she left, and I could hear her footsteps going down the stairs. I sat back on the bed and had some more coffee. My clothes were clean and folded on a chair next to the bed. She had gotten up, showered, dressed and cleaned my clothes all while not waking me. That was good tradecraft. Lying in bed all day, waiting for her to return, would be just short of ecstasy. I reached over to my pants and got out the cheap Nokia phone. I found the number in the contacts section and dialed.

"Post One, this is Cruz."

"Cruz, this is Dr. Porter. I need help with some things today. Are you on duty?'

"No, Doc. I was just waiting for your call"

"How did you know I would call?'

"You don't seem like the type who takes getting shot at lying down, Doc. I figured you might need some assistance today."

I hate being predictable and I am just the kind of guy to take getting shot at lying down. That is especially true if a beautiful woman is involved.

"Well, it's good you're there. Can you come pick me up?"

"Sure, Doc, be there in 30 minutes."

"I don't know exactly where I am."

"Doc, everybody in the Embassy knows by now that you stayed at Ms. Gonsalves' house last night. I know just where it is. See you in 30."

He hung up before I could say anything else.

Chapter 22

After drinking the coffee and eating two forkfuls of eggs, I showered and dressed. I went downstairs and had avoided the maid until I was almost out the door. She was about 35, tall, thin, with a narrow face but very friendly eyes. Having caught me near the front door, she tried to get me to go back upstairs. I think she would have forced me to go and in my weakened state it would probably have worked, but Cruz arrived. His honking roused the day guard, who opened the gate. The maid almost didn't let me out of the locked front door, but I told her I had a medical emergency at the Embassy. Reluctantly and with a stern look, she let me out, but I could tell she was going to call Felicity. Cruz was driving one of the Embassy motor pool Landcruisers. "Morning, Doc. How are you?"

"Good, Cruz, I slept all night."

"I hope you didn't sleep all night, Doc." He was smiling and he winked. I just let it pass. There was no way I could explain to him what had happened when I didn't really understand myself.

"We're going to do some more investigating."

"Sounds good. Where should we start, Doc?"

"Let's go to the Embassy and start there."

Felicity's house was far from my home in Bole and I wasn't sure where we were going. I didn't want to ask Cruz for fear he would want to know more about last night. The only thing that was familiar was the gray smoky haze that hung over the city with the smell of burning wood. We went in a northerly direction and uphill. Addis Ababa University was the first landmark I recognized. The Embassy was just up Entoto road. We showed our badges at the security gate and were waved into the parking lot. Cruz parked the Landcruiser next to an armored Suburban. The day was much brighter above the haze at the higher elevation that the Embassy occupied.

I didn't have a plan, so I thought it would be good to go to the health unit and think. Not wanting to appear clueless in front of Cruz, I

148

made something up. "Cruz, I'm going to the health unit to review some things, but I'll call you soon."

"Doc, whatever you think we need to do is OK with me. You pulled a rabbit out of the hat last time. How's your head?"

"It is fine, just a little sore." My head was hurting, but not as much as the night before. The double vision was almost gone, but it had become more blurry. We exited the Landcruiser and headed into the Embassy. The parking lot was located about 150 yards from the Embassy, just in case anyone put an IED in their vehicle. The Marine behind the thickened glass buzzed us in and gave me thumbs up and a wink. I was not sure what that meant but I returned the thumbs up. Cruz went to Post One as I went down the hall past the cafeteria and into the health unit. I said hello to Rhonda and went to my office.

She followed behind me. "Isaac, how are you feeling? You don't look so good. Did you eat breakfast?"

"I feel pretty good, considering what I went through last night. I had some breakfast this morning." Her concern was genuine and I was glad she didn't ask me about Felicity. Maybe she already knew.

"I'll take a look at your head later. I don't want you working too much today. The schedule is light, so you should go home in a few hours." I nodded and she continued. "I will need your signature on some forms later. Before you arrived, I had the authority to sign the invoices, but now that you are here you should countersign."

It made sense to me. "What are we ordering?"

"Just routine stuff, like sharps containers, vaccines and some drugs. You can review the list before you sign."

She nodded toward me and went back to her office. Dr. Lessing, I was sure, was working on how the buns were poisoned, but I didn't want to call. My stomach was nauseous enough without talking to her. Putting my feet up on the table, I leaned back in my chair and after a few spins, the room stopped moving. The buns had been contaminated by a needle or syringe or pipette or something long and sharp. Finding that instrument would help explain who was behind the whole thing. The fact that Rhonda had mentioned the sharps containers gave me an idea. The containers hold the used needles, syringes and scalpels that the office generates. It allows for proper disposal of the medical waste. It is safely collected and then incinerated. The ones in the office couldn't possibly be the disposal site of the needle or syringe used to contaminate the buns. No one besides Rhonda or me could get to them. My phone rang and I almost tipped over trying to answer it. It was Agent Solomon "Good morning, Doctor. I just wanted to see how you were doing. How do you feel?"

"Pretty good. Any progress so far?"

"I am glad to hear it. There have been some new developments. The buns may have been contaminated in Frankfurt. One of the bakery workers there has a record and his sister works at a clinic where they treat many cases of diarrhea. We think he may have acquired the E. coli there."

"It sounds like you have a good lead. Is Dr. Lessing helping on this?"

"Yes, she has been very helpful. It's looking like a terrorist attack after all."

"If I can help in any way, let me know." I hung up the phone, but was troubled by something that didn't make sense. I dialed Post One, the Marine Security Post, and asked for Cruz. "Cruz, when did the buns get here from Frankfurt?"

"They came in on Friday. It was just good luck that there was an Air Force C-17 dropping off some equipment for the DAT. Somehow he got the buns on the plane."

"Where were they stored?"

"They were in the commissary from Friday until the barbecue on Saturday."

"Where does the trash from the commissary go?"

"I think out to the trash receptacle out by the perimeter wall."

"We need some gloves."

"There are some in Post One. I will meet you in the health unit in a few."

Cruz came in a few minutes later with a couple of pairs of leather work gloves. After telling Rhonda I would be back in a few minutes, we walked out of the health unit and instead of going past the cafeteria, Cruz took me to the back door. We walked down a shorter hallway, past the mailroom and out the security doors. The back of the Embassy faced the Ambassador's residence. There was a small concrete driveway and the large lawn in front of his house. Large trees cast some shadows on the grass and the sky was clear and very blue. We followed a paved road to the left away from the parking area. The motor pool was ahead of us on our left but we took a concrete path around the Ambassador's house. The perimeter wall was about 300 yards from the back of the embassy and next to the wall was a large paved area. The trash receptacles were against the wall. They were not as small as in America but were large, European type, about 10 by 15 feet and 8 feet deep. Shaped like squared-off rowboats, they could hold a lot more trash. The two of them next to the wall were both full.

"So now what, Doc?"

"I don't think the buns were contaminated in Frankfurt. I think it happened at the Embassy. They probably injected them in the commissary and ditched the syringe or whatever they used in the trash."

"I don't like where this is going, Doc."

"It will be faster if we both do this. Look for a syringe or a long needle. If you find something, let me know."

I put on my gloves, climbed into the nearest dumpster and began going through the trash. It became clear to me that the only way to do this was to go through each bag and loose bit of trash. To do that properly, I ripped open the bags and went through the garbage one

151

rotting piece at a time. After looking at the trash, I would throw it over the side so that I could keep track of what had been sorted. I looked over at the other receptacle to see if Cruz had started. He was in his dumpster and muttering something in Spanish that didn't sound complimentary. We worked steadily at our jobs, motivated by a desire to get done so that we could get out of the smell and grime. The first thing I found was that the local guards were observant and came to check on us after about three minutes. Two of them walked up and began to speak into their radios. The Amharic I couldn't understand, but the gestures and tone of voice made me realize they weren't happy.

"Doc, I think they want us to stop."

"Would you climb into one of these to stop us?"

He laughed and we continued with the disgusting task. The trash was piling up in a haphazard fashion around both dumpsters. My pile was slightly larger, but I knew what I was looking for and Cruz didn't. Luckily the temperature was still reasonable and the odor wasn't too bad. It was a generic trash smell. The cafeteria used the same dumpsters as the commissary and the rotting spaghetti and tuna salad sandwiches were the worst.

"Hey, Doc what are you doing?" It was Billy. The local guards must have called him. He was dressed in brown slacks and a blue blazer with a cup of coffee in hand.

"Just going through some garbage, I lost my favorite pen."

He didn't say anything but took a sip of coffee and spilled some on the front of his shirt. After brushing it off and cussing he looked up at me again. I had continued to work since I was afraid he would make me stop.

"Doc, you've earned some slack, but the Ambassador thinks you are making a mess."

"I am making a mess."

"If you don't stop, he will be out here in a minute."

"I better work fast."

"Is this related to your head wound?"

"Only if I don't find what I am looking for."

He took a sip from his cup, more carefully this time, and looked over his shoulder. I followed his gaze and saw the Ambassador coming down the cement path toward us. His pace and body language indicated a certain animation, probably related to anger. I bent low in the dumpster. Out of sight, out of mind, I thought. There was still about half of the trash to go through in the dumpster. Time was growing short. I actually smelled it before I felt it.

"Doctor Porter, what in the hell do you think you are doing?" I didn't answer because I knew I was close. The black plastic trash bag I had just opened contained paper, plastic bubble wrap with the bubbles popped and some cardboard. The bag smelled like a sewer. Quickly reaching into the bag, I felt around for anything that might be a syringe. There was a small bundle of paper towels in the bottom with something firm in the middle.

"Lance Corporal Cruz, get out of that dumpster. Porter, this is intolerable. You cannot go on like this. Look at this place. It is a complete mess and I am not going to put up with your unorganized methods. I told you yesterday to notify me when you are going to be doing anything unusual. This is going to stop."

I stood up. There was a small crowd around the trash area. The local guards were the most amused. The Ambassador was standing with his hand on Billy's arm and speaking into his ear. Billy was looking right at me and nodding. He brought a radio to his lips and spoke into it in a low voice. Reaching for the edge of the dumpster, I jumped down to the ground, avoiding the pile of trash. Cruz was out of his dumpster and brushing himself off. There was a large dark stain on his pants from some kind of liquid. The Ambassador came up to me with a barely controlled rage emanating from his body. His fists were clenched, his face was red, and he was trembling. "Didn't you hear me? This is not going to continue. I am going to get you sent back to Washington. I warned you before."

I didn't answer. I just looked up and gave him a smile. He was about to really get angry when I showed him what was in my hand. There were two plastic syringes with four inch needles attached within a gray brown paper towel. Billy looked down and back up at me with a puzzled expression. The Ambassador was confused, too. Cruz was smiling, but I wasn't sure if he knew what I had found or he was just glad to be out of the dumpster.

"What is that?" The Ambassador's tone was changed. He was assuming a more diplomatic stance until he found out exactly was going on.

"These are the syringes that were used to contaminate the buns."

"How can you tell they were used, Doctor?"

"There is a small amount of fluid in the hub and if you smell it, it smells like E. coli. We will have to test it, of course, but this is it."

The Ambassador bent down toward my hand and stood up quickly when his nose registered the aroma coming from the syringes. "Of course, it smells, it was in the garbage. Agent Solomon has information that the buns were contaminated before they came here."

"It was too soon. If they had been contaminated in Frankfurt, the bacterial growth would have made the buns unusable. They would have smelled like this syringe and been discarded."

Everyone was quiet for a minute. Billy stood very still and didn't know what to do. He was waiting for the Ambassador to make a move first. Billy was uncomfortable and I felt sorry for him since I was making things difficult. The Ambassador had regained all of his composure and was contemplating what to do next. After about a minute he made up his mind. "Doctor Porter, you need to take this to Dr. Lessing and inform Agent Solomon. Your findings do not justify your methods. This investigation has to run in a logical and controlled fashion. You cannot be working independently. Do you understand me?"

"I'll make sure the syringes are tested properly."

He was not satisfied with the answer but he turned and left. As he walked away, Billy came up next to me and took his own whiff if the syringes. After he stood back up and held his nose in an exaggerated fashion, he touched my shoulder. "Doc, you're unorthodox but you get the job done. Upsetting your Ambassador is not a good career move, though. Be careful and let me know before you do anything else."

"OK, Billy, I will keep you informed."

I turned and started to put the trash back into the dumpster, when Cruz grabbed my arm. "Doc, you've done enough for one day and your head is bleeding again. You better have Rhonda look at it."

Foolishly, I reached around the back of my head and felt the sticky fresh blood. The wound was probably very contaminated by now. I nodded to Cruz and started to walk back toward the Embassy. As I approached, I could see Felicity looking out of a window. She didn't smile or wave as she slowly lowered the blinds.

Chapter 23

Rhonda knew I was there before she saw me. I could tell because she asked Mahedere, the receptionist, what that awful smell was before I turned the corner. The awful smell was me, of course.

"Rhonda, can you look at my head?"

"What have you been doing? You are filthy."

"I found these syringes in the dumpster out back behind the Ambassador's place. I think they were the ones used to contaminate the buns."

She looked at me with a combination of respect and confusion. "I'll look at your head."

I followed her to the room. It was still a typical examination room with an examination table, stainless steel and glass cabinets that held medications, sutures and equipment. It was very well lit but not well ventilated. The stench from my clothes was even too much for me "Isaac, take off all of your clothes and put on a gown. I am going to break the rules and wash them in the lab."

There was a small washer/dryer in the lab to wash lab clothes in if contamination occurred, but it was never to be used for routine laundry. The look on Rhonda's face had changed to one of mild anger and I did as I was told. She stepped out to give me some privacy. I stripped and piled the clothes in the corner. Before I put them down I peeled off an egg shell and what looked like spaghetti from the leg of my pants. Throwing that stuff in the trash, I put on the paper gown and sat on the table. Holding the syringes in my left hand like a treasure, I waited for her to come back inside. The delay was a little longer than I had expected, and when she came back Dr. Lessing, Billy and Agent Solomon were with her.

"Good morning, Dr. Porter, Rhonda and Agent Solomon tell me you have found something."

"Yes, Madeline. I found the syringes used to poison the buns." Dr. Lessing didn't like that I had called her by her first name and that made me feel good. Agent Solomon looked at Dr. Lessing and she looked back. They both slowly turned their heads toward me. Billy just looked at his shoes. The coffee he spilled out back had made a splatter trail down the front of his shirt. "I didn't think the buns could have been contaminated in Frankfurt and still be usable for the barbecue. I thought they would have to have been altered here, so I went looking for the source."

Agent Solomon looked very skeptical, but Dr. Lessing began to blush angrily. I had found another important fact in the case and I hadn't told her what I was doing first. "Dr. Porter, the Ambassador gave you specific instructions that I was to be the lead investigator in this case. Why did you ignore the chain of command? If you had a hunch about the syringes, why didn't you come to me?"

"I didn't want to bother you on a hunch."

Agent Solomon came forward and took the syringes from me. The gloves he wore were a light blue color, the same as my gown. "I will tag these as evidence and let you test them, Dr. Lessing. Do you think his theory about the buns is correct?"

Asking her if I was right and she was wrong was very bold. I waited to see what she would say. "My methods are organized and controlled. If you read the memo I sent you and the EAC this morning, you will see that I raised the same issue about the buns. If they were contaminated in Frankfurt and left unrefrigerated the bacterial growth would have been noticed here before they got on the burgers. I reached the same conclusion that Dr. Porter did, but I informed others and allowed the investigation to proceed in the proper fashion."

The investigation had proceeded in the proper fashion. The hierarchy and control had been maintained. She would not concede that she was wrong. I guess she wasn't wrong if she had sent that memo and I was sure she had done that. Her voice now was condescending and calm. "Dr. Porter, I must insist that you follow the proper protocol and inform me before you take any other steps in this investigation. There is a proper procedure in place for a reason, and I cannot allow you to continually ignore my authority. This investigation is too important to be left to a cowboy doctor who will not follow the rules."

"He didn't follow the rules, Dr. Lessing, but he did find the syringes." It was Billy riding to my rescue. He winked at me and Dr. Lessing just silently shook her head,

"Agent Solomon, I would like to get those syringes up to CDC for proper handling right away. Will you come with me?"

"Sure, Dr. Lessing."

They turned and left together. Billy came up to the exam table and stood next to me.

"Doc, I would warn you again about not pissing people off, but I don't think you'll listen. The Ambassador has called another EAC for 10:00, which is about one hour from now. You are requested to attend. Try not to get into any trouble between now and then. He's still upset at me for you getting shot at last night."

"I'll be there, Billy, showered and in clean clothes."

He just smiled a little and went out the door. Rhonda came back in and cleaned out my wound and gave me an injection of Ceftriaxone. The antibiotic was probably not necessary but I thought she wanted to give me the shot just to indicate her displeasure at my behavior. She certainly seemed to enjoy it. There was a small shower in the bathroom of the health unit and keeping my head as dry as I could so that Rhonda would not be angry I washed up. My clothes were ready by then and I left the blue paper gown behind as I went upstairs for the meeting.

The conference room was the same room as before but it looked completely different. The table was covered with papers, binders, pads, pens, pencils, laptops and coffee cups. The pictures on the walls had been knocked crooked by someone, and the Twin Towers were leaning toward Old Faithful in a threatening fashion. The

158

Ambassador had not yet arrived, but everyone else from the EAC seemed to be there. DCM Lawrence was sitting near the head of the table and talking to Agent Solomon in hushed tones. The DCM was dressed in a charcoal gray suit with white pocket square. His French cuffs were neatly pressed and he had silver eagle cuff links. Agent Solomon had a sport coat and slacks on but no tie. He had a radio next to him. Billy was on the other side of the table with his coffee stained shirt and a large cup of potential stains in his hand. Felicity was next to him. She did not acknowledge me as I came into the room. Dr. Lessing was on the same side of the table as the DCM and was talking to Constance Powers and Maria Katzakis. I took an empty seat on the same side of the table as Felicity but several spots away. No one had yet looked at me. That was fine with me.

The Ambassador walked in and we all rose. After we were again seated, he looked at a sheet of paper that must have been an agenda. Everyone else seemed to have one in front of them but I did not. The Ambassador spoke. "Let's call the meeting to order. Constance, can you take minutes for us? I want everything on the record today so we can send it to Washington."

"Certainly, Mr. Ambassador."

"Very well, Dr. Lessing can you give us an update about what we know so far and the new developments from this morning?"

"Mr. Ambassador, I have been in contact with my CDC colleagues in both Atlanta and Washington. It has been a team effort from the start and we have concluded that the source of the E. coli infection was the contaminated buns shipped from Frankfurt the day before the barbecue. Syringes were located today that have tested positive for E. coli. DNA sequencing will have to be done in Atlanta to confirm that the bacteria in the syringes and in the buns are the same. Agent Solomon and the FBI lab have been very cooperative and essential to the investigation so far. Since the buns are the source of the contamination, it is clear that this was a deliberate act."

The room was quiet and everyone was waiting for the Ambassador to speak. It was funny how her report sounded so complete. The Ambassador leaned back in his chair and loosened his tie before he spoke "Agent Solomon, can you tell us what the FBI thinks about this attack?"

"Mr. Ambassador, working in conjunction with Dr. Lessing, Mr. Spencer and Ms. Gonsalves, the FBI has come up with several likely scenarios. The most likely is that AQEA has infiltrated the Embassy, either through the local guard force or through commissary personnel. The barbecue was picked as a target because it is a quintessential American activity. The barbecue had been planned three weeks in advance, but we think the idea of poisoning the buns did not happen until the buns actually arrived. They were shipped along with some other Embassy items at the last minute. We think that AQEA was informed either by someone in Frankfurt, the Embassy or at the airport. The plan then just needed someone with access to syringes and the Embassy."

That sounded completely logical to me. Except that it assumed that Al-Qaeda in East Africa had the resources and people to penetrate the Embassy at will. Were they that powerful? Why not an IED or assault with AK-47s? Wouldn't that make the headlines faster than food poisoning? If it was a terrorist attack they got lucky. Al-Qaeda got lucky on 9/11 though too. Agent Solomon continued.

"In response to this threat, the FBI has dispatched 24 agents who will arrive in about 12 hours. The terrorists are also behind the attack last night at the Diplomatic Bazaar. It could be the same AQEA cell or it could be another cell taking advantage of the publicity generated by the poisoning and the Bazaar. We believe Dr. Porter was not specifically targeted, but was only in the wrong place at the wrong time."

Everyone looked at me but Felicity. She kept her head down and seemed to be focusing on the papers in front of her.

"Thank you, Agent Solomon and Dr. Lessing. I think that you and your teams have done an excellent job responding to this crisis. My cable to the Secretary will mention all of your cooperation and teamwork. The next thing we have to do is coordinate with

160

Washington on our public response to the crisis. Ms. Katzakis, what do you think the Ethiopian response will be?"

"Mr. Ambassador and fellow committee members, I have spoken with several people in the Ethiopian government, and they do not have a clear idea who was behind either incident. They are most concerned about the shooting last night and are happy that Dr. Porter was not seriously injured."

"Not as happy as Dr. Porter is." I thought it was funny but no one laughed. Not even Billy or Felicity.

The silence was getting uncomfortable even for me, and they were waiting to see what the Ambassador would say. He was starting to flush again and the paper he was holding in his hands shook. "Dr. Porter, we are trying to deal with a very serious situation here. Your attempt at humor demeans these proceedings and disrupts the flow. Your actions so far have been unorthodox and frankly unprofessional. In my cable to Washington, I am going to suggest that you be placed on medical leave and be recalled to the states."

Everyone looked at their papers now except for DCM Lawrence. He was looking at me and straightening his cuffs. Recall to Washington was the nuclear weapon of discipline in the State Department. It would ruin any career I hoped to have. The only good news was that I hadn't unpacked yet. "Mr. Ambassador, may I make a few comments?"

"Certainly, Dick."

"I think that this has been a terrible week for everyone here at this Embassy. The shock of the illness and death of a young child is very hard to take. Dr. Porter is new to the State Department and not familiar with the customs and protocols that we take for granted. Before any cables about recall are sent, we should take a step back and let our emotions cool. Dr. Porter has not been a team player here, but he did find the evidence that is helping us understand this case."

The DCM was coming to both my rescue and the Ambassador's. The DCM had explained away my faults and given the

161

Ambassador an out. An Ambassador should remain in control no matter what happened.

"Dick, you are right. I apologize for my outburst. Let us move on. Constance, can you coordinate with the DCM about a press release. I think we need to get something out to the media. I also think we can wrap up the meeting unless anyone has any questions."

I sat forward in my chair and Billy caught my eye and slowly shook his head. "How do we explain the note that was found in my house?"

The Ambassador began to flush again and Billy joined Felicity in staring at their papers. Dr. Lessing looked at me like I was a mental patient and wrote down some notes. It was probably her diagnosis of me. Agent Solomon cleared his throat and spoke. "The note was almost certainly left by your day guard, Eskander. He recently replaced the usual day guard. We are investigating him for any ties to known terrorists."

"Why would he leave a note? He is no more a terrorist than I am."

"How can you tell, Dr. Porter? People are not always who they claim to be." It was Felicity and her tone was icy and business like.

"I am a good judge of character and I trust him." It sounded weak even to me. Eskander wasn't a terrorist.   I knew that, it was just hard to prove.

"All of us can be easily misled." Felicity was mad at me. It wasn't about what I had said about Eskander. It was something else.

The Ambassador spoke again to take control. "Ms. Gonsalves is right and we need to end the meeting. We are still going ahead with the reception tonight as scheduled. I expect you all there at 7:00 PM."

He rose from his chair gathered his papers and left. We all stood and before I could catch up, Felicity bolted. I looked around and everyone was ignoring me the best they could. Even Dr. Lessing couldn't see her wayward pupil. I moved toward the door and tried to straighten the picture of the Twin Towers. The fastener holding it up must have been loose. It fell off the wall and left a three inch hole in the plaster board. They looked at me for a second and but they must have been expecting me to make a mess. No one said anything as I left the room.

Chapter 24

I went back down toward my office but stopped for a Coke and some cookies from the vending machine outside the cafeteria. The Coke bottle said Coca-Cola in English on one side and Coca-Cola in Amharic on the other. I wasn't really hungry but figured I should eat something. Real food didn't sound very appetizing. Rhonda and Mahedere were out to lunch, so I went into my office and shut the door.

Terrorist poisoned buns, death of an innocent boy, professional pettiness and whatever happened with Felicity were all unsettling events. Solomon, Billy and Felicity, the experts, were convinced that the entire sequence of events could be explained by terrorists but experts were not always right. Everyone at the meeting had experienced a loss since I arrived. The loss of a little boy, the loss of a feeling of security or the loss of professional pride. I had lost nothing, since I didn't have anything to lose, and with Felicity I had gained something. It was not clear to me what I had gained, but I felt I had turned a corner or closed a door. It seemed to me that because I was the only one to gain something in the last few days, I was the only one thinking clearly. But that could have all been my concussion. It was clear, though, that my time was running out. The Ambassador had already mentioned recall and everyone except the DCM had silently agreed.

The Internet has really changed the practice of medicine. Obscure facts that used to be memorized could now be retrieved in a matter of minutes. I decided I would go online and look into food poisoning and terrorism. The computer connection was slow, and it gave me plenty of time to think. Email and cables were waiting to be read but I wasn't in the mood. I only opened one from my brother, who asked if I was OK. He hadn't heard about the shooting yet, so I just played dumb and replied that I was fine.

When I got to the Google page I had every intention of looking up the cult in Oregon that had poisoned the salad bar, but somehow Felicity Gonsalves' name made it into the search box. I think it is called cyber stalking. There were things about her that I wanted to know and I didn't want to ask. It was harmless. The record had probably been erased by her employer anyway. Could they do that? The results of the search came back. Apparently they couldn't.

The first thing that came up was a website that listed the winners of a scholarship from the Portuguese-American club of Northern California. She had received a $1,000 scholarship her first year at Berkeley and was a speaker at the banquet in Sacramento. Other pages listed her participation in gymnastic events when she must have been in high school. There was an article in *The San Francisco Chronicle* that discussed a local job fair put on by The International Relations Club of Berkeley. Her picture was there. Her hair was longer then and her face had no scar. She looked very young but not nervous. The Facebook page linked to her name was set to private and had no pictures I could access.

The last thing I found on her was another article in *The San Francisco Chronicle*. It was the report of an attack on a student at Berkeley. The article said she had been burned by a Molotov cocktail thrown at her when she answered her door. The assailant, named James Edward Wong, had killed himself very near the scene. He was a math major at Berkeley with a history of paranoid schizophrenia. They had met at an Asian-Pacific Student Association dinner 2 months before. The story also said that she had had been burned on the face and chest.

The marriage certificate had been taken out in Monterey County, and I found her old wedding registry. She had good taste in china and housewares. His name was Christopher Lee Martin.

You can't technically cyber stalk someone you don't know, so I entered his name into the search field. There were quite a few Christopher Martins in the world. I guess it was a more common name than Felicity. It took about 10 minutes, but I found the right one. His Facebook page wasn't set to private and it hadn't been updated in over a year. He had more than 250 photos posted in about 20 different albums. He was tall, about 6'3" or 6'4", blonde, tanned and very fit. The album marked wedding day was the biggest, containing about 60 photos. The beach setting was sunny and romantic. Her family looked proud. She was beautiful in her off the shoulder, strapless dress and looked happy, with tears in her eyes in most photos. I could never have guessed by the photos that she was having second thoughts. The last photo was of the bride and groom toasting with champagne as the sun settled into the Pacific. It was a great picture that seemed to document the love story of the century. I looked in vain on his page for a bad photo of him. Maybe something taken when he was drunk or ill or just having a bad day. He was incapable of taking a bad picture. If she didn't want him, she would never want me. Not on a long-term basis.

I logged off and the clock said I had been on the computer for three hours. It was late afternoon and I had to go home so I could get ready for the reception. The Ambassador was hosting Pierre, the French-American chef who had restaurants in Beverly Hills and New York. He also had an empire of frozen French food and several cookbooks. His second wife was Ethiopian and they were sponsoring a local charity that educated orphans at a school about 45 minutes outside Addis Ababa. It was going to be quite a party. Many members of the local ex-pat community as well as people from other Embassies had been invited. When I was at the Foreign Service Institute learning protocol, the course was long and boring. I did hear out one valuable thing. Never be late to the reception when the Ambassador invites you. Not wanting to give him any more reasons to dislike me, I planned to be on time and cleaned up.

I told Rhonda I was leaving for the day and met my driver at the front of the Embassy. The sun was high and bright and there was no residual morning haze. The drive back to my house was pleasant and the traffic wasn't bad. The Ring Road was smooth and except for a few pedestrians who darted in front of us, it was an uneventful trip. Along some stretches, the road had been cut through an existing neighborhood. In a rather pragmatic fashion, instead knocking down the whole building, they had merely removed the part that would have blocked the road. That left several buildings cut in half or with corners missing, exposing beams, support columns and rafters. The wounds had been filled in with stone, brick, corrugated steel or fabric. It was if the buildings had healed themselves without interference from their owners.

Chapter 25

After eating some chili and watching some AFN, I showered and dressed in my best blue suit, white shirt, and red floral Zegna tie. The driver was right on time, and Eskander wished me luck at the reception. The ride back into the Embassy was interesting as the sun had set. The city has many street lights, but most didn't work or were too dark to give much illumination. Several people would try to cross the streets in front of the Landcruiser. Looming out of the shadows like deer on a country road, they made the driver, Edilu, swerve several times. We didn't hit anyone and that was good, but there were several close calls.

The Embassy was well lit and could be seen from several blocks away. We were waved through the security gate and Edilu let me off in the circular drive in front of the Ambassador's house. There were several cars in front of us and most were from other Embassies. The reception line was just inside the door and I got a glimpse of the Ambassador and Anita greeting people. I stood in line and didn't recognize anyone around me. The house was reinforced concrete with a large entryway that opened onto three large symmetric wings. The highly polished wood floor of the entryway was covered with a large area rug. The Ambassador and Anita were standing opposite the oversized double door I had entered and they greeted people as they passed. When I got next to them, they both smiled and acted like I was a long lost and beloved relative. It was not the welcome I had expected. "Good evening, Dr. Porter, Anita and I are very pleased you could join us tonight."

"Thank you, Mr. Ambassador. It is a pleasure to be here."

"You look very nice, Doctor, is that a new suit?"

"Anita, it is new, and I wore it because this is my first Embassy reception."

"How nice of you, Dr. Porter. Please come in and get a drink and again thank you for coming."

With that, they moved on to the next person in line and I was dismissed into the adjoining room. A waiter came up and offered me a choice of champagne, red or white wine. I chose the champagne and took a sip. The room was rectangular with a large buffet table along one wall. The table was filled with cut vegetables, cheese, crackers, cold cuts and a large basket of flowers in the center. I moved over to the table to get something to eat. I wasn't really sure how to act. No one seemed to be paying any attention to me and that was fine. The cheese was Cheddar and very good. The problem with having cheese and a glass of champagne is that you can't shake hands with anyone who comes up to you. DCM Lawrence approached. "Good evening, Dr. Porter. How are you tonight?"

I had to put down my champagne on the buffet table to shake his hand. "Very good, how are you?"

When I tried to pick up my glass, I knocked it over into a pile of Ritz crackers. As I cleaned it up with my cocktail napkin, the cracker tray unstuck from the table and clattered to the floor. All conversation in the room stopped, and the diplomats, guests and staff turned their eyes to me. The DCM took it in stride and reached down to grab the tray and placed my now empty glass on it. Some of the champagne and cracker bits had adhered to my pant leg. The DCM, unscathed, handed the tray to the waiter who had come to the table. Another waiter appeared with a second tray of crackers and another glass of champagne for me. I waved off the glass and the room returned to the sound of quiet polite conversation. No one was looking at me except Felicity, who was in a small group near the entry hall. I could see only her face but she was upset about something.

"I wanted introduce you to the RMO from the Russian Embassy." The DCM had assimilated the cracker chaos and was ready to move on with business.

"Dr. and Mrs. Lebed, this is Dr. Porter, our RMO."

It was Alexander and Irina from the Bazaar. He was now dressed in a blue suit, white shirt and blue tie. The suit was well cut, silk, Italian, expensive and fit him well. He looked quite different without his peasant garb.

"Good to see you again, Alexander and Irina."

"Oh, Isaac, you flatter me by remembering my name. I told Alexi that you were smart and charming. We are so sorry to hear about the shooting and hope that you are recovering."

"Thank you, Irina. I feel much better now." I put my hand up to the back of my head without thinking and felt the wound. It had started to bleed again.

"I'm glad you all know each other so well. If you will excuse me, I see some other guests I need to greet." DCM Lawrence bowed slightly and moved away toward the Felicity's group. I wanted to know what she was mad about but I couldn't leave the Lebeds right then.

"Tell me Isaac, why do you think this happened? Alexi and I were horrified when we found out it was you who was shot."

"I wasn't shot, Irina. I fell onto the ground when I was running away and cut my head."

"Still, you are wounded and with the other tragedy, this has been a terrible week for you."

"It has not been the best start to my diplomatic career. I don't think I was a target. They would have shot at anyone, at least any diplomat." They turned to each other and exchanged a look of skepticism.

Alexi had somehow acquired two glasses of a clear liquid. "Well, in any case, we are glad you are not seriously injured or worse. The terrorists should be hunted down like dogs. This vodka should make you feel better. It is Standart, the best, I brought it tonight myself." He handed me a glass that was very cold. The other he gave to Irina. From the table next to us he picked a bottle of Ambo, and poured himself a tall glassful. "To your continued health, Isaac."

We all drank. Irina took a sip of her vodka, Alexi a sip of his mineral water, and I emptied my glass.

"You don't drink, Alexi? You are shattering my stereotype of the Russian male."

He laughed and seemed very amused. "I don't drink, just like our Prime Minister. I do eat, however. Do they have any caviar at the buffet, Isaac?"

"There may be some. Before we look for it, may I ask you a question?"

Alexander smiled and seemed open but Irina was slightly cautious. "Certainly, Isaac, Irina and I will answer anything for you. Do you need some more Russian products for friends?"

"Why were Ms. Gonsalves and the Wollinskys at your place two weeks ago? Do you socialize with them often?"

They both paused and almost looked at each other but did not. They were trying to figure out what to say as I had caught them off guard. Irina recovered first and spoke in a light and matter-of-fact tone. "Felicity, Ms. Gonsalves as you said, is being posted to Moscow soon, and she had some questions about apartments, stores, cars and things like that. Bob, Travis and Jennifer came along to keep her company. Your CIA doesn't like its people to meet with Russians alone."

Luckily I had swallowed all of my vodka or I would have choked. It was my turn to be caught off guard. They knew the Wollinskys and Felicity were CIA and had met with them just two weeks prior to the death of Travis. How could that be? I didn't know how to answer but knew I had to say something. "Ms. Gonsalves is CIA? I didn't know that."

"Alexi, he is charming, handsome and gallant! He will not reveal what he knows about the lady even after they have been on intimate terms. You are a true gentleman, Isaac."

"Hardly a gentleman, Irina, I'm just a little confused, that is all."

Alexander spoke again as he winked at me and pinched my arm. "Love is very confusing isn't it, Isaac? Shall we go find the caviar?"

"I must go talk to the Ambassador but will join you shortly." I was lying because I didn't want to face the Ritz crackers again just then. The Lebeds smiled, shook my hand and went toward the buffet. They were speaking in hushed Russian as they left. The only words I understood were "Isaac" and "Samolet", the Russian word for plane. They must have been saying I should get on the next plane out of town.

I moved down the room away from the entrance and found a hallway. The hall had the same polished wood floors and area rug. There were framed documents on the walls that described how Haile Selaisse gave FDR and the United States government the land on which the Embassy was built in 1944. There were copies of the letters, signed affidavits, photos of the site and an Ethiopian flag under glass. Billy came up behind me with a woman about 50, tall with wide hips, a bright friendly smile, a baggy black dress and thin brown hair that looked like she cut it herself. "Doc, I wanted you to meet Laurie, my wife."

"It is a pleasure to meet you Laurie. How do you like the reception?"

She smiled and looked happy as she spoke. "I've been to quite a few and it's always a little trying to have to watch what you say all of the time, but I enjoy meeting the people."

I liked her right away.

"Doc, I have to go find Felicity. Could you stay with Laurie for a minute? She hates these parties."

He moved off and I was next to Laurie.

171

"Dr. Porter, Billy has told me a lot about you, and I was hoping to meet you here tonight. He really likes you and says you're doing a great job."

"Thank you, Laurie, and call me Zack. It has been quite a week. This is my first Embassy reception. How am I doing so far?"

"You look great, Zack, and I can see why Felicity is interested."

The vodka was making me blush. Billy came back into the room and motioned for us to come over toward him. There was no one else in the hall and I wanted to stay there to avoid people, but I wanted to find Felicity more. The hallway led to another wing where there were more people and someone was playing the piano. The room was large and, again, wood floored with an area carpet. The high ceiling and white walls made it feel impersonal. There were two seating areas marked by large sofas and some chairs. Constance Powers was playing the piano. It was a classical piece and I didn't recognize it, but she was good. Several other Embassy people stood around her but she stopped and they all looked toward the front entry hall. Everyone rose and a small group of people entered the room.

I recognized Pierre from his TV show and the tall Ethiopian woman next to him in a black off the shoulder dress must be his wife. He was shorter than I expected, gray haired and balding but his smile was broad and white. There was an entourage of five or six people following in his wake, like remoras follow a shark. The people in the room turned toward the celebrities and moved slowly in their direction. I stayed back and looked on as the crowd gathered near the piano.

Felicity was not with the crowd, but was standing closer to the entry hall. She looked great in a simple black dress with a short tasteful string of pearls around her neck. Her hair was up and she was distracted. She was not looking in my direction at all. In fact she looked in every direction but mine. My presence must have registered with her. I could go over and talk to her but I got the distinct impression that she was not up for that. Retreating to the buffet room seemed like a good plan, but the Ambassador had caught my eye and was gesturing to me. When I reached the Ambassador's side, he turned to Pierre and introduced me. "Dr. Porter, this is Pierre and his wife Adele. Dr. Porter is our new RMO and has been with us just a short period of time but he has made quite an impact. Like you, he is from Los Angeles."

"Hello, it is a pleasure to meet you and your wife. I have enjoyed your restaurant on several occasions."

Pierre smiled and his wife looked at him with love. The entourage was close but not in our circle of conversation. Felicity had moved over to talk to Billy and Solomon by the piano. "Thank you, Doctor. It is always a pleasure to talk with people who enjoy my place." He had a slight French accent and was a little overweight, but that's good in a chef.

"It is always a great experience to eat there. I want to congratulate you on your charity work in Ethiopia. How long have you been helping out here?"

He turned to his wife and put his left arm around her. "I met her in LA, but she has always been thinking about her homeland. She convinced me to help raise funds five years ago, and we have been coming here yearly since then."

"You should be very proud of your contributions."

"Thank you, doctor. We enjoy helping out."

Anita came up to me and was smiling. She looked terrific in a dark gray dress with a small gold necklace and gold ear rings. "Doctor, I have to steal these people away from you and introduce them to the Foreign Minister. Do you mind?"

"Not at all, Anita. It was a pleasure to meet you both."

Just as they began to move away, Pierre turned and handed me a business card. "Next time you are in LA, come into the restaurant and have dinner with your wife on me."

I took the card and put it in my pocket. Felicity had overheard. She gave me a blank look and took a large sip of her red wine. The distance that had developed between us was almost as surprising as the intimacy in the first place.

My cell phone buzzed, meaning I had a new message. I had the phone on silent so that it would not attract attention if it rang. The possibility of a medical problem that would take me away from the party and Felicity would be quite welcome. The phone was in my jacket pocket next to my Diplomatic Passport. I took the phone out and looked at the text message. It was the first one I had received in Addis.

"God welling. You well not be able to stop use."

Chapter 26

After looking at it for a minute or two, I decided it wasn't a joke and that I needed to tell someone. Billy was standing near the piano with several men whose suits were slightly too padded in the shoulders and whose lapels were wider than was quite fashionable. They must be the FBI agents Solomon had mentioned. Keeping the phone in my hand, I crossed the room and came up next to Billy. "Billy, could I see you for a second?"

"Hey, Doc, I was just telling these guys what a good job you have been doing here."

"I think we need to talk, Billy."

He was still smiling, but took me seriously and we moved away from the piano to the area near the hall connecting to the buffet room. I handed my phone to Billy and he looked at it like he couldn't believe it. "When did you get this, Doc?"

"Just now. What do you think this means?"

"Doc, I don't know for sure, but I think the party is over for you and me."

He left for a second and came back with the Ambassador, Solomon, DCM Lawrence and Felicity. One of the waiters came up to us and the Ambassador said something to him and he moved away. Billy handed the phone around and each of them took a look at the message. They had different reactions. The Ambassador, with a glass of red wine in his right hand, looked mad and confused. The DCM was concerned but did not look quite as upset as the Ambassador. Solomon showed no emotion but was grim. Felicity looked at the phone and looked at me with the first look of concern she had given me all night. Any reaction was better than the indifference she had been giving me. The Ambassador was flushed and as he turned to speak to me, he spilled some of his red wine onto the white carpet. The dark, blood red splatter hit everyone but me.

"Dr. Porter, how is it that you are the one who is chosen to get these messages? A note on your nightstand and now a now a text? This is frankly beyond belief." His voice was louder and higher pitched than usual. There was sweat on his forehead and the wine had stained his tan pants with an irregular dark mark that made it look like he had been cut. His voice and demeanor had attracted the attention of everyone in the room.

"I didn't choose to get these, Mr. Ambassador. I have no idea why I am the target." I sounded defensive but I didn't need to explain to him why I was getting the messages.

"Dr. Porter it has been nothing but bad news since you got here. Dick, what do you think we should do know?"

"I think we should move the discussion outside. No use in alarming everyone."

The DCM moved toward the door and motioned with his head for everyone to follow him. We complied and I was the last one out. Standing under the canopy that led from the porch out onto the driveway, we stood in a small circle.

The night was cool but it felt refreshing. Air filled with the full moonlight and the hint of wood smoke encircled me. Felicity was beautiful with her head turned to look at the DCM. I could see the elegant architecture of her neck and the scar on her face was barely noticeable in the low light. I wasn't thinking about Travis, the note, the text or my wife. I didn't care if the message was from terrorists, a practical joker or Russian spies. I just wanted to be back inside of her with my arms around her chest and my face buried in that neck.

The DCM handed my phone back to me and spoke. "David, I think this means the threat is not over. Felicity, we need to have your people trace all of the calls from this phone and see if any of them link to anyone involved in any activity detrimental to the US. Billy, we need to keep a close eye on the good doctor. Someone targeted him for some reason. Mr. Ambassador, we need to warn the Embassy and Washington of the new threat. Does everyone agree?" He was calm, almost matter of fact, and when he finished it felt like some control had been restored. Even I felt more reassured. Felicity spoke.

"Mr. Ambassador, I will send the cable to Langley tonight and get them to put a rush on the traces for Dr. Porter's phone. It will take about 24 to 48 hours before we get an answer. David, we need to get more people out here. This could be the beginning of a threat escalation that leads to more attacks."

"I agree, Felicity. We have extra agents here now, but I will ask for a complete tactical unit and a forensics team to fly out ASAP. We could use some of your ground branch people as well."

"The Ambassador and I will send a cable to Washington. Mr. Ambassador, we need to get Constance and Maria involved so that we think out the local political and media fallout. We need to be ahead of the chaos for once." The DCM finished speaking and was in control.

Everyone seemed to have a role in the response but me. They were all talking like I wasn't there and I got the feeling that I would not be missed. The next plane out would probably have an American physician on board heading back to Washington. It came as a relief when the Ambassador spoke again.

"Dr. Porter, would you excuse us for a minute. I want to tell the group something." The Ambassador was composed again, and his tone was more neutral than dismissive. I just moved down the canopy and out onto driveway in front of the Ambassador's house. Stars looked down upon me and I felt relieved to be away from the conversation. Tracing the contacts on my phone wouldn't help and the number that called was probably a disposable cell phone. If they were terrorists, they would know the first thing we would do would be to trace the call.

Doing nothing until I was expelled from the country by my own Embassy was not acceptable. I was angry at the Ambassador for being so diplomatic. Solomon had been too quick to back his theory about terrorists in Germany. Billy had done nothing wrong and was the one who had supported me since I arrived but I didn't need a full-time bodyguard.

Felicity was a mystery and yet I hoped to be with her again. The seduction and information gathering were cold hearted and cruel if she had no feelings for me.

I decided that I had nothing to lose and looked at my phone. I recalled the message and hit the button to dial the number that had sent it. I had no clear plan but I knew what I was doing was right.

The ringing began and at first I thought it was just from my phone as the ringtone was the same. The group was still talking under the canopy and the ringing was coming from a planter near Felicity. I walked quickly to a large terracotta pot that held a small palm tree and looked inside. On the dark soil was a cheap Nokia phone, the display was lit up and the number was mine. Picking it up would have been too dramatic but I thought about it. Instead I turned to the group and didn't wait for a break in their conversation.

"I found the phone." All of them turned to me and stopped talking. They could all hear the ringing now. "The phone in the planter is the one that sent me the text. Whoever is behind this has had access to the Embassy tonight."

As my words sank in, the group was silent. In the full moonlight I could see vulture slowly circling overhead. I felt sorry for everyone in the group and the vulture. I don't know exactly why, but from that moment on I knew Africa was going to be my resurrection after all. Confusion, loss and disorder were old friends of mine.

Chapter 27

The Ambassador went inside and made an announcement. He told the group that the power at the Embassy was in danger of being cut off and that one our emergency generators was on the blink. The party had to be cut short. I don't know if he came up with that story on his own or if it was a group effort, but it was really good. The power went out in Addis about five times a day. The government-run utility was not able to supply enough power to the growing city so it routinely cut the power to various parts of the city, much like rolling brownouts on a hot summer day in LA. Everyone believed him and after the obligatory comments about the lack of reliability on the continent, people began leaving. I waited by the drinks table and had another shot of vodka. It was quite good and I began to think that the Russians were on to something. The same group of people who had met outside to discuss the situation was now inside by the piano. No one expressly told me to stay away, but no one invited me to join in, either.

After I found the phone in the planter, Agent Solomon had taken both my phone and the planter phone into custody. He wore some yellow rubber gloves borrowed from the kitchen staff and examined the planter phone. The gloves did not fit well and he was having a hard time manipulating the buttons. After several minutes he was able to ascertain that the phone had been used only once to send that text to my phone.

The Ambassador and the others were still by the piano, and about every minute or so one of them would look over at me like one would look at the local malcontent. Felicity did not look at me at all, and I was getting angry about it. She had no right to be so aloof after we had been so intimate. I was remembering why I had given up on love since 9/11. To get my mind off of her, I began to try to figure out why terrorists were targeting me.

The whole scenario did not make sense. The barbecue had been the source of the food poisoning that had killed Travis. Dr. Lessing had blamed the meat and a faulty freezer in her report. The meat, the usual suspect, was not at fault - it was contaminated buns. The note in my house had said that it didn't need to happen. Agent

179

Solomon felt pretty sure that it was from a terrorist. The bazaar had been fun until I was shot at. Terrorists were blamed again and now I had found the phone that sent the misspelled threatening message. If I was a terrorist, I would get the spelling right. It was more ominous when spelled correctly. Much centered on me for some reason and I had only been in the country a few days. If they had the access and knowledge to target me, they could easily kill me or, better yet, get a bomb inside the Embassy. Their goal of terror, chaos and disruption could easily be accomplished. If they killed me, it wouldn't even make the papers back in the States. Well, not the front page anyway. Would Felicity care?

"Dr. Porter, could you come over here?" It was the DCM speaking from the piano group. His voice was calm and almost welcoming.

I moved toward the group and realized that I had lost count of the vodka shooters. The room wasn't spinning but it felt like I was traveling uphill. The trip across the room was short and I made it without incident, but the look in Felicity's eyes had changed. She was no longer indifferent. Her look had changed to open hostility, and that made me feel good. That was easier to deal with.

The group was in a semi-circle and I faced them like a schoolboy before the reviewing board. They all looked like they were going to kick me out and send me back home. The Ambassador spoke first, but only after looking to the DCM for approval. "Dr. Porter, we all want to thank you for the great service you have given the Embassy in the short time you have been here. It has been a very trying week for everyone, and you have not buckled under what must be a tremendous strain for you. That being said, we all agree that due to the circumstances and through no fault of your own, you should return to Washington."

I would have done the same. After the initial food poisoning, all of the other threats or incidents had revolved around me. I wasn't to blame, of course, but getting me out of there might calm things down. I should have thought more about what I was going to say next, but the fatigue, altitude, vodka and my need to be heard before I was dismissed took over. "This doesn't make any sense. The whole thing does not make any sense. Why would I be targeted and how is this related to Travis?"

No one spoke at first and it must have been the topic they had been discussing in my absence. The Ambassador began to flush and the DCM straightened out his pocket square. Billy was looking at his shoes while Agent Solomon slowly twisted the yellow gloves in his hands into a tight knot. I wondered if he wanted to do the same thing to my neck. Felicity looked at me with anger. I was going to ask her what her problem was when the Ambassador spoke again. "I have been in the Foreign Service for 33 years and I have never seen an officer who was less able to follow instructions, less able to be a team player and less able to work for the good of the mission than you. You should not only be sent back, but you should be terminated." His voice had risen to a guttural shout by the time he had finished. The DCM put his right hand on the Ambassador's shoulder and gave him a small squeeze. Everyone else had joined Billy in staring at their shoes.

My only thought was that if I am getting fired, then I'm going out with a bang. "This is ridiculous. You blame me for doing the job that you told me to do. Mr. Ambassador, you need to get a hold of yourself. Stop worrying about whether I'm a team player and start worrying about how you are going to deal with a real threat here in the Embassy. Agent Solomon and Felicity are selling you a bill of goods about terrorists, probably to ensure their own jobs. Think for a minute why I have been targeted. It's only because I have driven this investigation forward. It is far more likely someone on the Embassy staff has been responsible for it all."

The Ambassador was so mad that he could not speak. Solomon had dropped the gloves and his eyes were looking right at me. It was only self-control that stopped him from shooting me right there. Felicity looked hurt for a moment but then her face changed and the contempt and anger came back. She spoke with a cold and matter of fact tone. "Why should we trust anything you say? You are lying and deceitful even to those who are trying to help."

"That is completely untrue and you know it."

181

"Your wife is alive. She is living with her second husband and their two children in LA."

It was not a shock that she knew. It was a shock that she said it out loud. She must have told them all before I got to the piano. It made sense now. My lies about my wife had upset her. I would have told her the truth earlier that night but I never got the chance because of her distance -- the distance I had imposed on us by lying about the loss of a woman who never really loved me. Feelings of rage, guilt, anger and fear filled me and I felt cornered. It was good I didn't have Solomon's gun because I didn't have his self-control. "You can't use your tradecraft to spy on Americans. That is against the law. You have no right."

"I simply Googled you and it all came up. Why did you lie to me? What else are you hiding from us?"

"You Googled me? That is just crazy. Who does that? Are you some kind of stalker bitch? You have no right to do that, no right at all. This is all unbelievable. My personal relationships are none of your business."

There were tears on her cheeks and I was glad. I just wanted to do anything I could to hurt her. This was just what I had feared when I told her about losing my wife on 9/11.

The DCM stepped between us and spoke. "I think it has been an exhausting and trying day and that we should all go home and get a few hours of sleep. It will be a long day for everyone tomorrow. Billy, could you take the doctor home?"

I was so angry at her and so ashamed at the same time that I didn't say a word as Billy put his arm on my shoulder and led me away. I could hear Felicity start to sob as the DCM held her in his arms. It had felt good to be the source of the tears, but I wished I was the one holding her.

The ride back to my place was silent and because the hour was late there was no traffic and we made it in 15 minutes. The night guard opened the gate after Billy honked and I unbuckled my seat belt. As I opened the door to the Suburban, Billy spoke in a low but humorous tone. "You and Felicity sure had a fight tonight. This might come in handy, Doc. I will pick you up in four hours. Good night."

He handed me a small hip flask-sized bottle of Early Times whiskey as I got out of the truck. I was still feeling the effect of the earlier Vodka and had a hard time opening the steel grate and front door. Finally I got them open and was able to get into the house. I got a glass from the kitchen and poured some Early Times into it. After taking some deep hits and remembering how harsh whiskey can be, I laid down on the couch.

Chapter 28

I lost my wife on 9/11 at a family medicine conference at Disney World. We had met in the first week of Medical school in the Gross Anatomy lab. At USC, each body in the Gross lab had four students assigned to it. The Gross lab is so named not because it's a disgusting, but because it is large anatomy visible to the eye. That contrasts with micro-anatomy, which is the study of anatomy through the microscope. Gross anatomy is both disgusting and frankly bizarre. I was 22 at the time I first set foot in the lab, which is in the basement of one of the research buildings at the medical school campus. Every gross lab in the country is in a basement of some building, hidden away from prying eyes. It is almost as if some dark and evil ritual is performed there and the location must be kept from the uninitiated. The whole idea is to let the student learn about how the human body is put together. The best way to figure out how anything is put together is to take it apart. That's what happens in the Gross lab. The human body is systematically dissected like a vacuum cleaner at a repair shop. Not exactly like that though because at the repair shop the vacuum cleaner will be put back together. In the Gross lab the body is taken apart and the pieces are incinerated a little at a time. It's the ultimate in entropy.

Gross Anatomy is still included in the medical curriculum in these days of nuclear scans and 3-D computer displays for another reason. Once you have cut, chiseled, hacked, sawed and skinned a dead human body, nothing in medicine will faze you. You will have passed through the initiation rite and are a member of the tribe.

I was not looking forward to Gross lab. The idea of cutting up a dead body was strange and although I knew intellectually that it was good for my education, emotionally I was not ready. The lab instructors know that the average student may be put off by the idea of cutting up somebody they don't know. That is why they begin dissecting the back. The most emotionally laden areas of the body, the most human, are the face and the hands. Those are saved for the second semester. The back, however, is a vast broad plane that does not elicit the same emotions. There are no poems written about the romantic nature of the back. Most of the imagery is of work or labor, so the instructors feel that it is a safe place to start.

The lab was held on a Tuesday afternoon, and after a lecture about the sanctity of the body, we were ready to start. I think the part of the lecture about making sure we didn't take any body parts home may have started my anxiety and slight queasiness. We marched down the stairs like the good soldiers of medicine that we were. The chief anatomist, Dr. Winter, took the keys from the lab attendant, Mr. Parker, and opened the double doors to the lab. It was a little dramatic, like the opening of the Tower of London, and it didn't help my stomach. It made me wonder what they were hiding behind all the locks and the ritual.

I made my way into the room and two things struck me at once. It was freezing and it smelled of formaldehyde. After putting on my lab coat, getting my dissection kit and manual, I realized I had stalled long enough and looked for my table. The room was large and well lit by overhead fluorescent lights. There were 30 tables in six neat rows in the room, and my table, table 10, was at the end of the second row. Melissa Singh, Bob Goldman and a blonde woman were already there, and the shroud had been pulled back. A body wrapped in clear plastic was face down on the table. A small 3 x 5 card was on the cold steel gurney and it said that our body was that of a 75 year old woman who had died of congestive heart failure. The blonde woman was about 5'6" and slim, with her hair tied back into a bun and safety goggles on to protect her blue eyes. She was studying the manual and had her tools laid out in a precise fashion on a small metal stand next to the table. She was wearing jeans and a white blouse under her lab coat. Her breasts were not large, but her nipples were erect due to the cold and could easily be seen. It was the sole source of comfort I found in the otherwise alien room.

We started to dissect the back. It was hard to not think about cutting into a dead body, but I did pretty well for the first 20 minutes. We had been working on the back and were having a hard time holding the skin up while we cut away the underlying tissue. To this day I say a prayer for the woman who gave us her body. It was a form love and

185

sacrifice, but she was a little fat. The fat under her skin was slippery and it made the skin hard to hold. The skin, firm like leather due to embalming, kept flapping down, spraying us with bits of fat, flesh and skin like bellows spreading ash in a fireplace. A second year student came over to help. He simply cut a small round hole in one corner of the skin near the edge. It was about the size of a quarter and he put his finger through it. It allowed the skin to be held without much effort at all. We were all relieved, but treating this body like a flap on a suitcase was too much for me. I looked away from the body and down at my lab coat with the small flecks of fat and flesh on it. The vomit was already rising to my throat when I turned away from the table and to the medium sized metal trash can at the end of our row. It was a sanctuary of sorts. Puke in the can and then clean it up. People might not even notice.

I lifted the lid and peered down inside hoping none of the vomit would hit the floor. Unfortunately, the can was not empty; it was filled almost to the top with the discarded skin flaps my fellow students had successfully removed. They had been more efficient or had their finger holes cut earlier. Either way, it was full. Unable to hold the vomit in any longer and not willing to puke into a barrel full of human skin, I bent over and retched all over the floor. The lab was completely quiet when I was done and the flight reflex kicked in. I ran out of the lab, up the stairs and into the quad and the sunshine of a hot August day. Unlike Orpheus, I did not look back, so my Eurydice made it to the surface with me. She had followed me from the lab and her goggles were still in place when she came over to me. We had not exchanged any words, except for hello, in the lab. Putting her hand on my shoulder she spoke directly to me for the first time.

"I feel the same way, but if we're going to get through this thing, we have to go back and finish. We can get through it together."

I never forgot her words and I started to fall in love with her right there. We did go back and finish the lab. Dr. Winter kept close by the table and Mr. Parker had cleaned up the vomit. The other students didn't mention my reaction and she kept smiling at me throughout the afternoon. After we were done that day, she bought me beer and pizza followed by a ride home. After our divorce was final, she told me that she took such good care of me that day because she didn't want some lame student screwing up her chances of getting into dermatology. She was making sure I did well so she could do well.

We started dating in the second semester, and by then it was clear that she was the star of the class. She was attractive, smart, focused and hard working. I was in love with all of her and she was seemed to be in love with me. I was not as focused and hard working. The realization that the world of medicine was not as rational as I had thought was disturbing to me. The fact that the body worked in ways that we did not completely understand made me feel uncomfortable. Knowing the right answer to the right question had always been a source of pride for me. Now the answers on the tests were simple but they did not really reflect the uncertain world. The academic world of medicine and the real world of medicine were diverging for me. She never felt it. Her world was certain and predictable. The goals in her life were set and obtainable with hard work and concentration.

We married in the fourth year, after she found out that she would be going into dermatology at USC and I would be doing family medicine. By going into family medicine, I was trying to accept the unknown. The specialty that encompassed all of medicine was comforting for precisely the fact I couldn't know all of the facts. She wanted the certainty of a sub-specialty that at least gave the illusion of order. She also wanted easy hours to do research or raise kids.

I was as happy as I had ever been and even though we did not see each other a lot during residency, I felt that we had a good marriage. I finished a year before she did since learning how to take care of the whole body took three years and learning how to take care of the skin took four years. My residency was in a medium sized community hospital, and I took a job with a group practice nearby. To keep my license, the State of California requires me to get 25 hours of continuing education every year. There was a dermatology meeting in Orlando in September and she was going to attend. Luckily there was also a family medicine course in the same hotel a few days before. We decided to go together. She had been working long hours for about 6 months to complete some research, and it would be good to spend time with her.

We left on a Sunday and arrived at the hotel late in the evening. The next day I was in lectures all day but we had a nice dinner. She had stayed by the pool and was too tired and sunburned to make love that night. I loved her more that night than I had ever loved her. Her intelligence, beauty, drive and goal direction were all things I wanted in a spouse.

The next morning 9/11/01, I got up quietly and let her stay in bed. The lecture that morning was to be on acne. After showering, dressing and kissing her for the last time I went down to the ballroom for the lecture. The breakfast buffet was quite lavish and looked good but I just took a sweet roll and some coffee. The lecturer was very humorous and informative, but about 10 minutes before he was to conclude, a murmur arose in the back of the room. I was a little annoyed and didn't understand why people were being so rude. The lecturer made a joke about it, but I've forgotten what he said. The conference moderator stepped out onto the podium and whispered something in his ear, and then both men turned to the screen that had been showing the PowerPoint presentation about acne.

The screen went blank for about 30 seconds and then came on with CNN. I couldn't understand what was going on. It had a long shot of tall buildings, one of which was on fire. It was lower Manhattan and just as I was thinking that it was stupid to interrupt the lecture with a high rise fire, even in New York, the second plane hit the South Tower. There were gasps, sobs and moans in the room. I dropped my coffee and decided I needed to be with my wife. The elevator bank was just outside the ballroom and I went up to my floor. The Do Not Disturb sign was on the door but as I leaned in close, I could hear the television.

Letting myself in, I saw a breakfast tray and two people watching TV. It did not strike me as unusual. I figured my wife had been disturbed by the room service guy or one of her colleagues had come over to tell her about the attack. The fact that there were two people in the room did not alarm me. We all need human contact on a

188

day like that. The alarming thing was that there was only one set of pajamas. He was wearing a blue striped bottom and she was wearing the matching top. The shock could not have been greater. I could not understand how they could have gotten their clothes so mixed up. The breakfast tray had two half eaten breakfasts and the bed was a complete mess. The realization that she had invited this guy into the room for breakfast and sex was too much for me.

I left the hotel without speaking to her, got into the rental car and drove. The radio stayed off because I couldn't stand to hear any more bad news that day. I gassed up in Jacksonville and kept going. She phoned about noon and left a message, but the hurt and betrayal I felt would not let me answer. The anger I felt sustained me through New Orleans and a bad night in a motel. By the time I reached El Paso, I was regretting my actions. I had been too hasty. She still loved me and I still loved her. Marriage was not easy and I was not perfect. It could be worked out. I called her from Phoenix and was ready to go to Florida to get her. She didn't answer and the hotel said she had checked out the day I left. She was probably worried about me and unable to reach me. I turned the car around at the California-Arizona border and went back East.

There was no answer on her cell or our home phone. Planes had started to fly again and I took that as a sign of the resumption of normal. As I was driving through West Texas, my phone didn't ring but there was a voice message. It was her. She was sorry things had turned out this way and wanted to send me a letter. What was my address and where was I? I tried to call her back about 10 times over the next two days and got no answer. I got a room at a Holiday Inn. Driving back to LA might be the best way, but I had been on the road several days and needed a rest. I left her the address of the motel on her voicemail and the next day a Federal Express envelope arrived at the office for me. The young Hispanic woman at the desk was very nice and handed over the letter to me. I carefully opened it up and expected to find a letter explaining her actions and a path to reconciliation. The letter was dated 9/4/01 and was from an attorney informing me that my wife was seeking a divorce.

Chapter 29

He was a guy she had met in residency and it was not my fault. She had not been ready for marriage and I deserved someone who could love me like she could not. They had fallen in love and she intended to tell me on the trip to Orlando. She was so sorry I had to find out the way I did. None of her explanations made me feel better. I just wanted her back. I left long messages on her voicemail, sent flowers, bad poetry and long letters of love. She started to return them after about 2 weeks, unopened. The phone numbers and email accounts were all changed, and I was cut out of her life like an unwanted mole.

The last time I saw her was when we signed the divorce papers. She was wearing a large three carat diamond solitaire ring on her left hand and as I watched her leave in the Mercedes convertible with him, I knew she had moved on. The realization that I hadn't and probably never would was overwhelming.

There were other women after her, but mostly I was using them to make her jealous. I dated three women from our medical school class, hoping she would find out through the grapevine and be so upset she would come back to me. It didn't work. The women were nice enough but somehow they always knew that I was not interested in them.

The feelings of loss were mixed with feelings of competition and revenge. I am competitive and losing her to someone else really hurt my pride. If she had left me before finding someone else or if I had left her, which, of course, would never happen, it would have been easier to deal with. Those women from school were part of a revenge plot, but it never really worked because my wife didn't love me enough to be jealous. When I think about it now, I feel guilty about trying to use those other women to get even with a woman who didn't care enough about me.

I hadn't finished the bottle of Early Times. Thinking about losing her and the lost years of trying to get her back always takes so much time. I heard the honk and the gate opening up. Billy was coming with the Suburban. Eskander was closing the gate and I realized I hadn't slept much or showered in the four hours I had been given. Getting through a day, after a sleepless night thinking about her, was easy for me. However, I found myself less worried about her and more worried about Felicity. That was a good sign. I might spend the next 10 years worrying about losing Felicity, but at least it would be a change.

The door bell rang with a short industrial buzz. Straightening my tie and putting my suit jacket back on, hoping it would cover my wrinkled shirt, I looked in the mirror by the front door. I was tired looking, needed a shave and shower but I didn't look defeated like I had after other sleepless nights.

Eskander was holding the door to the Suburban open and smiling. "Good morning, Doctor. Are you OK?" He must have noticed my tired appearance and rumpled clothes.

"Good morning, Eskander, I feel very well, thank you. Is Kokeb coming over today?"

"Yes, Doctor. She will be here by 7:00 o'clock."

"Great, have her go to the store and buy some food for dinner."

I handed him about 1000 birr, about 60 bucks, and got into the Suburban.

"This is too much doctor." Eskander was trying to hand back the money. I moved the door so that it was open only a couple of inches.

"Nonsense, Eskander. You can give me the change later."

Closing the door all the way, I smiled as I saw the startled look on his face as he stared down at the money. Turning to Billy, I could see that he had not much sleep either, but he was at least showered, shaved and in fresh clothes. "Jesus, Doc, every time I see pick you up you look worse."

"I feel good, Billy. I also wanted to say that I am sorry I implied my wife was killed on 9/11. She left me for a better man on

191

9/11 and it's been hard to deal with. I hope you can accept my apology."

"Doc, marriage and love are the most complicated subjects that I know of. The way you deal with it is your business. I don't blame you for telling a half truth."

"Thanks, Billy, I won't tell anymore half truths."

"Like you just did?"

"Like I just did?"

He smiled and put the Suburban in reverse before he answered. "She may have left you, Doc, but I can't believe it was for a better man."

The Suburban backed into the street and Eskander waved as he closed the gate. We passed through my residential section but instead of making a right onto the Ring Road, Billy went underneath and made a left.

"I know I'm new in town, but isn't the Embassy that way?"

"The Embassy is that way, but we have to go over to Mexico Square and say hello to General Mulugeta."

"Who is he?"

"He is a very nice man in his middle fifties who is the head of the Federal Police and he has a few questions for you about your attempt to get shot the other night." We had crossed through an intersection and a traffic circle on to a four-lane road with a center median. The median had a fence with steel roses decorating the poles that held up the 4 strands of barbed wire. I guessed the barbed wire was to keep people off the grass. Ahead of us were two cars stationary in the right lane. There was a back-up. I figured that one of the cars had broken down and wasn't thinking much about it when Billy spoke. "Any time there is an accident here, the drivers have to stop where they are and not move until the police come. It makes for some interesting traffic patterns."

As he finished, the Suburban was slightly jostled. My first thought was that we had been struck from behind by another car in traffic, but when I looked in the mirror on the door, a thin cow was looking back at me. There was a small herd behind us and one of the cattle must have bumped into the truck. A small man, about 20, wearing black, dust-stained jeans and a LA Lakers T-shirt, was driving the cattle past our back bumper. The purpose of the barbed wire fence was clear to me. It kept the cattle off the center median. Ahead on my right I could see the Millennium Hall.

I heard the jets before I could see them and from the noise I could tell they were low. The airport was about a half a mile away. When I finally spotted them, Billy was leaning over the center console to get a better look. There were three Gulfstream Business jets about a couple of minutes apart, banking and approaching the airport. "That will be our colleagues from the FBI. They're sending over several agents. Getting that text last night, Doc, sure upset some people in DC."

"I am glad I can provide entertainment to two continents."

Billy laughed. The minor fender bender was still stuck in the right lane but after some polite honking and use of the bulk of the armored Suburban, we made it into the left lane and were moving again. The cattle had disappeared. As we passed the Millennium Hall, I involuntarily put my hand on the back of my head. The sutures stuck out through my hair and I could feel dried blood but there wasn't much pain or swelling. There was a multistory building on the left side of the road directly opposite the hall. The spindly wooden scaffolding and exposed cement block showed that it was still under construction, and there were windows only in the first few floors.

"The fifth floor facing the street is where we found the AK and shell casings the other night." Billy was looking straight ahead but must have seen me staring at the building.

"So, Billy, why does the head of the Federal Police want to see me?"

"I'm sure he is not pleased that you tried to get your head blown off in his country and probably just wants to ask a few questions. Of course, this could be the first step in getting you PNG'ed."

"PNG'ed?"

"Persona Non Grata. That is when the host government revokes your visa and kicks you out of the country. It would be a safe move on their part. If you, or another diplomat, get killed it would embarrass them. I don't think they will PNG you and it won't matter anyway."

"Why do you say it won't matter?"

"With PNG, they give you 72 hours to leave. I think you'll be recalled before that. You may be heading out on one of those Gulfstreams when they leave today."

"Billy, you know as well as I do that sending me home isn't going to solve this thing. If I had left after the note or I got shot at, we wouldn't know what we know now."

"Doc, it is the fact that you've been ramrodding this investigation that will get you the plane ride. The State Department is very good at a lot of things, but it does not like independent action. That goes against the diplomatic mindset of consensus and deliberation. You can't say I didn't warn you." He smiled and he was right.

He had warned me and if I looked at it from Washington's or Ethiopia's viewpoint, I would send me home, too. I had uncovered the tampered buns and had been shot at and texted to by potential terrorists. Having me around was getting to be embarrassing for everyone. In fact if I were a cop, I would think I was suspect number one. The facts of the case made no sense to me. Why was the food targeted? What was the point of the note? Who had shot at me and why was the text sent? It was keeping my mind off of Felicity. It was good not to think about her, but being preoccupied would make it harder to get her to talk to me again.

Billy made a left onto another four-lane street, and we were approaching a 10 or 12 story building. The quarter-circle-shaped edifice was built to conform to the circular plaza and was clad in a blue reflective glass. The sunlight was bright and it made the building almost ice-like in appearance. As we entered the traffic circle, I noted the broken fountain in the center. There was a large bowl, 30 feet across, with three cement structures rising from the base. They were curved, covered in multi-colored tile and pointed in three different directions. I couldn't decide if they looked more like cobras with their hoods extended or dolphins leaping in the air. The fountain looked forlorn and sinister without water.

Chapter 30

Billy pulled the Suburban up to a parking area just off to the side of the building. A uniformed man with black pants, black boots, sky blue shirt and white cap came up to Billy's window and saluted. Billy opened the door to speak to him since the bullet proof glass, which was actually plastic and bullet resistant, did not retract into the door.

"Hello sir, you cannot park here. This is a security zone." The officer was polite. Billy took off his sunglasses and smiled to the officer as he spoke.

"I am Mr. Spencer and this is Dr. Porter. We are from the American Embassy and are here to see General Mulugeta."

The officer looked at Billy and then at me and snapped to attention before he spoke again. "Yes, sirs, I have been expecting you. You may leave your truck here." He raised the radio in his left hand to his mouth and spoke a few words of Amharic. The radio replied and he saluted again. "Just go to the main gate and someone will meet you."

We got out of the truck. It was another sunny day in Addis. It really did remind me of LA, with the cool nights and warm days. Addis is dry most of the year but could experience heavy rains for weeks on end, also like Southern California. A steel fence about 12 feet high surrounded the courtyard outside of the building. There were two steel gates with a turnstile that allowed passage in only one direction at the entrance to the building. The gates were painted black, circular, about seven feet high, similar to ones in a football stadium or subway station in the States. There were two police officers in black pants and the sky blue shirts sitting at a folding table about ten feet in front of the gate. There was a small and disorganized line of people waiting to get into the building. Billy ignored the line and went to the officer nearest the gate. "Hello, I am Mr. Spencer and this is Dr. Porter. We are from the American Embassy and have an appointment with General Mulugeta."

The officer ignored Billy until he had mentioned the name of the General. With those words the officer rose to attention and in doing so had upset the table. The papers and clipboard on top slid to the side as the table tipped. It only had three legs and the officer must have been holding it up with his own leg. The second officer must have seen this happen before since he quickly balanced the table with his hands and put the papers and clipboard back in the center. "The General is expecting you. Go through and into the building."

Billy thanked him and we pushed our way through the gate. On the other side was a large cement plaza bordered by some potted trees. We approached the building and came to a small guard shack just outside the entrance. The guard, who was dressed like the other police but carrying an AK-47, came out of the shack and opened the door to the building for us. We passed through the door and came up to a large desk. Constance Powers and Maria Katzakis were seated off to the side of the desk, and I was surprised to see them. Billy must have known they were going to be there, because he wasn't surprised and seemed relieved.

They both wished us a good morning but didn't look at me at all. After our hellos, we turned to the attractive Ethiopian woman behind the desk. She smiled at us and glanced over her shoulder to a man. He was about 6'2", with close cropped hair like most Ethiopian men I had seen, dressed in a dark blue double-breasted suit and holding a small file.

He came around the desk and extended his hand as he smiled to greet us. "Good morning, ladies and gentlemen, I am Colonel Assefa. Welcome to Police Headquarters. The General is expecting you."

We said good morning and introduced ourselves. The five of us moved across the well-lit and very clean lobby to the elevator bank. We entered the elevator and the Colonel pressed a button for the top floor. In the elevator was a poster in Amharic with a smiling man and woman dressed in police uniform. It must have been a recruitment ad. The elevator doors opened directly into a large lobby with several chairs, a sofa and tables. There was no one waiting but there was another attractive Ethiopian woman behind a large wooden desk opposite the elevator. "Good morning, Colonel. If you ladies and gentlemen would have a seat, the General will see you in a moment."

We scattered to the nearest chairs and I picked up the *Ethiopian News*. The headline was about the construction of a new dam on the Blue Nile that was being funded by the Chinese. The chair was uncomfortable and the writing was too stilted for my taste, so I was happy when the woman behind the desk said the General would see us. The Colonel led the way with Constance, Maria and Billy next, and I followed. The woman behind the desk gave me full eye contact and a smile as I passed through the door. She did look good in her uniform, but I only wondered if Felicity would ever smile at me again.

The office was very large and took up most of the entire floor. The General was standing behind a large wooden desk that had several files on the top. He came around and greeted us with a warm and genuine smile. His hair was sprinkled with gray; his black silk suit was cut well and fit perfectly. He was about 60, tall, with a small bulge around his lower abdomen to contrast with his otherwise fit build. His handshake was firm, dry and lasted longer than I thought it would. "Good morning. It is so good of you to come see me this morning."

Maria took the lead and answered for the group. "We are all very pleased to be here and would like to help in any way we can."

"Please sit down and have some coffee."

The Colonel led us to a seating area near the window that had a sofa and several armchairs arranged in a semicircle facing the window. The view was of the square below and Mount Entoto in the distance. The morning haze from the cooking fires was lifting, and several high rises under construction were visible in the middle distance. The door to the reception area opened and the young woman receptionist came in with a silver coffee service. She poured us all coffee and the General spoke. "Dr. Porter, you have had a very interesting introduction to my city." It was an open ended statement meant to draw me out.

"It has been very interesting, to say the least." The General waited for more, so I complied. "The people have been so friendly and

198

the weather is very much like my hometown of Los Angeles. The death at the Embassy has been tragic, though." Billy gave me the "don't say too much" look, but I figured the General knew more than I did and answering his questions might just get him to answer mine.

"Very tragic. Who do you suspect?"

"The FBI and others suspect terrorists, but I think it was someone at the Embassy."

Billy spilled coffee on his tie but the good news was that the tie was already so stained that a little coffee would not be noticed. He sat forward and looked at me with some surprise. His face went from annoyance to acceptance. Maria exchanged silent signals with Constance before she spoke. "Dr. Porter is right that many theories about the incident have been put forth, but no conclusions have been drawn."

Maria and Constance had obviously been sent to ride herd on me. Everything that happened at the meeting would be reported back to the Ambassador. I was past caring about my career at the State Department or really even my own personal safety. I needed to find out what had happened to Travis and I needed Felicity. I spoke. "Ms. Powers is right, but if we look at the facts, it is clear to me that terrorists were not involved."

The General took a long sip of his coffee and sat back in his chair. The Colonel was not drinking, but was looking at me intently. Neither was taking notes so I assumed we were being recorded. The General set his cup on the table next to his chair and spoke again. "Tell me what you think happened, Dr. Porter."

"Someone with access to the Embassy contaminated the buns used in the barbecue. That would not be a good plan for a terrorist. The yield is too low and too uncertain. You can't guarantee people will get ill or that people will die. Also, if they had access to the Embassy, why poison buns? A car bomb or an armed attack would be far more likely to cause the panic and publicity they seek."

Constance just sat there with her mouth open like I was spilling the family secrets. Maria was trying to catch my eye, and Billy was just looking down at his tie. I was telling the family secrets but it was helping me to think out loud. Constance recovered and her voice had a controlled diplomatic tone. "Dr. Porter has his own ideas about what occurred at the Embassy, but others in our government do not agree with him."

The General was not buying it. "Ms. Powers, I agree with Dr. Porter. If the Eritreans or Al-Qaeda were targeting the Embassy they would not be so subtle." The General spoke in a calm but commanding voice. The Colonel silently nodded his head like the vizier to the sultan.

"I think I was shot at to slow down my investigation and to try to implicate terrorists."

Constance leaned forward in her chair and just looked at me with astonishment and disappointment. Maria was still trying to catch my eye and actually moved her left leg closer to mine as if to kick me. It was like we were married and I had said the wrong thing at the dinner table and she wanted to signal her displeasure with some corporal punishment. Billy was just sitting in his chair with a look of resignation on his face. Constance was silent only for a minute. "Dr. Porter, is of course, upset by the recent events and does not represent the views of the United States government."

The General gave a big smile and folded his hands together near his chin. He looked to Constance and then to me and spoke. "You are new to the Foreign Service, Doctor. I can see that. You will have to be more diplomatic in the future. I agree with everything you say, however. Will you be continuing your investigation, Dr. Porter?"

He was obviously well informed about the incidents at the Embassy.

"I hope to, but I think I may be recalled to Washington soon."

The General smiled again and put his hands into his lap. He looked at Constance and lowered his voice. "I think that Dr. Porter's
200

presence here in Addis Ababa is essential to the prompt and fair conclusion of this unfortunate affair. He seems to be the only one at the Embassy who is thinking clearly and not jumping to conclusions that would be detrimental to my nation. We are a poor country and are trying to raise our standard of living. Part of that effort depends on our ability to attract foreign capital. False reports of terrorism might slow down the needed investments."

Constance put down her coffee cup and looked at the General. Maria had retracted her leg and cleared her throat before she spoke. "General, we are all aware of the special relationship that our two countries are developing and the possible negative consequences the recent unpleasantness may have. We are acutely aware of the need for outside investment in Ethiopia and want to limit any negative publicity. Dr. Porter has been working very hard to try and solve this mystery. We are all grateful to him for his efforts, but it is clear that he has reached the end of his rope. Anyone in his situation would be stressed and not thinking clearly. His views clash with the official view of our government and we should all realize that. His personal view is not important and does not count."

She did not sit back in her chair but she was obviously relieved she had said what she came to say. It was clear they thought I had lost my mind and that I was the worst diplomat since Von Ribbentrop. No one could blame them. From an outside and balanced perspective, I was nothing but trouble. An element of chaos introduced in their controlled and diplomatic world. Constance had listened to Maria's speech with quiet approval, and it was her turn to pour dirt on my diplomatic grave. "Dr. Porter will be leaving today, General."

The General was quiet for about a minute. He looked very thoughtful. "I have met many people in my life and all of them are unique. God has given each of us special gifts and it is up to us to use them in the correct way. Ms. Powers and Ms. Katzakis, you are both diplomats and God has given you patience and a way with language. You are both very good at what you do. Mr. Spencer is a man who obviously wishes to protect others.

"When I was much younger, I knew things had to change in my country. The Derg was committing unspeakable acts in the name of their broken philosophy. As you may know ,doctor, the Derg, or the committee, in Amharic, were the Communist rulers that the present government swept from power. The Derg made Ethiopia a Soviet client state and adopted some of the Soviet Union's policies toward dissidents. They killed or imprisoned thousands of people. Many people told me and the others like me that we should not even try to stop them. They said that only diplomacy and discussion would work. They said that we were outnumbered, outgunned and outthought by their evil. I knew they were wrong.

"I have seen men like the Doctor before. He has an idea and he will hold on to it, no matter what may come. He will pursue what he thinks is right until he has changed things, he is fired or he is dead. My country now does not need revolutionaries or radicals like it once did. We need more diplomacy and cooperation now. Yet I must admit that I admire someone who will risk everything for what he believes to be the right course of action. It is true that many of the people who think like the Doctor have an almost religious zeal that is not welcomed by others. I have changed quite a bit over the years, and I am getting comfortable with the rules of diplomacy and teamwork. But I can still recognize a little of the dreamer and fanatic in myself. I see many of those same qualities in the good Doctor.

"I understand how difficult this is for everyone at the Embassy and my government. You have all been under tremendous stress and are very far from home. I would never even think of telling the government and the people of the United States how to run their affairs. The government of Ethiopia will support you in any way that we can and will not in any way impede your investigation. I know that many more Americans are on their way here to help. My colleagues at the Ministry of Foreign Affairs in conjunction with our Embassy in Washington have approved dozens of visas in the last few days. Visas are not always easy to get and the paperwork involved can be difficult to understand. If everything is not correct, it can slow down the process. With all of the recent visa requests, our colleagues in the Foreign Ministry have fallen behind in their work. If the doctor tries to leave before this is cleared up, he may find that his visa is not in order and that he will not be allowed to exit my country."

It was hard for me to believe what I was hearing. My Embassy wanted me out and the Ethiopians wanted me to stay. Constance and Maria just looked at each other but the General was right. They were born to be diplomats. Constance recovered quickly. "General, thank you for the candid and frank discussion. My government and the people of the United States are grateful for your cooperation and assistance in this terrible time. We are also pleased by your interest in the Doctor, his health and well being, but he needs to go home."

The General looked amused and I could see he was enjoying this far more than I could. "I wish the Doctor a good trip home as soon as the investigation is ended. I am only the head of the local police. I have no control over the exit of a diplomat from our country. It has been a very pleasant discussion but I am afraid I must meet with the Prime Minister soon to discuss the latest developments. Thank you so much for coming all the way down to my office."

Maria spoke. It was clear that she and Constance had agreed before hand to tag team their answers. "Thank you as well, General, we look forward to working with you in the future."

We got up to leave and said our goodbyes. The General wished me luck and shook my hand. Billy didn't know what to say and looked at me with pity. Constance and Maria did not acknowledge me in the elevator and were abrupt in their goodbyes when we left the building. I could tell they were upset, but it was a reprieve for me. I could stay and see things through to the end. Travis couldn't thank me and I wasn't sure Felicity would.

Chapter 31

The drive back to the Embassy was quiet. Billy tried to speak a few times, but I was too busy thinking about Travis to really engage in conversation. If I could understand who would want to tamper with the buns, I could figure it all out. It was clear to me that the same person or persons contaminated the buns, left the note, fired the shots and sent the text. Why would anyone poison a child? A terrorist would do it gladly, but who else would? If the motive was not to terrorize, and I was convinced it was not, what could it be? Was someone else at the barbecue the intended target, and if so, how did the culprit expect to poison only that person or if anyone would be poisoned at all? Not everyone at the barbecue got sick and food poisoning is a crude weapon. There would be distress and investigation, but the entire episode would have been chalked up to negligence on the part of a Marine who had volunteered to cook.

I wasn't going to get a lot of help at the Embassy. They were all tired of me. Even Billy was at a loss to explain or understand my behavior. It was ironic that the Ethiopians were the ones who had the most confidence in my abilities.

The street in front of the Embassy had been blocked off by cement barriers and there was a checkpoint manned by Ethiopian Federal Police. I had seen many of them on the streets in the previous days. They had looked bored, and casually held their AK-47s by the barrel, stock, magazine or strap. These officers held their rifles with the strap over their shoulders and hand firmly on the pistol grip. They didn't look bored but deadly serious.

"Ethiopians have increased the guards around the Embassy, as you can see, Doc. Most of the time they don't allow their guys to have loaded guns. All of those are loaded."

We had to show our badges before we were allowed to even get close to the driveway. We pulled up to the Embassy gate and the guard checked our badges again before he waved us through. Billy pulled into the nearest available space and turned off the Suburban. I was feeling guilty. Billy had been the first person to help me, and he had warned me about how the State Department worked. "Billy, I just wanted to say that I truly appreciate everything you have done for me. I'm not trying to make this difficult for you or for the Embassy. I'm just trying to figure out what happened and why a little boy isn't going home with his family."

Billy turned in his seat and gave me a small smile. He had missed an area on his chin while shaving and several gray and black whiskers were present. It was like a forest had been clear cut and there was one small stand of old growth left. He reached out and put his hand on my shoulder. "Doc, this has not been easy on any of us. The Ambassador has blamed me for not protecting you and for not guiding the investigation better. Agent Solomon is pissed because I let you get shot at and yet not let you get killed. Dr. Lessing is upset because you broke into her freezer space and I didn't stop you. The DCM is not pissed, which is the scariest because he's the most able person at this post. I think he will be drawing up my recall papers right after he gets done with yours. Did I miss anybody?"

"No I think that covers most of my sins. I think the Ethiopians aren't upset with me that's something."

"They don't know you like the others. Besides, they think you did the whole thing yourself."

"I shot at myself?"

"No, they aren't stupid. They think you paid me to do it. They say even a crossed-eyed assassin should have hit you at that range. The only explanation for a miss is that you were complicit in the whole event."

"Then why don't they kick me out of the country?"

"They are giving you enough rope to hang yourself. They can't accuse you and they don't want terrorists blamed because that would make investors skittish. They don't want you sent home because that would give more credence to the terrorism angle. They're hoping that you will be obliging enough to either uncover the person or persons behind this or get caught by us."

205

"Do you think I had anything to do with this, Billy?"

He squeezed my shoulder harder. "Doc, you're screwed up in a lot of ways. You follow your own rules even when you could work with others. You don't follow advice and revel in upsetting the system. You lie when it suits you and are incapable of following simple protocol." He didn't seem upset but had paused and let go of my shoulder. Turning to face the windshield he let out a deep sigh. "You couldn't be responsible for the poisoning you weren't here. You couldn't shoot at yourself and I know you didn't write the note or the text."

His body seemed to relax. "Doc, even with all of your bullshit, I'm glad you came here because without you we would never have known that someone killed Travis. I just wish your methods were more…collaborative, at least with me."

There was a long moment of silence. The morning sun was bright and the sky seemed very close. It was beautiful. Felicity was walking from the parking lot toward the Embassy, and she did not see us in the Suburban. Billy inclined his head toward her and looked at me. "I forgot one other person who is upset with you. She isn't angry at you because of your official duties, however. I don't know what you did to her, but she wants to kill me just because I like you."

I let out a sigh and slumped in my seat. It was crazy, but losing Felicity was worse than losing than my wife. It is true I loved my wife, but she didn't really love me. From the day in Gross lab to the day I found her with another man, there was always a cold calculus between us. She had used me and I had used her. We were a perfect professional couple on the surface, but I never felt the deep connection I had with Felicity. The closeness with Felicity was completely different and existed despite, in some ways because of, the uncertainty that surrounded us. There was no calculation or logic to it and it was far less stable. Although I had lost Felicity just as I had found her, the bond between us was stronger than anything I had with my wife. I spoke without thinking. "Do you think she will ever forgive me?"

"Felicity is a great woman. Obviously attractive, intelligent, loyal, determined, strong and yet there is something vulnerable about her. I have never seen her upset like this in the almost two years I have known her. She has always been aloof to a certain degree, but I think when you are as beautiful as she is, that comes with the territory. Every guy in East Africa fantasizes about her and half had tried to get her into bed. That has to be hard when you are trying to establish yourself in a business as tough as hers. She has never been intimate with any of them. My wife thinks she has had her heart broken and can't recover. I am not sure what is going on between you two, but you have hit her harder than anything else. Will she ever forgive you? My feeling is that she will not. Those who cross her have made a potent and powerful enemy."

He was right, of course. She was a woman that was charting her own course and could have her pick of men. Her ex was a recruiting poster for the CIA and he could not hold her. How could I compete with him or the next perfect physical and emotional specimen that came along? I could see all the qualities Billy mentioned in her as well. Our love was doomed as it began because I could not let go of woman who had left me 10 years ago. Why did I lie? I had lost everything before and survived. The problem was that just surviving was no longer enough.

Chapter 32

I entered the Embassy and went directly into the health unit. Rhonda was in the waiting room, straightening up some magazines and toys. She looked well rested and her white coat was crisp and fresh.

"Good morning, Rhonda. How are you?"

She looked at me closely before she answered. "Isaac. Are you OK?"

"Yes, Rhonda, why do you ask?"

"You look like you slept in your clothes and I heard about what happened last night at the Embassy reception."

"I didn't sleep in my clothes because I didn't sleep. Actually, I feel good. Better than I have felt in a couple of days."

She looked at me like she didn't believe me, but then she smiled a little. "That's good, because Dr. Lessing is here to see you."

"Rhonda, I think I am ready to handle even Dr. Lessing."

"Give me some of whatever you have been drinking!"

With that I went past the reception area and into my office. Dr. Lessing was writing some notes on a pad and did not look up as she spoke. "I need all you have on your investigation. The Ambassador has told me that you will be leaving for Washington this evening, and I will need whatever you have to assist in finding out what happened." Her tone was even but her voice contained a note of triumph.

"I don't have any notes. It is all contained on the hard drive." With that I pointed to my head and smiled. Finally looking up, she slowly put down her pen and gave me a smile. She was happy.

"You just don't get it, do you? Your career in the Foreign Service is over. The methods you have used have upset everyone at post and impeded the search for the truth. The lack of notes is indicative of the kind of slipshod attitude you have toward the Foreign

208

Service, medicine and science. You cannot respect the order and discipline that is necessary for the proper functioning of this organization." She let her words sink in and I think she was also waiting for me to cry or beg for forgiveness. After she got up and turned to go, I gave her one last shot.

"Everything you say may be true, but I am not leaving until this investigation is concluded."

"The Ambassador says you are going and you will go, unless you want to add insubordination to your other sins."

"The Ambassador may try to send me home, but I am not going yet, and it won't be insubordination."

She just stared at me with her blue eyes and her wrinkled lip as if I had just spoken in Russian or Martian. My words were incomprehensible to her; she could not understand someone who would not follow orders. Without another word she left the room and asked Rhonda for any of my notes. Rhonda told her there weren't any. Dr. Lessing scoffed and left the unit.

I sat down at my desk and turned the bobble-head of Manny Ramirez around so I could look into his eyes. He looked happy. The Empire State Building was tall and strong. I was dialing before I knew what I was going to say.

"Good morning, this is Emily."

She gave no indication of the name of the office. I guess they don't worry about branding or wrong numbers at the CIA station.

"Emily, this is Dr. Porter, I need to speak with Ms. Gonsalves."

"Ms. Gonsalves is preparing for this morning's EAC and asked not to be disturbed. I will let her know you called." She didn't say it but I could tell by her voice she thought I was a bastard. She hung up. My phone rang just as I replaced on the cradle.

"Doctor Porter, this is Dick Lawrence. How are you this morning?"

I wasn't sure why he was calling but he must have been informed of my meeting with the General.

"I am doing well under the circumstances. What can I do for you?"

"I would like to see you in my office. Could you come up now?"

"Should I pack first?"

He laughed. "You and I both know you won't be going anywhere soon. Can you come up now?"

"I'll be there in a few minutes."

I got up from my desk and told Rhonda that I was going up to the DCM's office. She didn't say anything but her one arched eyebrow told me good luck. I exited the health unit and went past the cafeteria to the stairs. The DCM was located on the third floor near the Ambassador's office. I paused at the top of the stairs to catch my breath. The Embassy was at about 8,000 feet and I had not gotten used to the lack of oxygen.

After a short rest I went to the DCM's office. His administrative assistant was a middle-aged white woman with a blue dress and a gold Ethiopian and American flag pin on her lapel. She showed me into the DCM's office. She said he had been called into a meeting with the Ambassador and that he would be right with me. I declined her offer of coffee.

The office was large and in the corner of the building. The view out of the window was down the mountain toward the airport. I could see a plane taking off in the distance and some donkeys strolling down Entoto road. His desk was large and well organized. There were pictures of him with a Hispanic woman and two teenage children on his desk. No bobble-heads or tiny skyscrapers needed. His bookcases contained a collection of Foreign Policy books and some fiction. The fiction was Stendhal, Joyce, Faulkner and Hemingway. There was a diploma from Yale for undergraduate studies in Foreign Relations and another from the Harvard Kennedy School. There was a small picture next to the diplomas that showed him receiving a plaque from the previous President. It was impressive and yet understated. The whole office was themed to let the visitor know a little about the man, but in a subtle and controlled way. I didn't hear him come in until he spoke. "Good morning Doctor, I am sorry to keep you waiting. I had to meet with the Ambassador about the EAC. Did anyone tell you we are having a meeting at lunch?"

"I had a meeting of my own this morning, so I haven't checked my email yet."

"I know how busy you have been. Well, consider yourself informed. I heard about the meeting from Constance and Maria. They seem to think you are not suited for the Foreign Service. I must tell you the Ambassador feels the same way." He paused and studied me. Even though he was slightly overweight, the black suit with white shirt and gray tie that he was wearing looked great on him. There was a sense of control that seemed to be just part of his being. He wasn't trying to project anything; it was just coming off of him like a mist from a pond.

I didn't want to respond and just waited for him to speak again. "I don't think they are being fair with you. You are brand new and the events of this week have been once in a career experiences for all of us. They blame you because your methods are very… disruptive shall we say. I never thought that something like this could happen at my Embassy, but it has. At first I thought that this was all too much for you but now I see that I have underestimated you. You were the only one here who could have started to unravel this thing. The others are afraid of you because you upset their concept of the world. Why do you think this happened?"

His statements were meant to gain my confidence. The praise he had given me would work far better than any threat and he knew that. The polish on him was not a veneer. He had true gifts of diplomacy and control. I answered as honestly as I could.

"I think someone in the Embassy has been behind the whole thing and that they are still out there. The food poisoning was a deliberate act, but I am not sure of the motive. The attack on me at the Bazaar, the note and the text, were all to lead us to conclude terrorists were at work. I don't think that is the case."

His face was a combination of concern and encouragement. "I can see your point. It does seem strange. Do you have any idea who could be behind it or why?" It was a good question but I didn't have an answer. All I had accomplished so far was to ask some questions and get everyone upset. I wasn't really any closer to understanding what was going on.

"I'm not sure. You know the people here better than I do."

"True enough. I can't see anyone here doing it. I thought Frederick may have been involved when I found the freezer malfunction, but it is obvious that was not the cause." He looked at me differently. I have seen the look before in patients. It usually occurs when they are about to leave the office but have something else they wish to discuss. The topic is always something embarrassing like erectile dysfunction, alcoholism or hemorrhoids. "I understand why you lied about your wife to Felicity. It is very hard to find out that your wife is unfaithful. I know from experience. You heard Frederick and me arguing outside the commissary, didn't you."

"Yes, I did and I mentioned it to him. Did he discuss it with you?"

"He did. I wanted you to know that I do not hold it against him and that I was just doing my job the other day. I also know the pain you are going through, not only about Travis but about Felicity and your wife. I would agree with the others that you should leave, but my reasons are not theirs. I don't fear you like they do. I feel like I know more about why you act the way that you do and it doesn't frighten me. I understand how things can spin out of control sometimes."

I didn't have anything else to say and neither did he. We did have things in common, but it seemed like he had taken his loss and betrayal better than I had mine. We just sat there for a few minutes until his phone rang. It must have been his secretary because he just said OK.

"Dr. Porter, thank you for coming in to see me and I want you to come to me if you have any questions or thoughts about the case or anything else. We were going to get you on a plane tonight, but it looks like we will have to wait until morning. Constance tells me she thinks your visa is not in order so she is talking to the Foreign Minister this afternoon. I will see you at the EAC at noon?"

"Yes, I will be there. Thank you for the meeting."

We shook hands. I walked out of the room and said goodbye to his admin assistant. Breathing going down the stairs was easier but I lingered hoping I might run into Felicity. She didn't show but I was probably in the wrong stairwell. After exiting the stairs I went back to the health unit. The waiting room was empty and the receptionist Mahedere was gone. I didn't see Rhonda, so I walked back to my office.

"Dr. Porter is that you?" It was Rhonda calling to me from the lab area. I walked into the lab and she was counting tubes and needles used to collect blood. She looked up as I entered and I leaned against a table holding the microscope.

"Yes, Rhonda, where is everybody?"

"Didn't you see the email? The Ambassador ordered all non-essential personnel home due to the possibility of a terror attack."

"It is good to know that someone thinks I am essential."

She snorted in disbelief and looked at me with a smile. "Billy told me about your meeting with the Ethiopians. You sure have things screwed up. That is so sad, I was just getting to like you and we need a Doctor around here with all this mess going on."

"I just wanted to see the world and get away."

213

She was silent for a minute and stopped counting the Red Top tubes. "I am sorry your wife left you, Isaac. I know that can be very hard."

"It was 10 years ago, Rhonda. It's time to move on."

She looked at me with concern mixed with some disapproval. I broke the silence. "Why are you taking inventory now? Is that part of the anti-terror preparation?"

"No, I just like to do things with my hands when I am thinking."

"What have you been thinking about?"

"Just the last few days and Travis. It is so sad and to think that someone did it on purpose." I felt some liquid run down the back of my head and I touched it. It was sticky and clear when I looked at it. Rhonda saw what I was doing and came over to look at the back of my head. "Isaac, you are the worst patient. This head wound is infected, probably from you dumpster diving yesterday. Come with me so I clean this up."

She grabbed my arm and took me into the exam room across the hall. After I was seated on the exam table, she let go and told me to lay on my stomach so she could clean out the wound. The hydrogen peroxide, cotton swabs and instruments were in a glass cabinet. The noise she made getting them told me she was upset. I could feel her gloved fingers probing the wound and it hurt a little. "Isaac, there is a small abscess here so I am going to pop a couple of stitches and clean it out."

"Is it going to hurt?"

"I hope so, you deserve it." Her tone was more motherly than mad but she was right. It did hurt. She was using a strange combination of caring and sadism. Maybe she was making me pay penance for my sins. The hydrogen peroxide stung as she dug the cotton swab under my scalp. The abscess was not a big deal and I was sure that I would feel better in a couple of days. "Felicity Gonsalves came in today to see me about you."

Involuntarily I arched my back and lifted myself up from the table so I could see her face. It was a mistake. Rhonda had been cleaning the wound with a wood shafted cotton tipped swab and I heard it break as I sat up. The wood buried itself in my scalp and it hurt. I didn't move, though, because I wanted to hear what she said about Felicity.

"Damn it, Isaac. You deserve that for moving and more for what you did to that poor girl."

"I shouldn't have lied to her about my wife, Rhonda."

"You be nice to her. She has been through a lot."

"What about me? I've been through a lot too, Rhonda."

"That is true, Isaac, but you are getting what you deserve and I am not sure she is."

"Why do you say that?"

"Lay down. I am trying to work here."

She pushed down on my back with a force more like a linebacker than a nurse. I resisted at first but gave up since I knew she would just keep pushing harder and she was probably stronger than I was. After I was back in my place, I decided to speak again.

"What did you talk about?"

"I can't tell you that. She came to see me, not you."

I could always look in the chart. Rhonda looked like she kept good notes. Unfortunately she also knew Doctors tricks.

"And don't try to look in her file. I didn't write down what she told me and I have her chart locked in my desk."

215

"Rhonda, I would never do that." There must have been a very deep pocket of pus that she was trying to get at because she seemed to pushing with all her weight on my head. It was hurting quite a bit. She let up a little before she said anything.

"You would do exactly that. You don't follow all the rules. She is a very nice woman and I like her. She just has bad taste in men."

"Am I that bad?"

"You are, but I wasn't talking about you. Her ex-husband, whom she doesn't lie to anybody about, came to see her about two months ago. He told her something and now she is going to Moscow in a couple of months to be with him."

My head stopped hurting and I felt like I was watching those damn towers fall again. It was the same thing the Russians had told me at the reception. The night I had spent with Felicity was probably just a last fling before she went back to him. She must not have experienced the same connection that I felt.

"You got quiet all of a sudden, Isaac."

"I think on that last probe you hit my speech center."

She snorted again and put her hand on my shoulder. The maternal instinct had taken over from the corporal punishment instinct. Maybe those aren't far apart. After a motherly pat on my shoulder she spoke again. "If that were true, the Ambassador would give me a medal. Your head is as clean as I can get it. You are getting a shot in your butt with some Ceftriaxone and you know that is going to hurt."

"It isn't the pain that I mind, it is the fact that you're enjoying it that bothers me."

"Isaac, someone has to look out for you, Billy Spencer can't do it all himself."

Chapter 33

Rhonda had put a gauze turban over my wound, but I didn't want it on my head. It was too dramatic and I was afraid it would make me look ridiculous in the EAC. However, the memory of the pain Rhonda could inflict made me afraid to take it off while she was around. My plan was to go into the men's room, near the cafeteria, and remove it. As I went inside, I was getting ready to remove my bandage when Cruz walked in. "Morning, Doc, nice bandage."

"Rhonda cleaned my wound and she got carried away with the dressing. I was just going to take it off."

"I don't think that is a good idea, Doc."

"I wanted to take it off before the EAC."

I really wanted it off before I saw Felicity. There should be no distractions when we talked and a head wrapped in gauze is a distraction. Looking too wounded in front of her would not help. Her sympathy or pity would just make losing her worse. We needed to talk even if was just me apologizing for being rude last night.

Cruz was just looking at me and then he smiled. "Doc, chicks dig the wounded warrior look. Ms. Gonsalves will be hot for you again."

"I think it will take more than some gauze to get her to notice me again. Besides, who said she was ever hot for me?"

"Doc, the Embassy is like a small town. Everybody knows you two are fighting. It will blow over. All great loves are tempestuous."

"Are you a warrior philosopher?"

"Nope, I'm a Marine who knows a lot about women. Let me take you up to the EAC, Doc, you don't want to be late." He came over to put his hand under my arm like he was afraid I was going to faint.

"Cruz, I appreciate the escort, but you don't have to hold me up."

He laughed and let go. "I just wanted to make sure you knew I was serious."

We exited the bathroom and went to the nearest stairwell. Cruz didn't say anything else and the altitude did not seem to bother him like it did me. When we exited the third floor I was breathing very hard and did not see Felicity at first. She was standing by the stairwell exit, almost as if she had been waiting there. I became paranoid and wondered if this was all a plot by Cruz and Rhonda to get me to see her.

It took her a minute to notice me, and when she did the look on her face was mixed. At first there was contempt and anger, but it soon turned to concern and then indifference. It was interesting to see but would have been more interesting if I wasn't the cause of the change. It is interesting to watch the lions feed on the zebra as long as you aren't the zebra.

"Good morning, can we talk?" I was so out of breath that my voice sounded like an old man with emphysema. It was weak, gasping and with a sound of defeat that did not impress Felicity. I should have waited to catch my breath.

"Why do you have a bandage on your head, Dr. Porter?" Her tone was flat and emotionless.

"Rhonda cleaned out my wound this morning. I am sorry that I lied to you about my wife and I hope you can forgive me."

She looked at me and at Cruz. He was looking down the hall like he expected a bus or taxi.

"You shouldn't have lied to me, but I don't want to discuss that here. We should go to the meeting." She turned toward the meeting room, and I tried to grasp her arm to stop her. It felt like I was drowning and grabbing for a life ring. I reached across my body for her arm. She pulled away violently and I was thrown off balance. There is always that point when your brain knows that you're going to fall and there's nothing you can do. My body spun around and I fell to the floor. My skull made the satisfying ripe watermelon sound as I hit. I didn't think I passed out, but somehow Cruz and Felicity were kneeling beside me when I opened my eyes.

"Zack, are you alright?" There was concern in her voice, but who wouldn't be concerned about a guy passed out in front of you? Anyway, it felt good, even if it was going to be temporary.

"I'm fine, I just slipped."

"You were out again. You should see a doctor."

"I see one shave every day."

She smiled in spite of herself for a moment and then her face was impassive again. Pulling hard on my arm, she sat me up. My head was throbbing and I felt like throwing up.

Cruz looked worried. "Doc, how are you feeling? Like Ms. Gonsalves said, you were out for a minute."

"I feel great Cruz, and we need to get to that meeting, Felicity."

It was good to say her name out loud. I pulled myself to my feet and started to walk down the hall toward the EAC when 2 hands grabbed me under my arms. "Conference room is the other way, Doc."

"It's OK Cruz, I'll make sure he doesn't get lost." With that, I turned around under my own power and headed for the meeting with Felicity on my right. I wanted to say something else, but when I turned to speak she just shook her head. It was clear she did not want to talk, at least, I told myself, not now.

We could hear the voices before we got to the conference room. They were loud and angry but unintelligible. There was a small table outside the room with a large coffee urn and paper cups. I stopped at the table, hoping to hear more before I entered, and also to prolong my time with her. My offer of coffee went unanswered except for a shake of her head to indicate no. She waited for me to pour

219

myself a cup a before she opened the door and held it for me. The room was a mess. There were about 25 people either standing or sitting around the table that was littered with coffee cups, pads, laptops, pens, paper and even a couple of maps. Everyone was talking at once and no one seemed to notice us enter. The picture of the Twin Towers was gone but the hole in the wall remained. The Ambassador, at the head of the table, was talking to the DCM. The Ambassador caught sight of me and stopped talking. The DCM followed his eyes to me and slowly, like a contagion of interest, everyone stopped what they were doing and turned to me. It was eerie, as if they were all shocked that I was even there.

The room was completely silent for a moment before the Ambassador spoke. "I am glad you could join us. The DCM and I were just discussing your performance at Police Headquarters this morning. I am sure you are very proud of yourself."

It was clear he didn't want an answer but I didn't care. "I am just doing my job, Mr. Ambassador."

He was about to speak again when the DCM just barely touched his arm and spoke. "We should get the meeting underway."

The Ambassador was mad but under control as he looked at the DCM and then at me. "I hereby call the Emergency Action Committee to order. We will need all of you to give Constance Powers your names, affiliation and contact information so that we can have an accurate record of attendance."

It was like taking roll at school during a tornado. I could see why a guy like me who is more interested in outcome than in process could really upset them. Even in adversity they could fall back on procedure. Maybe they were right. I hadn't followed the rules and what did I have to show for it?

With the housekeeping announcement out of the way, the Ambassador was ready to get down to business. "As you all know, last night a message from a terrorist organization was sent to one of the Embassy staff. The phone that sent the message was later discovered inside the Embassy compound. We are here to decide how best to proceed. I will tell you that an Ordered Departure of all non-essential personnel and all dependents has already been authorized. I spoke with the Secretary this morning and we agreed that it was a necessary step."

Ordered Departure meant that people were ordered to leave. It didn't mean things were in order. No one spoke and everyone was listening to the Ambassador, but many eyes were on me. I was standing near the door. Felicity had taken a seat near the DCM and Billy. The people looked at me with a mixture of hostility, pity and anger. Billy looked slightly amused and Felicity's expression was blank, but she was looking at me. My head was throbbing and the coffee was making my stomach hurt. The Ambassador continued. "I want to go around the room and hear from the other professionals as to what they think our next steps should be. Agent Solomon, perhaps you and your colleagues can start."

Agent Solomon was seated opposite Felicity and several of the men with the slightly too large suits were seated next to him or standing behind him. "Thank you, Mr. Ambassador. The FBI has sent out several field agents and technicians to help us evaluate the evidence so far and to plan a proper response. We have some information about the letter Dr. Porter found. The paper was standard and it was printed on a popular brand of computer printer. The only fingerprints on it were Dr. Porter's. We have no other facts about the text or the letter at this time. More agents are on the way as we speak and should be here within the next 12 to 24 hours. I am going to let Agent Wong speak for a moment since he is the lead agent from D.C."

Agent Wong was Asian, about 45, with a short, almost military haircut, and a black suit with red tie. He had some papers and a Blackberry in front of him. His voice was clear and full of confidence. "Thank you Agent Solomon, and thank you, Mr. Ambassador for the warm welcome we have received from the Embassy. My team and I are here to help you get to the bottom of these threats, find out who is responsible and bring them to justice. The FBI is putting its full resources to bear to mitigate this situation."

The Ambassador nodded towards the FBI and was getting ready to move on when Agent Wong spoke again. "One more thing. Did Dr. Porter get on the plane to D.C. yet? Washington is very anxious to speak with him. We feel he is the key to the entire situation."

The Ambassador didn't know what to say for a moment. Agent Solomon looked in my direction, as did everyone who knew me. It was awkward but not as bad as being shot at.

The DCM stepped into the breach. "Agent Wong, Dr. Porter is still here and standing there at the end of the table with the bandage on his head."

Agent Wong looked like he had seen the corpse stand up at the funeral. He turned to Solomon. "My mistake. Agent Solomon said he was going back this morning. I am sorry that I did not know who you were, Doctor." He said it with a smile and a nod of the head.

The Ambassador spoke next. "Thank you Agent Wong. Ms. Gonsalves, can you tell us about your end of the investigation?"

"Mr. Ambassador, we have done a preliminary trace on all activity from the phone that sent the text. The text was the only time it has been used and it was acquired locally, but we don't know where yet. We are working with our Ethiopian and other East African liaison partners and although we have a few leads, there is no hard intelligence as to who is behind the threats. My team and I think getting Dr. Porter out of the country as soon as possible will also help the situation."

"How will my departure help the situation?" My voice was louder than I had anticipated and I was angry about being told what to do but it was a fair question. I should have stopped there.

"I think we're on the wrong track here and need to get some questions answered. Ms. Gonsalves, can you tell me why you and the Wollinskys met with the Russian Alexi Lebed at his house two weeks before the barbecue? "

Her mouth actually dropped open, and she stared at me in disbelief. It was a stupid thing to say in front of everyone, but I needed to know. I didn't really believe she met them to find a dry cleaner in Moscow. Felicity recovered quickly and she looked directly into my eyes. It was the look an audience member gives to the lion tamer at the circus just before he steps into the cage. It was amusement, horror and amazement. She was trying to figure out why someone would ask such a foolish question.

I recognized Dr. Lessing's voice before I could find her at the table. She was close to Billy. "Dr. Porter, please. Even I know not to ask certain questions, even here in the EAC. I know you think are helpful, but really you are impeding the investigation. It is clear that you are under a great deal of personal stress and feel guilty about the death of the boy. Dr. Porter, as a fellow professional, I think for your own health, you should go home."

The Ambassador and the DCM wanted me out because I wasn't good at following orders. Agent Solomon and Billy wanted me to leave so that there would be one less target for the terrorists. Dr. Lessing wanted me out so she could run the investigation the way she wanted. Felicity had had her fling and was ready to return to her ex. They all had separate reasons, but the main goal was the same. Get me out of town. Dr. Lessing was right. I was fed up with being told what to do, but I didn't want to get thrown out just yet.

"Dr. Porter will go home, but we should all think about Travis for a moment and put aside our differences to try to figure out what happened." The DCM was calm and in control as he spoke. The meeting went on for another two or three hours but nothing really happened. They should have changed the name to the Emergency In-Action Committee.

Chapter 34

I went back down to the health unit and took off the bandage. The Embassy was quiet. Most of the people were at home getting ready to ship out on the next flight. Did they regret leaving or were they relieved?

Rhonda was in her office doing paperwork, and she saw me as I passed the door. "How did it go?"

"The meeting was another example of why I don't belong in the Foreign Service. They all want me to leave."

"I meant, how did it go with Felicity? I knew you wouldn't do well in the meeting."

"It went OK up until I slipped and cracked my head on the floor. I took off the bandage, it was bothering me."

She laughed with a mixture of amazement and humor. Slowly shaking her head, she looked at me. "I'm not worried about you anymore. Your skull is too thick to break. My middle son, Thomas, is just like you. He won't do anything he doesn't want to and is always getting into some kind of scrape at school, or in sports or in Boy Scouts. I used to worry about him all of the time. He is so different from my other kids. I've just grown to accept him."

"Well, look at the bright side Rhonda; he'll probably grow up to be a doctor in the Foreign Service."

"Maybe, or he may wind up in jail somewhere. I still love him though. He can't help who he is." It sounded like a compliment and I waited for her to continue, but she simply went back to the paperwork she had been doing. My head was spinning a little but it stopped when I started to walk to my office. The office was bright in the afternoon sunshine. I sat down at my desk and got out some paper to help organize my thoughts.

The problem was simple. I needed to figure out who contaminated the buns and why. That would tell me about the note, the

224

shooting and the text. There were about 300 Americans at the Embassy, including all the Federal Agencies and dependents. They all had access to the Embassy as did the 700 or so local employees. All of the Americans had access to the commissary where the buns were stored. The local employees could go there to buy things, but the prices were too high for most of them and they really didn't want Cheetos like the Americans did anyway. Anyone in Addis who could shoot an AK-47 could have shot at me at Millennium Hall. The phone that sent the text had been used only once and had been purchased locally. On my rides back and forth between my house and the Embassy, I had seen that cell phone stores were on every block. It would take time to run down where it was sold but even then it would be hard to track the buyer. The phones were a government controlled monopoly but I doubted they kept very good records on each sim card sold. The syringe that I had found in the dumpster was available in the health unit or any pharmacy in the city. All the Americans had access to the health unit and although it might be tricky, they could all steal a syringe. Nothing really pointed to one person. They would need more agents.

Finding the phone that had sent the threat on the Embassy compound helped narrow things down. The MSG kept an afterhours log of everyone who entered the Embassy during non-work hours. Unfortunately, there must have been 100 Americans and 200 Ethiopians and other Diplomats there that night. Still it was a start.

The note was placed by someone with access to my house and that was a more exclusive list. It had been printed on a standard printer of which there must be a hundred in the Embassy. Printing logs might show which computer it was from but maybe not and it could have been printed at home or at an internet café in the city. Those were more common than cell phone stores. The note itself did not help. The fact that it was found in my house did. I didn't think Eskander would do it unless someone paid him. He didn't seem like that kind of guy, even if I wasn't completely sure what kind of a guy he was. If he placed the note, he didn't have access to the Embassy to send the text.

In medicine we look for the single unifying diagnosis that will explain all of the facts. It was Sherlock Holmes' favorite thing as well.

All the disparate and seemingly contradictory facts could be explained by the proper theory. In reality medicine is not ordered and a lot of the time does not make sense. Just like life.

Management Officer Frederick Stevenson would have the keys, to the house because he oversaw the housing department. The Ambassador and the DCM could theoretically get the keys but I was sure that would raise some eyebrows. The Marines had keys to everything. Could Cruz have put the note in my house as a way to relieve his guilt? I didn't think so, but it could have happened. Agent Solomon could get the keys from the Marines or from housing. Why would he leave the note? Was he trying to make a terrorist attack seem plausible? As RSO, Billy could have placed the note but I couldn't understand why. Felicity worked for the CIA and presumably there was no key she could not get. Why did she meet with the Russians two weeks before the incident? Could she be in league with them in some way? Dr. Lessing didn't like me, but I didn't think she could do this. She had worked hard to close the investigation. Was that to cover up something?

My head was really hurting now. I glanced at the clock and saw two hours had passed during my musings. It was getting late and I needed to get home for dinner. Maybe more thinking later, after I ate, would help. My brilliant notes were a disappointment. There was only one thing written on the page. Felicity?

I said good night to Rhonda and told her I was going to the communication office to get another phone and radio. Agent Solomon had taken my old phone and I needed the radio in case of emergency. She wished me a good night and reminded me to keep my head out of any dumpsters on the way home. The communication office was in the basement of the Embassy and I got another cheap Nokia phone and a Motorola radio with charger. Going back up to Post One, I stopped so that the Marine could record my new cell phone number and to pick a call sign for the radio. The name badge on his shirt said Stanger and he was a Lance Corporal. He explained that the call signs were used so that anyone listening could not identify the person using the radio. He said most people choose something related to them that was easy to remember and handed me a list of call signs already assigned. Post One was Home Plate, Billy was Cowboy, Cruz was Romeo, The DCM was New Haven and the Ambassador was Alpha. Rhonda had chosen Nightingale and Felicity was Macau. I briefly considered Flat Tire or Wrecking Ball but settled for Glasscutter. I worked in a glass shop in high school.

The motorpool driver was new and spoke very little English, but he knew my name and seemed to know where he was going. As we went down Entoto road through the roundabout and onto the Ring Road, I noticed that the road crossed a very deep ravine. Addis Ababa has two rainy seasons. The little rains come from March till June and the big rains from July through September. The bottom of the ravine was 30 or 40 feet below the road and there was not much water there. The rocks were well worn, about 10 to 20 feet above the present water level, so it must fill up with the rains. Other than a wayward donkey or two, the traffic was not bad and we were outside my house 20 minutes after leaving the Embassy. Eskander let us in through the gate and I got out. The driver wished me a good evening and backed out.

After the gate was closed, Eskander came up to me. Kokeb was sitting on the front step with several bags of food. "Good evening, Doctor. Kokeb is waiting to cook your dinner."

Turning to Kokeb I spoke. "Hello, Kokeb, how are you doing? Ready to start work?"

She smiled, stood up, turned toward me and took the ear buds from the iPod out of her ears. The modest brown dress was gone and she was dressed in jeans, white top and blue Adidas shoes. Her hair was tied up, revealing her high forehead and she gave me a genuine, warm smile. "Yes, Doctor, did you have a good day at work?"

Not wanting to tell her yet that I was about to get fired, I changed the subject. "Eskander, will you be joining me for dinner?"

"Oh no, Doctor, I should stay out here and watch things until the night guard arrives."

227

"Eskander, you don't want me to eat alone for my first real meal in Ethiopia, do you? I insist you join me."

"Thank you, Doctor, I will wash up." He smiled. I think he was hoping I would insist. It was also a good sign that he liked Kokeb's cooking. Eskander had gone to the little guard shack/bathroom that was in the front yard near the fountain. After I unlocked the security gate and door, Kokeb carried the bags into the kitchen and declined my attempt to help. She was opening and closing drawers looking for pots and utensils. When I entered, she was pulling some pots out of the bag she had brought. "My uncle told me you may need pots, so I brought my own."

"Your Uncle will join me for dinner and I hope you will, too."

"My uncle likes my cooking, especially when someone else is buying. We do not want to intrude."

"Like I told him, you don't want me to eat my first real meal in Ethiopia alone, do you?"

She smiled and put down the spoon she had been holding. "It would be a pleasure to join you, Doctor."

"Great. I will just go and get cleaned up."

She nodded and moved back over to the stove. I went upstairs and the altitude took the usual toll on my breathing. The warm water of the shower felt good and woke me up. Putting on a clean shirt, jeans and my casual shoes, I went downstairs. Eskander was waiting by the table and when he saw me he said something to Kokeb who was in the kitchen. She looked out at me and nodded her head. They must have been wondering what had kept me. There were three plates on the table, with glasses and napkins but no silverware. I sat down at the head of the table with Eskander on my left and a place for Kokeb on my right. She brought in a large platter and set it down. She then returned to the kitchen and brought in a basket with rolls of gauze before she spoke. "We are going to eat Ethiopian style tonight, Doctor. My uncle and I are very grateful for what you are doing for me and we will treat you like family."

"That is most gracious of you both. I'm hungry and it smells good. Where is my fork?" They both laughed and looked at each other and then back to me before Kokeb spoke.

"We will eat Ethiopian style and no silverware to clean afterward." She was quite pretty and seemed more American than Ethiopian. "We will use this flat bread called njera to pick up the wat from the platter and eat. Let me show you."

She picked up a roll of what looked like used gauze from the basket and unrolled it. It was flat, spongy bread with a pale gray color. Tearing off a small piece, she dipped it into the platter. Scooping up some of the wat with the bread, she took it to her mouth and ate it. She looked at me while she was chewing and motioned with her hand to follow her lead. Eskander had beaten me to the punch and was already enjoying his dinner. The njera was cool and very elastic. The gray color was off-putting, but I tore off a piece and picked up some wat that looked like spinach. The bread had a mild malty flavor and the spinach was good. I took some more njera and tried the other wats. Kokeb was a good cook and the food tasted delicious. My fingers were very messy by the third or fourth round, and I tried not to think about the hand hygiene of my fellow guests. Eskander had some of the juice from the spicy chicken wat on his chin while he spoke. "Kokeb will get more weight on you, Doctor."

"The meal is excellent and I'm glad we don't have to clean the silverware." It seemed as good a time as any to tell them the truth.

"I need to tell you both that I will be leaving here in the next few days. I am sure you both know about the death of the little boy at the Embassy."

They both stopped eating and looked at me. Eskander was shocked but Kokeb looked upset. I think she was worried about me but just in case she was worried about the money, I wanted to put her mind at ease.

"I'm going to loan you the money so that you can get back to New York and I am not going to argue about it. If you don't take it, I am going to get Eskander fired."

I smiled so they would know I was joking about Eskander but not the money. Kokeb reached out to touch my hand and to mouth thank you because she could not speak. There were tears streaming down her cheeks. Dinner must have been over because she got up and started clearing the plates. Eskander tried to get in one last bite but in his haste the njera and wat landed in his lap. He quickly scooped it into his mouth but Kokeb gave him a disapproving look. The table in front of me was littered with small bits of food and my white shirt had several brown, red and yellow stains on the front. It looked like I had been sprayed by a multi-colored rain. Eating Ethiopian family style was good but messy.

"She looks just like my sister, her mother, when she was that age." Eskander had gotten up from the table while I had been surveying the damage to my shirt front. He was standing to my left as he spoke.

"Your sister must be very pretty, Eskander."

"She is with God now. She died soon after Kokeb was born. The Derg killed her just before the revolution."

"I am sorry for your loss, Eskander."

He paused and was silent. Kokeb reappeared from the kitchen and said something to Eskander in Amharic. He nodded and they both turned to me. "My uncle and I want to thank you for your kindness, Doctor. I deeply appreciate the loan you are giving me and I will pay you back as soon as I am able."

"Kokeb, it is a pleasure to be able to help you out and you can pay me back when you can. There is no hurry."

"Thank you for the meal, Doctor, and for what you are doing for Kokeb. You are a man of honor. I will go outside to wait for the night guard and Kokeb will clean up."

"Thank Kokeb for the meal, Eskander, she did the cooking."

They both smiled and he moved toward the front door. I opened the door and the security screen. The night was clear and cool probably around 55 degrees. The street light was out and I could see the stars and Milky Way. There was less illumination than in LA and the stars were very close and clear.

"I need to get my hat." Eskander had moved off toward the small cement block building in the corner of the front yard that was both a shelter against the rain and a bathroom for the guards. I was going to say something but the evening seemed to demand silent respect. A few familiar constellations, such as the Big Dipper and Orion, let me know that I was on a new continent but that the stars were the same.

There was no shock when a shooting star came over the front gate. It was spinning like a pinwheel on the 4th of July and I followed it with my eyes until it hit the ground right near Eskander. He was standing just in front of the guard shack when the star exploded and sprayed him with burning gasoline.

Chapter 35

The second shooting star hit the shack. Eskander's legs and torso were covered in bright yellow and orange flames. I could see his eyes and they were not scared or in pain, they were angry. Kokeb screamed and came running from inside the house toward Eskander as the third Molotov cocktail sailed over the fence. The burning rag in the bottle's mouth escaped and fell onto the lawn, while the bottle traveled farther to hit a bush near the house. Kokeb had gotten only a few feet when I knocked her to the ground with my arm. I think I was trying to protect her, but maybe I was just mad.

Eskander ran toward the house, and I met him near the fountain. The smell of burning hair, flesh, clothes and gasoline were actually worse than the heat. There was no plan in my mind when we collided. He almost knocked me off my feet, but I was able to keep my balance, grab him and spin into the fountain. There was pain in my hands and face.

The base of the fountain was five feet square, with about a foot of water in it and a patina copper rod in the center shooting water into the air. I hoped I was going to miss the pipe. Impaled as well as burned seemed too much for one night. The two foot high edge of the fountain hit me in the legs as we fell.

The fire was stubborn and did not go out immediately. Locked in an embrace tighter than when I made love to Felicity, we rolled back and forth until the flames died. The anger in his eyes was illuminated by the flames of the guard shack. He did not pass out, but I felt I should. Still holding him tight, I lifted and dragged him out of the fountain. The burns on his face and chest were not too bad but his legs were blistered and the flesh was split like an over done hot dog from his ankles to his thighs.

Kokeb was kneeling next to us on the lawn near the fountain. She held his head in her hands and stroked his brow. She was not weeping and her uncle's anger had spread to her somehow.

"I'll get some towels and call Post One." It was my voice and it sounded much too calm for the moment. I think it is OK to panic in some situations, but Eskander's anger had spread to me as well. As I stood, I heard the racing of an engine just outside the gate. I thought the security patrol or a passing American had seen the flames and was waiting for me to open the gate. I walked quickly but could not run because my left leg must have been burned. The main gate was locked and I couldn't find the key but the small door-sized gate was unlocked. I opened it and stepped into the unpaved street. There was a Toyota Landcruiser about 100 feet away with the lights on and Diplomatic plates. As soon as I had turned toward the truck the driver stepped on the gas and it sped away but not without spraying me with gravel first. I had been shot at, concussed, burned and now had gravel kicked in my face.

I stepped back into the yard, moved quickly into the house and retrieved a couple of towels from the kitchen and went back outside. Kokeb and Eskander were arguing in Amharic when I reached them. She had placed him with his back to the fountain so he could sit up. He was not having any trouble breathing and was talking to Kokeb in hushed but hurried tones. She kept shaking her head as he talked. I placed the towels onto his legs and examined his face to discern if he had breathed in any flames. There was no charring around his nose or mouth, which was a good sign. His voice showed some pain when he spoke. "Doctor, thank you for saving me. I will never forget what you have done tonight."

"It was nothing, Eskander. I need to leave you here for a minute and call the Embassy."

He reached out to touch my right hand which was burned. The skin was already blistered and it hurt when he grabbed me. I knelt beside him and felt a blister over my left knee burst into the grass. "Tell Kokeb to make the call I requested, my fingers do not work well."

I looked at her and she nodded. That was what they had been arguing about, but it seemed like a trivial thing. She stood, hit a number on the cell and spoke in a calm but hurried manner to someone on the other end of the line for a couple of minutes. When she was done she came back and began to stroke his brow tenderly again. "They will be here very quickly, uncle."

He relaxed and seemed almost at peace. It was very strange, because he had to be in a great deal of pain. As the adrenaline rush was wearing off, I could feel the burns on my hands, face and leg. Mine were nothing compared to his. Something about the call gave him great comfort

"Kokeb, stay with him and I will get the Embassy to send some help."

"Help is on the way, Doctor, but you should call the Embassy for you." Her words didn't make much sense to me but I figured that she was upset. I got up and hobbled my way toward the house. My left leg from the knee to the ankle was really starting to hurt and it slowed me down. I went upstairs as fast I could but it took several minutes between the pain and the altitude. My radio was on the dresser in my bedroom and the call sign sheet was right next to it. The radio was not heavy, but it was an effort to lift and my blistered hands were stiff and still felt on fire. I set the radio to position two and pressed the button on the side to talk. "Home Plate, this is Glasscutter, do you read me?"

After a pause of only a few seconds there was a response. "Glasscutter, this Home Plate. I read you loud and clear."

"Home Plate, there has been an explosion and fire at my house, I need assistance." My voice broke at the end and I felt nauseous. The room began to spin and I grabbed the dresser for support. The pause was longer this time and I wondered if he believed me.

"Roger that, Glasscutter. Cowboy is en route and should arrive in 10 minutes." Cowboy was Billy Spencer.

"Home Plate, this is Glasscutter. I am going back outside, so I need to leave the radio."

"Glasscutter, the radio is portable."

234

"Right." I had just associated the radio with the bedroom and thought it should stay there. Of course, it was portable. That was the point. I recognized the voice on the radio now. It was Cruz and in the silence I could hear him calling me dumbass again.

I held the railing tight as I came down the stairs and was very surprised to see that the main gate was open. An Ethiopian police van was sitting in the driveway and several men had gotten out. They were all near Eskander. Another van pulled up and more police with fire extinguishers entered the yard. They went to work on the guard shack and shrubs on the wall that were burning. Some other police were using the garden hose.

By the time I got close to Eskander, one of the police, who was armed with an AK-47, stopped me by putting his hand on my chest. I must have burned there as well because it hurt. Eskander had been placed on a gurney and when he saw the guard stop me he spoke in Amharic in a low voice. The guard let go and jumped back. It was strange. I bent down toward Eskander. "I am sorry, Doctor, the officer did not know who you are."

"Eskander, it doesn't matter. We need to get you to the hospital."

He smiled and nodded but did not say anything else. The men lifted his gurney, three on each side and carried him to the police van. They put him in the back, Kokeb climbed in, and then the van slowly backed into the street. I thought about hitching a ride but knew that Billy would be there soon. The flames were beginning to die down, not due to effective fire fighting, but because they were running out of fuel. By the dying light, I went over to the shrubs near the house and found the third bottle that did not break. I picked it up and poured out the remaining gasoline. I held it up to the light to read the label. The label said Standart Vodka in Cyrillic and it fit. The diplomatic plate on the Landcruiser outside the gate had been CD10. That was the code for the Russian Embassy.

Chapter 36

My burns were killing me. I went back into the house and was standing in the living room trying to assess my injuries. The bathroom on the second floor would have been a better venue but I didn't want to face the stairs again. The backs of my hands were raw, my left forearm was red, and my left leg was red and blistered on the shin from the knee to the ankle. There was a hole in my shirt over my heart. Without a mirror, there was no visual inspection, but the skin was hot and raised. I went into the kitchen, filled a pan with water from the distiller and, standing near the floor drain, poured it over my hands and leg. The first aid books say that is the thing to do but it hurt like hell and my head began to spin. Sitting down to avoid passing out for the second time that day, I dropped the pan next to me. The sound it made was hollow and lost.

"Hey, Doc...you look like shit." Billy was kneeling at my side, and offering a medical opinion or perhaps fashion advice. My pants were torn and burned below the left knee exposing my blistered leg. The sleeves on my shirt were torn, burned and stained.

"Hey, Billy, how are you doing?" Obviously he was doing better than I was, so I handed him the Standart vodka bottle that was sitting next to me. He picked it up, read the label and took a sniff from the mouth of the bottle. He turned away involuntarily when he smelled the gasoline.

"Jesus, Doc, have you switched to high test?"

"Three Molotov cocktails came over the wall. Two exploded near the guard shack and burned Eskander pretty bad. The locals just took him away. The third bottle didn't break and the burning rag fell out onto the lawn. I just got the bottle out of the bushes and came in here to get cleaned up when you came."

He set the bottle down on the floor and looked at me with concern. "Probably should have left the bottle until I got here. The FBI guys will want to check for fingerprints, DNA, type of gasoline and such. How did you get so wet?"

"After I grabbed Eskander we took a swim in the fountain. Then I went into the house to get something to cover him up. When I got back there was a truck right outside the gate. When I went out to look, they took off, but the plate said CD 10. That is the Russians, right?"

Billy just nodded. "I'm just going to call this in, Doc, be right back."

He stood, went into the living room and must have been talking on his cell phone because I couldn't hear a radio. Where I had put mine? It must be outside by the bushes. Billy came back in the room, and put his right arm around my shoulders and helped me to my feet. He was wearing khaki cargo pants, Merrell boots and black jacket. The wind breaker had a white stain on the front, but he looked better than I did. "I'm going to take you over to the Korean hospital. Rhonda and some others are going to meet us there."

"Do you know where they took Eskander?"

"He will probably be there, too. It's just about three minutes away." We walked out of the kitchen and into the living room. Billy wasn't holding me up, just guiding me like a Boy Scout would guide an old man across the street. I tried to speed up him up by walking more quickly, but my leg almost buckled. Billy held me up. "Even for you, you look bad. And you smell like a restroom at an Exxon station, gas and bad water."

He was right. The water in the fountain was not clean and the gasoline from Eskander's clothes must have soaked into mine. There was a sudden feeling of panic. I couldn't see her like this. Our last meeting had been a disaster, with me fainting outside the EAC and then asking her about the Russians. Now I was a complete wreck and burned. I needed to clean up and be more presentable before I could talk to her. When we got to the base of the stairs, I grabbed the wooden knob on the top of the hand rail and stopped. Billy tried to move me in the direction of the door but I held firm.

"Maybe I should shower before we go. I look and smell bad."

Billy looked at me with a great deal of concern, and then his natural, easy smile came over his face. "You don't want to look bad in front of Rhonda? She treated me for amoebic dysentery a couple a months ago and I looked worse than you do now."

"But what about the Ambassador and DCM? They will be there, too."

His smile broadened and he let out a derisive laugh. He knew what I was thinking; I could see it in his eyes. "Since when do you care what the Ambassador and DCM think about you? Don't worry, Doc; Felicity won't mind you looking like a bum. It may bring out her maternal instinct or whatever it was that kicked in the other night. That turned out pretty well for you, didn't it? Let's go, Doc, I don't want to carry you, but I will if you don't start walking."

He was right. The hospital was the best place for me, and it was stupid to worry about how I would look to Felicity. I let go of the banister and started walking, stumbled and almost fell. Billy was taken by surprise and caught my left arm. I could feel my burned skin tear as he grabbed me. "Damn, that hurts, Billy."

"Doc, if you would tell me when we're moving I won't have to guess. First you stop to worry about how you look and then you take off like a wayward calf. Just work with me this once." After the scolding I felt bad, just nodded my head and motioned with my unburned hand to have him lead the way.

The fire was completely out and the Ethiopian Police were all over the yard. They were measuring something on the lawn and one of them was taking pictures. Billy's black Suburban was parked in the driveway, facing the street. He opened my door and helped me in. That's when I thought of the bottle. The police would be in my house next and get the bottle. As I moved to open my door to get out, Billy got in and grabbed my left arm, above the burn this time, but it still hurt because he was squeezing hard. "Doc, now where are you going?"

"I need to get the bottle before the police do."

"You mean this one?" In his left hand was the bottle. He held it by the neck with a white handkerchief.

"Don't smudge the prints too much, Billy."

He snorted a laugh and dropped the bottle behind my seat. We left the driveway and drove onto a street new to me and unpaved. Several times my burned left leg bounced against the center console of the Suburban and each time it hurt like hell. I closed my eyes and thought I passed out, but wasn't sure. Billy abruptly stopped the truck under a covered entrance. The hospital was four stories tall, painted blue and white. There were a number of people in the lobby as we walked in.

The normal buzz of conversation stopped as Billy helped me through the room. He was on my right side and had draped my arm over his neck and shoulder while his left arm was around my waist. Everyone stopped what they were doing and turned to face me. Several pointed and a few crossed themselves. It did not inspire me with confidence. The ER was over to the right, and Billy guided me in that direction. An Ethiopian nurse came up to us and I thought she was going to stop us. Instead she smiled, took my left arm above the burn and told me I was going to be fine. It has been my experience that if you are going to be fine, no one tells you; they figure you know that. The nurse was trying to reassure me, Billy and her. I must have looked bad even to an ER nurse.

We went through a double wooden door and into a large room with several beds separated with yellow curtains. No medical equipment could be seen and the room smelled of burned meat. There were 20 to 25 people standing, sitting or lying around. Several people were eating from dishes or plastic containers. In one corner, the curtain was pulled back and I could see Kokeb standing next to a gurney with a pair of badly burned legs on it. An Asian man, who must have been one of the doctors, was doing something to the legs, and I could see that Kokeb was crying. I tried to get over there, but Billy held me firm. "Let's take care of you first, Doc, you can visit him later."

239

I just nodded because my strength was starting to fail. Rhonda was close by with another Asian man.

"Isaac, you look terrible. What happened to you?"

"I had a few too many Molotov cocktails this evening."

She ignored my humor and spoke again. "Does it hurt badly?"

It was hurting like I had stuck my hands and leg in a deep fryer. "It stings a little bit."

They laid me on the gurney and cut off what was left of my clothes, including my underwear, which seemed like overkill. Rhonda started an IV and gave me some morphine so I didn't really care though. The Asian man looked me over quickly then spoke with a heavy accent. "Dr. Porter, I am Dr. Kim. I am sorry I have to meet you under these circumstances. These wounds will have to be cleaned and dressed." He was telling me that because he knew it would hurt.

"Thank you for your help, Dr. Kim. Rhonda, stand by with the morphine." Then I laughed and she looked at me like I'd had enough. Rhonda was on my right, along with the Ambassador and the DCM. Billy was on my left. Felicity was near Billy and had appeared before I was ready, but it was good to see her. "Could I talk to Felicity alone for a minute?"

The Ambassador and the DCM were going to object when Billy and Rhonda nodded and moved away. Dr. Kim followed them. The Ambassador and the DCM, left reluctantly, but kept looking at me. Felicity stood closer to the gurney and touched the burn on my chest with her fingers. "Does it hurt?"

"Only if somebody touches it." I smiled and winked to let her know it was a joke. Instead of withdrawing her hand she placed her palm flat on my chest. It was warm and felt good. The morphine had helped my pain but not as much as her hand over my heart. I was naked but didn't care. "Felicity, I'm sorry I lied about my wife being dead. I should have been courageous enough to tell you the truth, and I'm sorry that I upset you so much."

240

"Zack, you are so stupid." She pinched the burn and it hurt but then she bent down to kiss my cheek. The scar on her face was very visible in the harsh Halogen light of the ER, but she was so beautiful. I didn't know what she meant, but at least she was talking to me. There were no tears in her eyes but she looked very sad. I reached up to touch her face with my burned hand, and she bent forward so I could reach her. "We can talk later, Zack. We have a lot to discuss before you leave. I am going to get Rhonda and the doctor back here."

It sounded good to me. I needed more morphine.

They call it debridement. In medicine, a confusing or odd sounding name for a procedure is common. Debridement means cutting out all of the dead tissue from the wound to limit infection. Burns can devitalize (doctor-talk for kill) large sections of skin and tissue. That is bad because the skin is damaged, which leads to infection and the dead tissue just feeds the bacteria. Think of burns as an all-you-can-eat buffet for germs that want to kill the patient. It isn't personal; dead flesh just tastes better to bacteria.

Rhonda came in and gave me more morphine. They must be getting ready to start. I dozed off after the morphine and woke up when Dr. Kim started scraping my left leg with steel wool. Someone had put a blanket over my groin, but I sat up a little to see what was going on. It had felt like steel wool, but Dr. Kim was just using gauze to remove part of my pants from my leg. The room spun, clockwise I think, and I felt like I was going to throw up, so I lay back down. Rhonda put her hand on my shoulder to comfort me.

It was like being at the dentist's office. I knew they had to do what they were doing; I just wished I was somewhere else. More steel wool to the leg made me break out in a cold sweat. Luckily, Dr. Kim put down the steel wool and started with the sandpaper. The morphine cut the pain and I decided I should doze off when Dr. Kim put away the furniture refinishing tools and began to gently wrap my leg in gauze.

The dream I had was bizarre like most dreams on morphine. (I say that but it was the only dream I ever had on morphine and it wasn't as weird as some I have had.) I was sitting at my desk in the health unit

241

of the Embassy and it was daytime. My computer displayed a map of Macau, and Travis walked in, pulling a red wagon behind him. Travis looked good, healthy, warm and alive, and yet I knew even in the dream that he was dead. He let go of the wagon and sat down on the floor. I stood up to see what he was doing. There were several toys in the wagon, and he was pulling them out to play with them on the floor. His hand held a note and I took it. It was the note I had found on my nightstand.

"Doctor make me well?" He looked right at me when he said it and handed me a shell casing from a rifle. I put the note and shell casing on my desk. Someone was coming down the hall, and it was a man by the sound of the steps. He stopped outside the door and called to Travis. "Time to go, Travis."

Travis looked at me, gave me a mischievous smile and shook his head. Reaching into the wagon he pulled out my phone with the threatening text on it. The room had grown dark because of a cloud passing the window. It was very black and looked like it was going to rain outside. Travis had stood up and was standing next to me. He reached up to put his left hand into my right and smiled again at me. There was a small glass object in my hand when he let go. I looked at it. It was a small bottle of Standart Vodka like you would get on an airline.

"Time to go, Travis." A hand appeared in the doorway. It was a man's hand and he was wearing a blue blazer, white cuffed shirt and State Department cufflinks. Only the hand and forearm of the man were visible. Travis walked away from me and took the man's hand. He waved with his left, as four year olds do, with an exaggerated movement of the hand and arm. The smile was back on his face as he went around the corner. I moved to the door and into the hallway. It was completely dark and I searched for the light switch with my hand. The hall was briefly illuminated a white flash. The thunder came immediately afterward. There was no one in the hall. I gently whispered to Travis to come back, but he did not answer.

Chapter 37

"Doctor Porter, wake up, everything is going to be OK. You were having a nightmare." DCM Lawrence was shaking my shoulder with his hand. Billy and Rhonda were also around my gurney.

They all looked very concerned and Rhonda spoke. "Isaac, you must have been dreaming. You will be fine."

"I don't want any more morphine, Rhonda." She patted me on the shoulder and gave me a motherly nod of the head. "How is Eskander doing, Rhonda?"

She put down the blood pressure cuff that she was about to place on my arm and waited for a few seconds before she answered. "He has been badly burned on his legs and chest. Even in the States it would be difficult for him."

Billy spoke next. "General Mulugeta is here and wants to ask you some questions. Are you up to it?"

"Sure, Billy, as long as I can see Eskander afterward. What is this all about?"

"Doc, there is no easy way to tell you this, but the Federal Police have had you under surveillance since you got here. We're not sure you were just being directly observed or if there was electronic surveillance as well."

"Why were they doing that?"

"They suspected foul play with the poisoning and needed to monitor our investigation. You were new, so it was easy to put someone into your household. Their goal was to minimize the damage to Ethiopia from the incident."

It seemed to make sense if I looked at it from their perspective. As the doctor at the Embassy, I would be involved in any investigation. Putting someone into my house would be the best way to get the information. They would know that I was single from the housing

243

report and that I might like some feminine companionship. Using Kokeb was a perfect plan. She was American, young, attractive and had a compelling story about being jilted. It would be easy to get the information. All she would have to do is smile and ask how my day was going. I was feeling like an idiot and didn't like the way she had used me. I wasn't going to give her any money, that was for sure. "I can't believe that I didn't see that Kokeb was put there to spy on me."

Billy wrinkled his brow and looked confused. He then smiled and reached out to touch my hand like people do when their senile Grandpa makes a pass at the nurse. The look was bemused, fatherly and concerned all at the same time. "Felicity is right, Doc. You are a smart guy when it comes to medicine, but don't know anything about women. It wasn't Kokeb. It was Eskander. We should have run a better background check on him but he came with great credentials. It turns out that Eskander and General Mulugeta go way back to the days when they were guerrillas fighting the Derg in Tigray."

I just stared at Billy and regretted telling Rhonda that I didn't want any more morphine. My head was hurting, my hands were burning and my chest ached. "So what do they want to ask me, Billy?"

"I'm not sure. The DCM and I will be here and I don't think you have anything to worry about. Eskander has been talking to the General for quite some time and the subject was you."

"How do you know they are talking about me?"

He smiled again. "I can't understand Amharic that well, but every other sentence contained the words 'Dr. Porter.'"

I laughed. It was funny. Billy smiled and took his hand off my shoulder.

The curtain around my gurney opened and Colonel Assefa and General Mulugeta entered. The General spoke. "Dr. Porter, I am sorry that you have been injured. My country is usually more welcoming to visitors, and I am truly sorry that you have had so much trouble here. I also want to thank you for what you did tonight for Eskander. I have known him for over 40 years, from the time when we were both just boys. He explained to me how you risked your own life to save his. His wounds are very bad, but the he has told me that he would not be alive if you had not put out the fire that was consuming him. Thank you for helping him." He paused and wiped a tear from his right eye and blew his nose. I wasn't sure if I should say anything or not. He spoke again. "Dr. Porter, when we spoke this morning, you said that you believed that someone in your Embassy was behind this whole affair. Have the events of this evening changed your mind?"

It was a great open ended question that I could answer in almost any way I wanted. A cop, like a physician, needs good interview skills. "The events of tonight have convinced me that it was someone at our Embassy." The General just waited for me to continue. DCM Lawrence pulled on his sleeves so that his shirt cuff was the proper length beneath the sleeve of his blazer. It was two in the morning, but he was still dapper. Billy was looking at the ceiling like he was waiting for it to fall on us and Rhonda was just looking worried. No one said anything, so I just started to talk again. "It makes no sense to firebomb my house. What is the point? The only point was that I would find a Russian vodka bottle and see a license plate with the Russian diplomatic code on it. Those things are to divert suspicion away from the real culprit. I am more convinced than ever that someone inside our Embassy is behind all of this."

ERs are usually very noisy, but it seemed like all of the noise in the room stopped after I finished speaking. It was quiet enough to hear a pin drop. It wasn't a pin that dropped, though. It was one of the DCM's cuff links. He must have been trying to refasten it when he lost his grip and it hit the floor. Bending over, he picked it up and put it in his pocket before he spoke. "General, Dr. Porter has been shot at, has injured his head and is now burned. He has held up very well and has served his country with distinction. However, his theories are not the official position of the United States government. I know that you said earlier that you are thankful for his actions tonight. As the Ambassador and I told your Foreign Minister today, we do not want this incident or the delayed departure of Dr. Porter to affect the strong and warm relations of our two great nations or the aid that we are providing."

The DCM would be a terrible guy to play poker with. He had great skill at the understated, diplomatic threat and I couldn't tell if he was bluffing. Would the U.S. really cut off aid to Ethiopia because of me? It seemed odd that the delayed departure of one diplomat could be so serious. The United States had to protect the diplomats abroad vigorously though. It even had to protect them from themselves sometimes.

The General nodded and reached out to touch my right arm just above the bandages. "Dr. Porter and I have many things in common. He and I do not always speak in the hushed and measured tones of the Diplomat. Our theories, emotions and threats are open like a book. I have also met with the Foreign Minister today. I told him that we should not allow the United States to threaten us and obscure the fact that the death of the child was directly related to the actions of someone in its own Embassy."

"General, the Ambassador and I are not threatening anyone. We are only pointing out that diplomats must be treated with respect and that their departure from the host country should not be delayed. We have worked closely with Ethiopia to improve bilateral relations by emphasizing the many strong bonds…"

The General held up his right hand and motioned for the DCM to stop talking. "Mr. Lawrence, I want to inform you and Dr. Porter that in the light of his actions tonight, that he is free to leave the country any time he wishes. I and my officers hope that he makes a speedy recovery and that he is able to return to my country soon and in good health."

"On behalf of Dr. Porter, the Ambassador, myself and the government of the United States, I want to thank you, General, for being so understanding in this difficult time. I hope that our countries will continue to cooperate on the many important issues that we face."

The DCM shook the General's hand and they both smiled but neither of them seemed to mean it. The General turned to me. "Dr. Porter, thank you again for your honesty and your help. Eskander and I will always be in your debt. I wish you safe travels and a quick recovery."

"General Mulugeta, thank you for your kind words. May I speak with Eskander?"

"Of course, Doctor, he wishes to speak with you as well."

With that, he bowed slightly and shook my hand but he was very gentle and it did not hurt my burns. He and the Colonel then left. The DCM looked at me and winked for some strange reason. He moved away from the gurney and starting dialing his phone. No doubt he was calling the Ambassador or the airport. Both would be happy to know that I was cleared to leave the country. I sat up on the gurney and flung aside the sheet.

"Rhonda, help me get up, I need to speak with Eskander." I slid off the gurney and as I was standing, it rolled away from me. There was a split second when I thought I could stand on my own, but the pain from the burn in my leg and the dizziness from the morphine made that impossible. I fell onto my butt on the cold concrete floor of the ER. Billy and Rhonda quickly lifted me to my feet and I was ready to get over to Eskander. I started to walk in his direction when Billy pulled forcefully on my arm. It hurt.

"Whoa, Doc, where are you going?"

"I need to speak with Eskander."

"You can speak with him in a minute. You need to get your britches on first, though."

I'd forgotten that my clothes had been cut off me and in an instinctive reaction I covered my genitals with my hands.

Rhonda burst into a derisive laugh. "It is a little late for modesty at this point, Isaac."

She was right, but I still covered myself with the sheet when I got next to the Gurney. Billy had pulled it close and locked the wheels so it would not roll away again. He also grabbed a paper bag from the

247

floor and handed it to me. "Put these on, I had Cruz pick them up at your place."

I looked inside and there were a pair of jeans, shirt, underwear, socks, running shoes and T-shirt. With Rhonda and Billy making sure I would not fall again, I got dressed. It took about 15 minutes. Just as I was tying my shoes, I heard Kokeb shout in Amharic and a loud slap. The sounds came from the direction of Eskander's gurney. She was standing in front of Colonel Assefa. He was holding his left hand to the left side of his face. It was clear to me then that he was the former fiancé who had betrayed her confidence. At least she had found out before she was married.

"Love is never easy." I said it to no one in particular and Billy looked at me with some concern.

I walked toward Eskander with a slow and deliberate pace. Billy and Rhonda were on each side. They didn't hold on to me but both were ready to pounce at the least sign of a wobble. When I got close to Eskander, Kokeb spotted me and smiled. Colonel Assefa turned and walked away. Eskander had his eyes closed and may have been asleep or passed out.

Kokeb spoke. "Hello, Dr. Porter, how are you feeling?" She came over to me and took my arm above the burn and guided me to the side of her uncle's gurney.

Eskander opened his eyes and smiled but looked like he was in a lot of pain. "Doctor, I hope you are not too badly injured. Dr. Kim has told me that I will recover but that it will take many months. I am sorry I will not be able to be your guard anymore."

I reached down and touched his shoulder. "General Mulugeta will make sure you get work when you recover, I am sure."

"I am sorry I had to deceive you, Doctor. I was just doing my job and I hope you can forgive me. We all have to serve, do we not?"

"Yes, Eskander, we all have to serve. I wanted to tell you that you can email or call me if you have medical questions about your course of treatment. And as I said before, I will be loaning Kokeb the money she needs to get back to New York."

Kokeb was next to me. She simply nodded and hugged me. Her small arms were very strong, much stronger than I would have imagined based on her size and build. It was a good tight hug that you give a loved one when you are not sure when you will see them again. Eskander had passed out and as she let go, I kissed her on the cheek. It was time to leave, so I turned toward the door, and with Rhonda and Billy as my wingmen walked to the exit.

Chapter 38

We got into the Suburban and Billy took us up on the Ring Road and headed toward the Embassy. It was just after dawn and the familiar smoky haze was lightly applied to the air. Several people crossed in front of us on the road at a half trot. My hands were hurting and I was still somewhat groggy from the morphine. Rhonda was in the front seat. They were talking about me but I didn't care.

The thoughts in my head were all about Travis and Felicity. It was clear to me, even in my foggy, groggy state that I would not be in Addis much longer. Travis had been a random target. They might have known he would get sick but they couldn't have known he would die. No one could have. The attacks on me were different. I was the sole target. Even burning Eskander was a side effect of the bombing aimed at me. I hoped no one believed the Russians were involved. Whoever was behind the fire bomb attack was behind everything else. The Russians could not have tampered with the buns and left the note in my house. They could have shot at me and texted me but why would they do that? Even if Felicity or Bob Wollinsky were their agents, and that I couldn't believe on several levels, what could they gain? They would have no motive to attack Travis and they were not that subtle.

Entoto road was closed off by the police about three blocks south of the Embassy. A Russian made tank was sitting on the side of the street. The tank was green, with a rounded almost soft looking turret, and the gun barrel pointed downhill at the passing traffic. The Suburban had to slow to turn right, left and right again to get around large concrete barriers that had been placed to foil any truck or car bombs. Whoever killed Travis would be waved right through the barriers. They had an Embassy badge.

After passing through the gate, Billy stopped the Suburban outside the main entrance to the Embassy and I spotted Cruz in battle fatigues and body armor. He came over to my side of the truck and opened my door. "Good morning, Doc. Rough night, I hear. How are you feeling?"

"I'll live, but I think I should go to the health unit and lie down for a while."

Billy looked at me and spoke. "Doc, the EAC is meeting as we speak and I think you should go. However, if you think you need to rest, maybe we can get Rhonda to give you a note."

Time to think was what I needed more than rest. The meeting would get in the way but I couldn't see how I could get out of it. "I doubt I will be invited to the next one, so I guess we should go."

I walked toward the Embassy with Billy still holding onto my arm. Cruz and Rhonda followed us at a very close distance. I felt like the wayward uncle who has finally lost his marbles and is being escorted into Shady Acres. If I had been in bedroom slippers and a robe, the image would have been perfect. Cruz left for a moment to place his M-4 rifle in the Marine guard post. He still had his Glock on his belt. The Marines didn't usually carry firearms in the Embassy.

We took the elevator to the third floor and made our way to the conference room. Even before we got close, I could see a distinct change. There were several people in suits, blazers and combat fatigues outside of the conference room huddled around a phone that was on speaker. They were the extra FBI agents and CIA officers that Billy had said were coming. No one paid any attention to our little party as we approached. The voice on the phone was Felicity's and she was talking about me. It felt good to know she was thinking about me again. We had broken a barrier in the hospital when she touched my chest. Confidence about our future was increasing.

"Dr. Porter is a liar, a danger to himself and others, and I want him on the next plane out of here more than anyone in this room." It wasn't what I had expected, but I couldn't really disagree. She continued. "He must go before he gets himself or someone else killed. However, my Agency and I are convinced that this entire episode would never have been properly investigated if he hadn't been here."

It wasn't a warm endorsement of my actions, but she wasn't saying she hated me either.

Dr. Lessing sounded uncontrolled when she spoke. Her voice was high and trembling. "My colleagues and I in the CDC would have come to the same conclusions that Dr. Porter reached and we would not have been as disruptive. I disagree with the conclusion of Ms. Gonsalves and her Agency. They know nothing about the investigation of food poisoning and should stick to things they know, like waterboarding people."

A commotion started in the room and the speaker phone was turned off by a young Hispanic male who was wearing khaki pants, a blue blazer and Merrell boots. The shouting in the room was getting louder and someone knocked over a chair and a glass was broken. Billy, Rhonda and Cruz were busy discussing something among themselves behind me. It was the perfect time to make my entrance. The door to the conference room was only about 15 feet away but it took me a minute to get there. Like a drunk on ice, I kept my feet wide apart and moved slowly. Luckily the young Hispanic man was arguing loudly with a short, overweight white male in khaki pants, a blue blazer and black leather shoes. The portly gentleman's hair was dyed an impossibly black color and it made him look like an Elvis impersonator. As I passed, Elvis told the Hispanic man that Dr. Lessing was right and that the CIA were a bunch of undisciplined spooks who did more harm than good. A large redheaded man in combat fatigues was separating the two of them as I passed. Cruz, Rhonda and Billy had finished their conversation and had realized that I had escaped. Billy called after me like I was going to miss the Bingo game at Shady Acres. It was a plaintive cry, somewhere between anger and disappointment. "Doc! Wait a second."

He crossed the room in a hurry, but it was too late. I made it through the door of the conference room. Every chair at the table was taken and there were two people standing for every person seated. The table was a mess, with spilled coffee competing for space with notebooks, note pads, computers, maps and dirty dishes. Dr. Lessing was standing opposite Felicity and yelling at her. Felicity was yelling back and the scar on her face was bright red. No one was really running the meeting but the Ambassador stood up when he saw me.

Flushing and stuttering, he looked like he was about to have a stroke. The DCM to his left followed the Ambassador's gaze in my direction.

Everyone stopped talking and one by one they all turned to look at me. Felicity's mouth dropped open and she quickly brought her right hand up to cover it. Dr. Lessing gave me her best dirty look, which was, I admit, very good. The room was warm and there were so many people. My head laceration and my burns were really starting to hurt and I hadn't eaten anything for about 12 hours. The cold sweat and nausea came on me fast and I knew I was going to pass out. Two things came into my mind just as I started to collapse. First I wished I was closer to Felicity so she could catch me or not. It would be a good indicator of her feelings. It sounds ridiculous but that was what came into my mind as my knees gave way. The second thing was that I needed to make an announcement.

The pressure to speak was so great that I could not control it. It was as if I had been suddenly struck with Tourrette's syndrome. I was going over backward, and tunnel vision was quickly making the room small and dark. "I know who killed Travis."

Arms grabbed me before the floor did and I was smiling as I lost consciousness. I was sure now that I was back in Felicity's arms. At least until I heard a male voice very close to my ear as the final crumb of consciousness was swept away.

"Dumbass."

Chapter 39

I have a memory of being lifted onto a gurney and a trip down to the health unit but I may have dreamed it. Full consciousness did not return until I heard the Ambassador screaming at the DCM. His words were not intelligible but his anger was apparent. The tone and delivery of his voice were sharp and rapid like a hammer on nail. The pounding was continuous. When I opened my eyes I expected to see them, but Rhonda was the only person in the room. She was sitting with her back to me, writing and the door was closed. The Ambassador and the DCM must be in the hall. I could only imagine what she was writing.

"Forty year old male with concussion, head laceration, extensive partial thickness burns to legs, chest and hands had syncopal episode while proclaiming he had solved the mystery of the death of Travis Wollinsky. Advise immediate medical evacuation for medical and psychiatric care."

She turned slowly toward me with a look of exasperation and fatigue. "Pretty close, Isaac, pretty close. How are you feeling?"

My head was foggy, my arm, hands, leg and chest hurt. The laceration on my head was leaking. The scent of gasoline lingered as a mute reminder of the previous evening. "I feel much better. I just need to sit up and have some water."

Raising one eyebrow, she stood up and came to my side. She gave me a small bottle of water and helped me sit up on the edge of the gurney. The bandages on my hands were still relatively intact. I was going to feel the back of my head, but I didn't want Rhonda to touch it, so I just sat there with my legs over the edge. The hammering in the hallway had stopped. I drank the water and it tasted good. "I think I'm getting better. I feel hungry now."

Rhonda put her arm around my shoulder. I couldn't see her face but she was concerned. "Isaac, you're a mess. I think by the time you are done here, they will have a seminar named after you at the Foreign Service Institute."

"How to destroy a Foreign Service career in seven days or less?"

She squeezed my shoulder in support. I had been physically wounded in various ways, failed to save a little boy's life, upset everyone and found and lost Felicity. It was quite an achievement for first tour officer. The plane was probably already fueled and waiting at the airport. I needed to wrap things up very soon or I would be out of the equation.

The door opened and the DCM came in alone. He looked somewhat worried, but his pants and coat looked great. The blue blazer even had a white pocket square. He was the kind of guy who would look good in any emergency. The contrast between us could not been clearer. He didn't even smell like gasoline. Rhonda excused herself and left. "Dr. Porter, it is so good to see you up and about. How do you feel?"

"Better. How did the meeting go after I left?"

"The meeting was very productive and frank. The Ambassador and I have been discussing your situation and have come to some conclusions. You have done a great job here but in light of your injuries, it is time for you to go home. There is a flight tonight to Frankfurt and you will be in D.C. tomorrow. It will be easier for you to get proper medical care there."

I couldn't argue with his logic, but I wanted to stay. He had stopped speaking, and I thought he was going to ask me who was behind all of the mess, but if he was interested he wasn't acting like it. Curiosity would have made me ask, but I didn't have the control he had. I wasn't a career diplomat. "Thanks for the update. I just need to get a few things together here before I leave. It shouldn't take too long."

"Take your time, Doctor. I will talk to Rhonda and Billy so they can help."

He came closer to the gurney and gave me a firm handshake, which hurt through the bandages. Without saying anything else, he

255

left. Rhonda came back in with more water and some crackers for me to eat. She didn't say anything, put them down on the gurney and left. I opened the crackers and dropped only one onto the floor as a symbol of my career. The survivors tasted pretty good. My office was just down the hall, but I decided to stay where I was for a while. One more fainting episode and they might not wait for the Lufthansa flight.

I was still confused. Despite my announcement in the conference room, I didn't know who was behind it all. At the meeting, I thought my statement would buy me some time and frankly, I'd hoped to impress Felicity. It had not worked on either account.

The events after Travis' death had been an attempt to stop my investigation or at least derail it. Who would benefit from that? Obviously whoever was behind the poisoning. Why was he poisoned? Was it a specific attack or just random? It had to be random. No one could be sure a food poisoning would hit a particular individual. It had started out as a general attack and had only become specific after Travis died. I had been targeted to impede my investigation and their aim, though not perfect, was pretty good. There were a few things I had uncovered but Dr. Lessing would have found them eventually, especially after I found the tampered buns. Now the FBI, CDC, CIA and State were using massive resources to get this cleared up. Somebody would figure out the whole thing even if I was sent home or killed but the attacks had continued anyway. I finished my crackers and water. It was time to get to my office and contact Felicity.

I slipped off the gurney and, after a momentary wobble, felt pretty good standing up. I moved to the door and slowly opened it to see if anyone was in the hall. It was empty, but Rhonda was working on her computer in her office. She was playing some music as well and that was good. It would make my transit down the hall easier to conceal. Moving with stealth and a slow pace to avoid detection and falling down, I made it to my office.

Sitting down in the chair, I felt like I had run about five miles instead of walking 25 feet, but I had made it. After pausing for a few minutes, I started my computer. The first thing I did was to open my State Department email account and draft a letter to Felicity. The first draft was about 100 words long and full of apology, excuses and regret. Even I didn't want to read that so I deleted and started over. The second draft was about the same length and was defiant, angry and confrontational. It was worse than the first one. Deleting that one as well, I just sent her a note that said I was leaving tonight and would like to see her before I left. There were other emails from The Office of Medical Services Foreign Programs Division and from various CDC, FBI and State Department people located both in the Embassy and in Washington. Leaving those unopened, I left the computer on just in case and turned around to look out my window and think.

The morning was very bright and cheered me up. There were dozens of people walking around outside on the grounds. Most of them were local Ethiopian guards, but there were several people with black windbreakers. Most of those had FBI in large yellow letters on their backs but there were CDC, State and FEMA jackets as well. What was a FEMA guy doing here?

"How is our patient doing, Rhonda?" It was Billy's voice. He was standing just outside Rhonda's doorway. I didn't turn to face the door because I didn't want to make any noise that would let them know I was listening.

"He's resting in the exam room right now. The DCM just left and he told me that Isaac was going to be leaving tonight. Is that true?"

"Yes, it is, Rhonda. We have to get him out of here before he does permanent damage. He's going to be OK, isn't he?"

She laughed before she spoke. "He will be OK, but he has some issues that have nothing to do with his physical injuries. He is a very strange man, but I really like him."

"Me, too, Rhonda. Did he say anything else about who he thought was behind all of this mess? That statement of his at the EAC really has people talking."

"He hasn't said anything else to me but maybe he told the DCM."

"I hope he has solved this thing so that we can put it all behind us and get back to semi-normal life."

"Listening to other people's conversations is not really a very doctor-like thing to do, is it, Zack? That's more in my line of work." I recognized Felicity's voice and turned to see her standing in my door way. Her arms were crossed against her chest and she had a mock look of anger on her face. There was friendliness in her eyes to let me know she wasn't upset. She was dressed in a tight black skirt with pale yellow blouse and her hair was tied up. She looked so beautiful it felt like a dream, so I wondered if I had passed out again.

Chapter 40

Billy popped his head around the corner, and I was sure I was awake since he wouldn't be in any dream I had about Felicity. Standing would have been the gentlemanly thing to do but I decided I should sit. The room had begun to spin and my head wound was sending a trickle of fluid down my neck. She uncrossed her arms and the look on her face changed from open and friendly to serious and concerned. Thinking she was alarmed by my appearance, I stood up to show her I was OK. It was an effort but I didn't faint.

"What do you think Billy? Should doctors listen to other people's conversations or should they leave that to professionals?"

"Felicity, I've come to the conclusion that the Doc does things his own way and we're just going to have to put up with it."

She had turned to face Billy when he spoke but faced me to smile at Billy's statement. Even though she had been up all night and must be as exhausted as I was, she was fresh and alluring. Worn out, wounded and almost broken, I regained my strength just by looking at her. My attraction was undiminished and I would have made love to her there in my office. I just had to get Billy out of the room and talk to her. The CIA must have taught her mind reading.

"Billy, Zack and I have some things to discuss, could you excuse us a moment? I would take him up to my office, but I think he is going to faint soon and I don't think Rhonda would be very happy with me if she has to stitch him up again."

"No problem, Felicity, just make sure he doesn't crawl out the window. The Ambassador made it clear to me that my pension is dependent on no further trouble from the Doc before he leaves tonight."

They both smiled at me and I felt again like the senile wayward uncle that everyone had to watch. Billy closed the door after Felicity had stepped fully into the office. She crossed the short space from the door and sat down in a chair that was directly opposite my desk. Now that she was closer, I could see some wrinkles around her eyes and sense her fatigue. "You can sit down now, Zack, I have duly noted that you're strong enough to stand on your own for several minutes."

"I'm glad that you came by and doubly glad to sit down."

"You know you're going to be leaving tonight."

"The DCM told me that I had done a great job here, but that it was time to move on." I smiled a little but I was trapped and broken. The realization that I had lost her by lying to her was worse than all of my physical wounds. Those wounds ceased to exist as a dull ache began in my heart. She crossed her legs and put her hands in her lap. It was visual confirmation that she was not as receptive as she had been in the hospital. The interrogation had begun when she walked into the room.

"That was quite a show you put on at the EAC. It was very dramatic and got everyone's attention. I can't say that I wasn't impressed. It took great courage to do that." She was flattering me to make me feel more secure and to help me open up. Her techniques were subtle, professional and effective. I knew I was being manipulated, but I didn't care and just wanted her to keep talking to me. I hoped the conversation would stay on Embassy matters. That way the fact that I was losing her would not come up. My plan was to keep the conversation light and professional.

"Felicity, the truth is I went there hoping you would be there. I need to talk to you and apologize for what I did to you."

She didn't say anything at all for a minute and just stared at me. Turning her head to look at the window she let out a sigh. "Zack..." I couldn't tell for sure but I thought she was crying. The dull pain in my chest deepened and widened and I knew the next words out of her mouth would be about me never seeing her again. It was clear that she felt she had made a mistake the other night and that she did not love me. I knew I would not spend 10 years mourning her like I had my wife, but the acute sense of loss was worse. It was like losing a newborn baby, something only partially formed yet full of potential. The silence lasted for several minutes before she turned back to face me. She wiped her eyes and smiled. "You don't really know who killed Travis, do you? That was all a ploy. Did you do it to impress everyone or was it is some kind desperate attempt to have someone confess?"

I was concerned that she was able to shrug me off so easily. I smiled. "You're right. I don't know exactly who is behind it, but it has to be an American who has access to the Embassy, the storeroom and my house. There can't be that many people with that kind of access. It was someone who was at the bazaar and the Diplomatic reception."

Her face was professional but not cold when she answered. "Billy and the FBI have been looking into it, and they have concluded the same things. There are about 10 people at the Embassy who fit the criteria, including me. Do you think I did it, Zack?"

"You didn't shoot at me, leave me notes or texts or burn me with gasoline. All of the physical pain I feel is nothing compared to the pain I feel for lying to you. Is there some way we could go back to the other night and I could tell you the truth? You are a beautiful, intelligent woman and I love you. I know you think that this is all due to my concussion but it isn't. For the first time in 10 years I'm glad my wife left me and the thought that I'm losing you because of a stupid lie about a woman who never loved me is almost too hard to bear. I wish that you would give me another chance."

Felicity just stared at me and smiled. "Zack, you are without a doubt the hardest man to interview I have ever come across. If I didn't know better, I would swear that you were behind all of this and that you would say anything to avoid answering my questions."

She was changing the subject, but I didn't feel like letting up. I just stared back at her. A tear from her left eye crossed her scar and chased the smile from her face. Looking down into her hands she spoke again. "You're not the only one who will be leaving Addis soon Zack. Chris, my ex, and I have been in contact over the last several months. We both think we should give things another chance. I have accepted a position in Moscow and will be leaving in six weeks."

The cavity of pain in my chest was increasing and it was hard to breathe. I just wanted to get up and run to the airport to get on the next plane out. It was clear to me now that I had been just a way to pass the time until she went back to her husband. I would have yelled at her but I couldn't speak. There were tears on my face now.

"My plan was perfect. It would mean that my life was stable and back on track. My parents would be happy, Chris would be happy, and I would be back with a man who loves me." There was another pause and the tears were flowing steadily down her cheeks and dripping onto her hands. "Then you come along and screw everything up. You think I was mad at you because you lied about being divorced instead of a widower? Grow up, Zack. I'm not a child and don't care about your past. It was just an excuse to push you away. You were upsetting my plans. You are screwed up in so many ways, Zack. You lie and deceive with ease. There isn't a rule you won't break if you think it is getting in your way. The CIA should have hired you instead of me. I follow the rules, Zack, and don't like it when others don't.

"Yet when I saw you take care of Travis... You cared for him when he was alive and have been caring for him, even more since he died. Without your determination and compassion for him no one would have known what happened. The passion for life that you possess is something I want that in my life too. I felt a deep connection between us the other night. We were so close and yet I know so little about you. Is that love or are we just mourning a loss and seeking solace in each other? It was more than just sex but how much more? Being close to you scares me because I've always wanted stability with my personal relationships.

"Life has so many challenges without looking for more. Getting involved with you would be exciting and maybe wonderful. I'm just not sure I can handle all of the chaos that would bring. Chris is familiar and safe. He and I are so much alike and I need to know if we can make it work. You and I have so little in common and you are so much older than I am. I'm not getting any younger and I need to make a good decision about love for once. You are great in many ways but that might not be enough to sustain a relationship over the long run even if I love you."

The shock I felt was worse than the one I had experienced in the hotel room in Orlando. My wife had left because she didn't love me and Felicity was going to leave me despite being in love with me. She had felt the connection and it was too chaotic?

"Felicity, you're right about our connection and believe me, I know how frightening love can be, but you can't judge me by the last few days. If we had time together under normal circumstances, you would see that I am very stable. We should just give it a chance and not rush into anything. True love lasts forever, there is no hurry."

"Zack, as long as I'm in this job, things will never be completely normal. I don't think life with you would ever be normal either. You embrace the chaos of life. You will follow your own path and don't care about the consequences. I'm just not that way. Maybe if there was no Chris… but there is. He wants me back and I need to know if it will work with him."

"I know this week has been hard for us but I wish you would reconsider."

"Zack, I've thought a lot about it and talked to my parents, Chris and my brothers. I even talked to Rhonda. They have different opinions but they all want what is best for me."

"I want what is best for you too, Felicity, I just think that is me."

"I have to find out if it is Chris…"

She stood up and waited for me. I tried to speak but there were no words to say. I stood up and walked around my desk. My chest ached but there was no dizziness or weakness in my stride. I stopped in front of her and she leaned into me and held me tight. It was farewell. She kissed me full on the lips and I tried to hold her but she just shook her head. Dropping my arms to my side I watched her go out the door and close it quietly behind her. She was gone.

Chapter 41

I just sat there and waited for more bad news. Billy knocked and entered the room 10 minutes after Felicity left. His blazer was wrinkled and his khaki pants looked like he had slept in them. After standing quietly for a minute he spoke. "Doc, you have the strangest effect on people. I can't say exactly why, but I like even though you have gotten me into more trouble than anyone except my older brother. Rhonda is bawling her eyes out because you won't take care of yourself and Felicity looks like she's never going to smile again. What is it with you?" He just shook his head in amazement. "You ready to go back to your place and pack?"

"Sure. Can I print some stuff up here first?" There wasn't really anything to print, but it was a good way to stall for a little while longer. Once I left, I wouldn't be able to come back to the Embassy and there was no way I could solve this thing from my house or Washington, D.C. Of course, I didn't really have a plan at all. All of the information needed to be put together into a coherent pattern. Billy had drifted off to speak with Rhonda, and I felt that the best strategy would be to sneak out the back door. Wandering around the Embassy would stimulate my thinking and Billy couldn't take me to my house if he couldn't find me. I decided to print a few emails that had nothing to do with anything so the printer would make some noise and help cover my escape. Maybe hanging around Felicity had made me paranoid, but if I was caught I also could claim I was going to get more paper. I wasn't really sure where it was kept but there were several storage cabinets near the back entrance to the health unit so at least it was plausible.

While the printer was working on a 32 page email about malaria prophylaxis in Africa, I slowly and quietly got up and moved out of my office. Rhonda and Billy were still talking in her office. The trip down the hall to the back door was uneventful and except for a headache, dizziness and pain in my arms I felt pretty good. There was a slight feeling of deceit like I was sneaking out on my parents on Saturday night, but I was very happy that my escape plan was going so well. With stealth and caution I opened the door and stepped into the hallway. I had made it.

"Hello, Doc, how are you feeling?" It was Cruz standing 10 feet down the hall in camouflage fatigues and with his Glock on his belt.

"Hello, Gunny, I'm feeling much better. I thought I would just go for a walk. I need some time to think before I leave."

"That sounds good, Doc. Did you tell the RSO in your office you were leaving?"

"I didn't want to bother him, he seems busy. Maybe you don't have to mention it to him?" I turned and saw that Susan Bell was behind me. She was dressed in khaki slacks, white blouse and holding a clipboard like a hall monitor at school.

"I don't like bothering the RSO, either, Doc. I don't think you are a threat at all, but Ms. Bell has orders to report me if I let you leave. So do you want to go back in the back door or the front?"

My guards needed guards.

"It will have to be the front, Gunny, I don't have my keys."

"Doc, you are a unique individual, I am going to truly miss you."

I had the feeling he would miss me like he would miss a flat tire or a toothache. I thanked him and nodded to Ms. Bell as I passed her to go back in the health unit. The door was open so I didn't have to knock. Billy and Rhonda were still in her office and I briefly thought of trying to sneak past them and go back to my office unnoticed, but I was too tired for more games.

"Cruz and Ms. Bell say hello." Billy turned to me and had a small smile on his face.

"The DCM wasn't sure the Gunny would prevent your escape, so he had Ms. Bell as a backup. Are you ready to go yet or do you have more printing to do?"

There was defeat in my soul. I had let Travis down, lost Felicity and there wasn't going to be a solution before I was forced to leave. No messy investigation and revelation about the murder of Americans by Americans. It would all be hushed up. Billy was looking at me with some pity and regret.

"Let me take you home, Doc. You've done enough for everybody, including Travis. The plane leaves in four hours and you probably want to pack. If you think it is too much for you, don't worry about it. Rhonda and I were just talking it over and we could pack your stuff after you leave. We would be happy to help out."

"Thanks, Billy, but I never really unpacked so getting ready will be easy."

I turned to Rhonda to tell her I would see her later but then I realized I probably wouldn't. "Rhonda, it has been great working with you. The Embassy is very lucky to have someone of your caliber here. If you ever get to LA look me up."

"It has been great working with you too Isaac, but we can say our goodbyes at the airport. I'll make sure you are OK before you leave."

"Rhonda, I don't want to put you to any trouble. I'll be fine."

Billy spoke up. "Doc, it is not that Rhonda doesn't trust you. The Ambassador asked her to see you off along with me, Katzakis and Bell. Hell, the DCM and the Ambassador may be there, too."

"Sounds like a good party, I wouldn't want to miss it."

Billy's voice turned serious. "You won't. Shall we go through the front door this time?"

We exited the health unit and went out of the Embassy past the cafeteria and Post One. The ride to my house was uneventful. The main gate was open and an Ethiopian Police van was parked in the driveway. Police and my Ethiopian neighbors were in the yard looking at the damage. The guard shack had burned down and the generator was also damaged. The house looked intact and Billy helped me inside. He told me he would pick me up at 18:00 for the short trip to the airport and the flight home. After seeing him out, I went upstairs and took a shower to wash the gasoline out of my hair.

It didn't make sense to change clothes later for the plane, so I put on my new blue suit with a white shirt and red print tie. My instructor in diplomatic etiquette at the FSI said we should always travel in business attire since we were representing the United States. The saleswoman at Barney's told me the suit brought out the blue in my eyes, which may have been true. If Felicity came to see me off, which was unlikely, I wanted to look as good as possible.

The mirror showed me that I didn't have to worry about the suit. It was well cut and fit perfectly, but with the tired look in my eyes, the bandages on my hands and the persistent smell of gasoline coming from my hair, I wasn't anyone's idea of a good date. Felicity would take one look and after laughing or worse, feeling pity, would give me a handshake or a kiss on the cheek. Even though it would be humiliating, it would be worth it to see her again.

I headed down the stairs. A black Suburban was in the driveway. The DCM was behind the wheel. I went out the door and opened the passenger side of the armored truck.

"So what brings you down to see me? Has my departure been moved up?" He turned toward me and smiled. He was wearing a black windbreaker over a crisp white button down shirt with no tie and black jeans. I spoke again. "Even when you dress down you look good."

He laughed a little. "You look better than I have seen you in a few days yourself, Doctor. Red tie, white shirt and a blue suit? Have you finally decided to do things the State Department way?"

It was my turn to laugh. "I just thought I should look good for the trip home. Has the itinerary changed?"

"No you are still scheduled for the 9:00 PM Lufthansa flight but the Ambassador wanted me to bring you back to the Embassy for one final meeting. Would it be OK for you to come see him now?"

"You are being very diplomatic. Do I really have a choice?"

"We all have choices. Sometimes not very good ones, but we all have choices."

"We might as well go. Should I bring my bags or can I pick them up later?"

"Leave them here, we can get them later. Shall we go?"

He backed the Suburban up after I got in. Just as I was closing the door a loud roll of thunder came down from Entoto Mountain. The sky above me was bright and blue but as we got out into the street I could see a heavy black cloud over the higher elevations of Addis. "Looks like we may get wet at the Embassy."

"No problem, I can drop you off underneath the awning. I wouldn't want to ruin your good suit."

We were traveling down the gravel street in front of my house and made a left onto the paved road that ran through the large field closer to the airport. After the field, we drove through another residential section of Bole homes and took a right to pass the small shops and furniture store on our way to the Ring Road. We stopped just before the off ramp to let a man drive a herd of goats in front of us.

"Have you thought any more about who was responsible for the food poisoning?" I didn't hear him at first and he had to repeat the question. That must be what the Ambassador wanted to ask me as well.

"It has to be someone at the Embassy. They are the only people who had the access to my house and the compound."

"So the statement you made during the EAC was not true."

He had me there. I knew it was someone at the Embassy. I just didn't know who it was exactly. I locked the door to the Suburban

268

and started to think about who had the key to the lock on my house. The realization that the DCM had a key to my house because he had lived there for 6 weeks came to me. It was like making the diagnosis just as the patient dies in your arms. It was too little too late. "Why did you put the note in my house?"

"It was the third time. They say the third time's the charm. I think you're guessing now but you would've figured it out eventually."

I was still trying to figure out what he meant by the third time when he let go of the wheel to grab something with his left hand. It was a Glock pistol. There must have been another threat to the Embassy and he was armed to make sure we got there in one piece. He noticed me looking at the gun and then looked at me with derision. It was the first time I had really felt any emotion coming out of him.

"You don't understand, do you? For all of your intelligence and training, you mostly stumble onto your findings. I truly admire your ability to deal with the vagaries of life but you are mostly just lucky. You have no method or process. You are the anti-Sherlock Holmes but you're the only one who could have figured it out."

The mocking yet jovial tone of his voice was actually reassuring. He had a gun but at least he was in a good mood. "It was the third time I had tampered with the food for a barbecue. The other two times I just contaminated the meat. That was the best plan and should have worked fine, but Cruz always made sure the burgers were well done. Very few people got sick and Dr. Lessing or Rhonda wouldn't look into it. I needed to get that bastard back."

The unreal feeling I had at that point was the same one I had had in Orlando when I found my wife and her lover sharing one pair of pajamas. "You used to live in my house and so you had the key. You put the note there to make sure someone investigated this time. You didn't know Travis was going to die. You did this to discredit Frederick Stevenson because he slept with your wife."

We were traveling on the Ring road at about 45 miles per hour and there was a bright flash of lightning over Mt. Entoto. In the white light he was smiling like a teacher who finally has explained calculus to the dumbest kid in the class.

"After Cruz and I found the buns, it was a different game though. It was no longer shoddy rat control that caused the poisoning. The buns had been deliberately tampered with and all the rest, the shooting, the text, the firebomb, were all meant to mislead me and everyone else away from the truth." I was completely stunned. It was all so clear and he was right, I just stumbled onto the truth.

The DCM's voice shook as he replied. "I never meant for Travis to die. The whole point was to get that bastard demoted or recalled. He had no right to do what he did."

"You had no right to kill Travis." A blind fury was coming over me and any control I had was slipping away. My voice was unsteady. It had trailed off and sounded unsure, but I knew that retribution was coming to him no matter what he did to me. I thought of Felicity. "You killed the son of a CIA officer. Do you think Felicity, Bob Wollinsky and the National Clandestine Service are just going to forget about that?"

An involuntary shudder ran through him like he was cold. It had begun to rain but it was still warm in the Suburban. "You think Felicity is burning a candle for you? You idiot, she is just like every other woman. She used you and is now going back to Moscow to be with her husband. Bob is a nice guy. Too nice. He will be too torn up about his loss to seek revenge. No one will mourn you and no one will retaliate against me. The paper will take care of it."

The statement may have been true. She probably had used me but that didn't bother me as much as him saying it. Who was he to pass judgment on her? I needed to stay calm though because it was now clear that he was going to kill me.

"Pick the paper up."

For the first time he was pointing the Glock in his left hand at me. His tone was still derisive and mocking, but I obeyed, not knowing what else to do. The paper was on the dashboard. No letter or

270

statement could get him out of this, but I picked it up. I could see it was a short paragraph in English but it was now too dark in the truck to read.

"I can't read it. There isn't enough light."

"It's your suicide note."

Chapter 42

The fact that I was trapped in an armored Suburban with a man who would kill because he lost his wife almost made me laugh. I had been fleeing the loss of my wife for 10 years and had been too ashamed or too stupid to deal with it. He was eager to deal with it and to handle all of the consequences.

"I have to admit it's a good plan. It won't work, but it is a good plan. How did you get the AK-47?"

He sat back in the seat and lowered the pistol. "This is Africa. They are everywhere. I got it as a gift when I went to visit a Somali warlord near the border with Felicity. I was supposed to turn it in, but I kept it."

We had reached the British Embassy on the Ring Road. He must have been planning to take me to Entoto Natural Park, just north of the Embassy, and have me kill myself there. It all made sense now when it was too late. He started this all for revenge but it had spun out of control. I almost understood it. I understood the pain he felt and the desire for revenge, but I did not understand his need to hurt people who were not directly involved.

He continued. "When Travis died, I felt terrible. My plan was simple, direct and would punish Stevenson for sleeping with Marisol. It would have worked if you would have followed the rules. The shooting, the text and the firebomb were just spur-of-the-moment things and can't be traced to me. When you kill yourself, everyone will be relieved and the investigation will stop. There will be too many loose ends and no way to wrap it all up. It will be just like the anthrax attack in 2001. There will be no solution and everyone will blame the guy who isn't around. The guy who killed himself. I wouldn't be surprised if Dr. Lessing blames you for tampering with the buns in the freezer and goes back to her original theory about the beef. Stevenson may be blamed yet."

In LA we get strong Pacific storms that will dump large amounts of rain over a short period of time, but it had begun to rain like

I had never seen before. The Suburban was cloaked in rain that came down in layers like paint on a canvas. The simultaneous flash of lightning and roll of thunder meant we were in the center of the disturbance. The street had disappeared underneath the runoff, and people were under any awning, tree or building that could offer minimal protection. He slowed the Suburban since I was the only one going to commit suicide. The windows grew thicker with the water and everything outside was distorted like looking in a funhouse mirror. Donkeys had enormous bellies that expanded and contracted as we passed. Storefronts melted into the colors of their signs or awnings. The side mirror wavered like it was on a wave. Two small lights were spinning in the reflection.

Someone was following us. "Your whore is behind us, but don't worry, you'll be dead the next time she sees you. Admit it, I'm doing you a favor, you could never keep her. I tried to get her but she was too much even for me."

It wasn't a conscious action and I'll never know what my intent was. Anger, jealousy, revenge and desperation all came upon me at once. I grabbed the wheel. Pulling hard over to the right, he lost his grip and the Suburban heaved to the side of the road. We went through the guard rail and were airborne over the ravine. Three bolts of lightning followed immediately by thunder erupted inside the truck. The second one hit me in the leg.

Chapter 43

The problem with having a gunfight inside an armored Suburban is that there are multiple chances for the bullet to hit its target. That's good for the casual marksman but not so good for his intended target. If we had been in a regular Suburban, any bullet that missed the mark would simply sail out the window or be lodged in the bodywork. In an armored truck, the bullets got a second or third chance to hit the target. The second bullet hit the window to my right and then traveled down into my thigh. It did not hurt and, except for the concern about the small fountain of blood, I felt relieved that I had not been shot in the head. The Suburban had smashed through the guard rail on the bridge like the 6,000-pound uncontrolled force that it was. We were at the top of the arc over the river and the DCM had gripped the wheel with both hands and was standing on the brakes as we nosed over and started down.

It could only have been a few seconds since I grabbed the wheel, but I had a great sense of accomplishment. It was clear to me that I gone from the hunted to the hunter. We hit the roof of a corrugated metal shack and the riverbank before we hit the water. The truck was filled with a burning smell and powder. It was like being in a fire at a baby powder factory. My seat belts tightened around me and the truck turned over two or three times. When the motion had stopped, I opened my eyes again was suspended above the DCM. The air bags were deflated and I could feel the burns they had left on my face. The truck was lying on the driver's side.

He must not have taken the same driver safety training course at the State Department that I had taken because he had not been wearing his seat belt. He was unconscious and bleeding from the nose and ears. I hoped he was dead. I was disappointed when he took a deep breath and tried to move his right arm. The Glock was not around. There was a mark on my window where the bullet had hit and the driver's door was slightly ajar but otherwise the interior of the truck was intact.

A loud banging noise was coming from the roof of the truck and tailgate. At first I thought it must be some rescuers who had seen the wreck and were trying to get us out. When I looked out the windshield, I could not see a thing. A shaft of lightning, followed by thunder that drowned out all other noise, gave me enough light to realize that we were underwater. The continued pounding on the roof and body must be rocks or logs hitting the truck driven by runoff from the storm. I was not immediately alarmed since I knew that I could get out of the truck relatively easily even if we were submerged. The key would be to wait until the truck was almost full and the pressure inside and outside the truck equalized. The door would then open easily and I could get out.

The problem would be trying to get the DCM out of the truck. He could be badly injured and I wasn't sure I could lift him with a bad leg. I released the seat belt and braced with my left leg, my good leg, on the side of the center console. I had only burned my left leg; the bullet was in my right. Dark brown water was entering by the DCM and the banging and pounding on the outside was increasing. The river must have been rising from the storm and the detritus along the banks was flowing down on us like a liquid avalanche. Waiting for the water to fill up the truck sounds like a good idea when you're in a dry classroom, but not so much when you are in a submerged Suburban. I unlocked the door and pulled down on the handle while I pushed with my shoulder against the door. It did not move a millimeter.

The lecture about the armored vehicles came back to me. They always stressed the weight of the doors so that we would not let our foot or leg get caught in them. I realized that the same armor that kept me safe from bullets made the door weigh several hundred pounds and trapped me in a sunken truck. I had to laugh, it was such a potent symbol of my life since 9/11. The only way out was through the door so I braced myself as well as I could and pushed with all my strength. The door lifted about two or three millimeters, which I took as an encouraging sign. My breath was rapid and ragged both from fear and pain. My latest wound was beginning to hurt and I could feel the blood running down my leg. Getting out of the Suburban was my top priority and I could bandage the leg after that.

Pushing again, I felt a sharp pain in my right leg and right ankle. At first I thought my foot had slipped and my ankle was caught on the center console. A brilliant flash from the storm illuminated the truck for a moment and I could see the DCM looking up at me. His face was covered in blood and burns from the airbag, but he was awake and staring. There was a level of hate in his eyes that I didn't think could exist in a human being. Every primitive emotion he had was funneled into an intense expression of contempt and loathing, and he was using his last bit of strength to keep me in the truck. My body shuddered and I knew then I could not save him because.

The world consisted of only the two of us. More precisely my leg and his head. Something deep and primitive in me opened up as well. The kicking began before I realized it. I felt his nose break, then the bones around his orbit and then one of his eyes burst. I kept kicking him with my left foot and the grip he had on me grew tighter.

With increasing force I continued to bring my foot down onto his face with a gruesome and vengeful rhythm. Nothing else existed. Travis, Felicity, my wife, Billy and Cruz were distant and forgotten. The grip on my ankle began to weaken and I could feel water when I kicked down onto the bloody, broken mass that had been his face. There were several more flashes as the storm intensified. The rocks, logs and debris continued the symphony of chaos outside the truck. His face no longer was recognizable and even after he lost his grip I kept pounding away at it with my foot. I stopped when the water got to my knee and I couldn't generate enough force to do any more damage.

I took several deep breaths and tried to focus on moving the door. A bright light, less intense but more steady than lightning, was now pouring through the back window. The sun must have come out again as the storm passed. The truck was about three quarters filled with brown, foul-smelling water and some floating paper cups. One of the DCM's handkerchiefs was floating near the back seat. It was monogrammed with his initials and spots of blood. The rising water made bracing myself more difficult, but I hoped the pressure inside the truck was equalizing. It didn't really matter. The water was at my chest and I would soon be underwater if I couldn't move the door.

Lifting with the panic of a near drowning man, I pushed with my shoulders and legs against the door. The pain in my right leg was bad but the bone was not broken because I could generate force. The door moved a few inches and then was ripped upward as I was forced down back into the truck by more water. Taking only a second to recover, I pushed myself into the gap between the door and the truck. The river was flowing from the back of the truck toward the front and had lifted the door open. The surface of the water was only inches above me and I was able to get my head above and take a breath.

The door slowly came down on my back in a gentle and almost reassuring way. It was like the arm of a lover wrapping around you in the night to let you know you are not alone. As the door descended, it squeezed the air out of my lungs and pulled my head under the water. My legs were kicking inside the truck but had nothing to brace against. I tried to grab the door frame and pull myself loose but I couldn't move. The need for oxygen was getting intense and I drew in a breath. The brown river water filled my mouth and I began to choke. Someone was calling my name. The door was pressing down. More coughing and struggling for air. Pain in my leg and hands. Cold. Darkness except for a single dim light. Consciousness slipping. Water. No air. Darkness. Cold. Struggle. Water. Peace.

Chapter 44

FOR IMMEDIATE RELEASE

FROM: ETHIOPIAN NEWS SERVICE

TO: ALL PRESS OUTLETS

SUBJECT: AUTO ACCIDENT CLAIMS THE LIVES OF TWO AMERICAN DIPLOMATS

Two American diplomats were killed last night during a heavy rainstorm. The truck they were driving went off the road and into a local river. Police at the scene say that the truck was traveling at excessive speed when it left the road and that the two diplomats were killed instantly. The barrier over the bridge has been repaired and traffic has resumed. Combined with the recent food poisoning, related to undercooked meat, brought in from the USA, it has been a difficult week at the American Embassy. The National Police and the Foreign Ministry expressed deep regret for the accidents to Ambassador William Winston.

ALL ETHIOPIANS ARE ENCOURAGED TO SUPPORT THE GRAND ETHIOPIAN RENAISSANCE DAM.

END OF PRESS RELEASE

UNITED STATES DEPARTMENT OF STATE

CLASSIFIED: CONFIDENTIAL
CABLE: AA 2011-156-A
FROM: ADDIS ABABA
TO: WASHINGTON
CABLE PRIORITY: URGENT

SUMMARY: DEATH OF ADDIS ABABA DCM RICHARD C. LAWRENCE

BEGIN MESSAGE: DCM Lawrence was killed in a motor vehicle accident today. Also injured and not expected to live was Isaac Porter M.D. RMO Addis Ababa. The Suburban they were driving (VIN 3546YT728D) left the road during a storm and landed in a river. The DCM suffered extensive injuries during the crash and appears to have not been wearing his seat belt. He will be sorely missed by everyone at the Embassy and was an outstanding Foreign Service officer.

Porter was extricated from the vehicle but appears to have suffered brain damage due to near drowning. Porter has been the source of extreme difficulty since he arrived in Addis Ababa and was in the process of being recalled when the accident occurred. (Reference Cables AA-2011-135 through AA-2011-143)

Dr. Madeline Lessing, from CDC, has been instrumental in leading the current investigation. She believes that undercooked meat was the reason for the food poisoning and that the buns were cross-contaminated. She is confident that subsequent incidents were not related at all. FBI Agent David Solomon does not completely agree but has no explanation for the subsequent events other than opportunistic terrorist or related groups taking advantage of the situation. CIA Deputy Chief of Station Felicity Gonsalves has not been consulted on this cable but her judgment has been called into question because of her personal involvement with Porter. The body of DCM Lawrence is being prepared for shipment to his home leave point.

AMBASSADOR WINSTON

END MESSAGE:

CENTRAL INTELLIGENCE AGENCY

CLASSIFIED: TOP SECRET

CABLE NUMBER: ADDIS 3441

REF CABLES: ADDIS 3401, 3402, 3410

TO: DIRECTOR CIA, DIRECTOR NATIONAL CLANDESTINE SERVICE, DIRECTOR AFRICA DIVISION, ALL AFRICA STATIONS.

FROM: ADDIS ABABA

CABLE PRIORITY: IMMEDIATE

SUBJECT: FURTHER INSIGHT INTO DEATH OF DEPENDENT SON OF C/O ROBERT WOLLINSKY. NO TERRORIST LINK FOUND.

1.   IT HAS COME TO THE ATTENTION OF ADDIS STATION THAT THE DEATH OF THE DEPENDENT SON OF ROBERT WOLLINSKY, TRAVIS WOLLINSKY, WAS A DELIBERATE ACT BY THE DCM OF ADDIS ABABA RICHARD LAWRENCE. ALTHOUGH A CLEAR MOTIVE MAY NEVER BE FULLY UNDERSTOOD, THIS STATION BELIEVES THAT THE DCM TAMPERED WITH BUNS USED IN THE BARBECUE THAT RESULTED IN THE ILLNESS AND DEATH OF TRAVIS. IT APPEARS THE DCM WAS TRYING TO EMBARRASS OR IMPLICATE THE MANAGEMENT OFFICER FREDERICK STEVENSON, WHO MAY HAVE INSULTED THE DCM IN SOME WAY. THE DCM WAS RESPONSIBLE FOR THE NOTE, ATTEMPTED SHOOTING, TEXT AND FIREBOMBS THAT AFFECTED THE EMBASSY AND STATE RMO ISAAC PORTER. BOTH THE DCM AND RMO WERE INVOLVED IN AN MVA WHICH RESULTED IN THE DEATH OF THE DCM AND THE INJURY OF THE RMO. THE RMO SUFFERED A GSW AND NEAR DROWNING BUT IS EXPECTED TO FULLY RECOVER. IT IS CLEAR TO THIS STATION THAT IN A STRUGGLE AFTER

THE ACCIDENT RMO PORTER WAS FORCED TO KILL THE DCM.

2.   RMO PORTER HAS BEEN INSTRUMENTAL IN UNDERSTANDING THE FOOD POISONING AND LEADING THE INVESTIGATION. WITHOUT HIS DILIGENCE, PROFESSIONALISM AND COMPETENCE THE TRUTH BEHIND THE RECENT EVENTS WOULD NEVER HAVE BEEN UNCOVERED. HOWEVER DUE TO CONSIDERATIONS RELATED TO LOCAL TERRORIST ACTIVITY THIS STATION FEELS THAT THE OFFICIAL EXPLANATION FOR THE EVENTS SHOULD FOCUS ON UNDERCOOKED MEAT AND ACCIDENTAL CONTAMINATION. IT SHOULD NOT BE PUBLICLY ACKNOWLEDGED THAT THE DCM HAD ANY ROLE IN THESE EVENTS. ALTHOUGH THE FINAL DECISION RESTS WITH D/CIA AND SECSTATE THIS STATION STRONGLY ADVISES AGAINST IMPLICATING AMERICAN OFFICIALS IN THIS EVENT. IMPLICATING AMERICAN OFFICIALS WOULD WORSEN INTELLIGENCE GATHERING IN THIS AREA FOR YEARS TO COME. THE DEATH OF THE DCM SHOULD BE DESCRIBED AS RESULT OF THE ACCIDENT AND NO MENTION OF RMO PORTER'S ROLE SHOULD BE ACKNOWLEDGED. ALTHOUGH IT WOULD HAVE BEEN BETTER FOR THE DCM TO RESPOND TO HIS CRIMES IN COURT, SEVERAL OFFICERS HERE, SHARE WITH CIA-HQ THE SIMPLICITY AND JUSTICE OF RMO PORTER'S INTERVENTION. THIS STATION ALSO ADVISES THAT ALL EXTRA CIA PERSONNEL, INCLUDING SPECIAL ACTIVITIES DIVISION OFFICERS, HERE OR EN ROUTE SHOULD BE RECALLED SINCE THIS EPISODE IS NOW CLOSED. ALL SATELITES AND DRONES CAN RETURN TO NORMAL TASKING. REGARDS.

GONSALVES DCOS ADDIS

Chapter 45

Shivering, cold, coughing, light, voices, chest pressure. Hands on my hands, on my chest. The waters from the source of the Nile pouring forth from me. Pain in my leg, head, chest and stomach. Vomiting and more vomiting. Someone is holding my head. My eyes are closed or at least I cannot see out of them. It is cold. Voices are discussing me and the Suburban. Someone says I am dead. No, they say, he is dead and I just assumed it was me. They must be talking about the DCM. Several people were hanging around, some are Ethiopian and some are Americans. My eyes begin to work and I am on the ground. I am soaking wet. Billy is standing about 10 feet from me and talking to Felicity. Both of them are wet and I can see Cruz a few feet from them. He is wet but unlike Billy and Felicity he is staring at me. The look he has is one of shock and bemusement. Rhonda has been holding my head and after one last episode of throwing up the river I decide it is time to say something. "How did I get out of the truck?"

"I'm glad you are awake. You have been out for about 30 minutes and it sounds like you almost drowned. I am not sure how you got out of the truck. When I got here you were laying here with Cruz, Billy and Felicity doing CPR. How do you feel?"

"I feel terrible but not as bad as I look."

"It would be hard to feel as bad as you look."

I glanced down and could see that my shirt had been torn off and my suit jacket was nowhere to be seen. Luckily my tie was still loosely around my neck. My left shoe was missing and my belt had been tied around my right leg as a tourniquet. The blue pant leg had a jagged hole in it that revealed a nice round hole in my upper, outer thigh. The smell coming from my clothes was a mixture of sewage and vomit.

Billy knelt beside me before he spoke. "How are you feeling, Doc?" His voice was tired but concerned.

"I feel OK. How did I get out of the truck?"

"We were following you and the DCM. We were coming down to your place to help you get ready and just happened to see you drive by. Felicity decided to see where you were going. After you went over the edge, we stopped. Cruz went in first, without a safety line, but was knocked over by the current. I went in after him with a safety line so he wouldn't drown. By the time I got him to shore, Felicity had pulled you out of the truck and got you to dry land. You weren't breathing but she got you going again in no time. You started babbling after that and we just watched you until Rhonda arrived."

"The DCM poisoned the buns, shot at me and sent the note and the text."

Billy touched my shoulder and nodded. Felicity had knelt beside me as well and gave me a warm smile. She spoke with a combination of concern and anger. "You told us the whole story in about 30 seconds. It was amazing how lucid and angry you were. I think you thought you were dying and wanted to get the story out before you expired."

"I don't remember any of that. How did you get me out of the truck?"

"It wasn't easy but I had good leverage. How did you get shot?"

"The DCM was going to shoot me and leave a suicide note. I grabbed the wheel and he shot me while we were in the air over the river."

Cruz was standing at my feet, shaking his head. Rhonda and Billy looked worried. Felicity spoke. "We can get the rest of the details later. Rhonda says you have to go to the hospital. Billy and Cruz will go along. I have to get back and send out some cables. Zack, I won't ever forget what you did for Travis."

She bent down, kissed me on the cheek and left. Billy and Cruz carried me over to another Suburban and put me in the back.

Rhonda sat next to me, gave me some morphine and started an IV. I passed out in about three minutes.

I must have slept for some time. It was a deep and dreamless sleep and when I woke up I realized that I was back at the hospital and that Dr. Kim was working on my leg. It was either that or St. Peter was Korean. There wasn't as much pain as when he worked on my burns. I was naked except for a towel covering up my groin. There were fresh bandages on my arm, hands and left leg for the burns and on my right leg for the gunshot wound.

Just after Dr. Kim left, the curtain pulled back and Anita, the Ambassador's wife came in to stand next to my gurney. "Dr. Porter, I wanted to come personally and let you know that the Ambassador and the entire Embassy community are deeply saddened by your accident. I have been assured that you will make a full recovery." She looked great. Her hair was tied up and she was dressed in a gray business suit that fit very well. The pearls around her neck shined perfectly under the ER light. They probably hadn't looked that good since they had been out of the jewelry shop. It was hard to hate her because she was so good at feigning concern. It felt like she really cared about me.

"Thank you, Anita. Is the Ambassador coming to see me?"

"He wanted me to let you know that he is very concerned about you, but that he will not be able to come right now. He is in consultation with the Secretary who will be briefing the President soon."

"Does he know the DCM was behind the whole thing?"

She learned toward me and touched my shoulder. He hand was warm and soft and it reminded me of my mother's touch when I was younger and ill. It was comforting and reassuring, a tactile sign that everything was going to be OK. "Dr. Porter, if there is anything that I or the Ambassador can do for you, let me know. I have to go back to the Embassy now."

I couldn't understand what she meant or why she left. Obviously she did not know the DCM was behind it or she would have said something. How could she be so ill informed? Billy was standing above my head and I had not seen him before. He must have heard the entire conversation.

"Billy, when is she going to be told what happened and that the DCM was behind the whole thing?"

"She already knows, Doc. State and CIA think that it would be best if the whole story doesn't come out. The Wollinskys have been told and they have agreed to a cover story. The ground beef will be blamed and the shooting, text and note will be attributed to terrorists trying to take advantage of the situation. Everyone thinks that revealing the DCM was behind the attack will only encourage the terrorists. Besides, he's not here to defend himself. You took care of that. There isn't a lot of evidence anyway." He sounded half-hearted but I had to admit it made sense. The DCM was dead. Very little of what I had found out, besides the hole in my leg, would stand up in court. It was the cleanest and most tidy ending.

"How many people will know the truth?"

"Besides me and you? Not very many. Felicity, the Wollinskys and the CIA. The Ambassador and the higher ups at State. Solomon and the FBI will not be told too much but I think they know already."

It didn't really seem fair to me, but it wasn't my decision. I could go to the *LA Times* but what would be the point? The DCM would still be dead and that was more justice than he would have gotten if he had lived. The Wollinskys would be traumatized again and Felicity would still be leaving to reunite with her ex-husband.

"I guess it makes sense Billy, but I don't like it."

"I don't like it either, Doc."

A chant of USA! USA! USA! arose in the ER. It was a chant for an Olympic basketball game not for an ER in Ethiopia, and it confused me. Cruz and two other Marines in battle fatigues and body armor were chanting but several of the patients, their families and staff had joined in. I just looked at Billy and he spoke. "It has been a big night for the good guys, Doc. You eliminated the DCM and the SEALS eliminated Bin Laden. The President just confirmed the raid."

I was not expecting it, but I guess no one was expecting it. The head of the terrorists behind 9/11 was dead.

Chapter 46

I got dressed with some clothes Billy had brought. Jeans, shirt, socks and running shoes. We drove back to my house and there were several Ethiopian police around there. He helped me inside and upstairs. The plane was leaving around noon which gave me about three hours to get ready. I had missed the previous evening's flight while I was in the hospital.

Billy said goodbye and I told him to leave the door open. The bullet had gone through my leg but left two nice round holes. Dr. Kim had assured me that the femur (thigh bone) was intact and that there was no major arterial or nerve damage. He had placed my leg in a knee immobilizer that did just what the name implied. It was a long nylon and plastic tube that went from my upper thigh to above my ankle. It made walking very difficult so I took it off. It took about 15 minutes for me to get undressed and make the 20 feet from the bedroom to the bathroom. The shower felt wonderful and I didn't get out until the electric water heater, on the wall next to the shower, ran out of hot water. It took another 30 minutes to bandage my burns and my bullet wounds. The bullet wounds were just oozing blood and the burns looked pretty bad but not infected.

I threw the few clothes I had unpacked back into my suitcases and wrote out the check to Billy for the money Kokeb needed. Going back downstairs was a struggle but I made it without falling or bleeding too much. I had my briefcase with my laptop with me and dropped it only once. The morning was bright and cool so I decided to wait outside. Unlocking the door and security gate brought two young Ethiopian police to meet me. They saluted and snapped to attention. I wasn't sure why or if I should salute too, so I just smiled. They helped me over to the fountain and I sat down. They then retreated a respectful distance and watched me like they expected me to burst into flames. An orange-billed bird flew by my head and then started pecking at its image in the glass of the front room window. There was still a smell of gasoline and burnt wood in the air.

A horn honk broke the silence of the morning and one of the policemen opened the gate. Billy drove a Suburban into the driveway. Rhonda was in the front seat. They both got out.

"Hello, Isaac, how are you feeling?" Rhonda looked very tired but relieved as well.

"Pretty good, Rhonda. It's a beautiful morning. I'm ready to get out of here."

Billy took off his sunglasses and spoke. "I'll go get your bags. The rest of the wheels-up committee will meet us at the airport."

In the State Department, when a difficult dignitary leaves the country the Embassy personnel have a "wheels-up" party to celebrate. It is a going-away party where the guest of honor makes the party a success by not showing up. The party they would have after I left would be epic.

Rhonda helped me and we walked over to the truck. The step into the truck took all of my strength, Rhonda and the two policemen lifting to get me in place. Billy brought down the bags and loaded them in the rear. He got in and backed the Suburban out and we made the short trip to the airport. As we passed the traffic circle near the Ring Road, I saw the large pothole had been repaired and the pavement was smooth but darker than the surrounding asphalt. It looked like a scar. The large rock road barriers were gone. I was anticipating a long walk from the parking lot but when we got to the airport Billy drove up to the gate blocking the road up to the terminal. He simply waved and the gate opened. After we were parked at the curb I spoke. "Getting true VIP service today?"

"General Mulugeta called and said there wouldn't be any problems getting you on the plane and he didn't want you to have to walk too far."

We got out of the truck and Colonel Assefa met us. He took my passport and my luggage and told us to proceed through security. He said Billy and Rhonda could come along. We entered the large departure hall. The roof was supported by white steel tubular columns and had a large glass front that allowed in the morning sunlight. It was really very modern and comfortable.

The security people did not want to let Rhonda and Billy through until Billy mentioned Colonel Assefa. The name had a magical effect and we sailed on without any problem. Colonel Assefa met us in front of Immigration control and escorted us up the escalator to the diplomatic lounge. The Lounge was on the second floor and was not big but was well appointed with comfortable leather chairs and tables. A large Ethiopian flag stood against the back wall. The Colonel turned to me after I sat down. "Dr. Porter, General Mulugeta wanted me to wish you a pleasant voyage to the United States and also hopes you have a speedy recovery from your injuries."

"Thank you, Colonel. Tell the General I appreciate the help he has given me. Do you know how Eskander is doing?"

"He is recovering with the help of his family."

I wondered if I should ask about Kokeb, but decided it was not a good idea. He excused himself and left. Rhonda and Billy wanted to help themselves to the small buffet that was provided and I gave Billy the check for Kokeb.

The lounge had Wi-Fi so I decided to send my brother an email. It didn't take long but I didn't write much. I only said that I would be back in the States soon and didn't go into why. The explanation would have to be in a face-to-face conversation. It was late evening in LA, but he replied back quickly with several questions. Without answering the questions I told him I was all right and would be back in LA soon. I scanned the rest of my inbox, deleted a few items and shut the computer off. I was distracted by the hope that Felicity would come to say goodbye. There was a small breeze of perfume from my left and I turned to see Anita there. She was in a black pants suit with her hair still up and the same pearls. Constance Powers was with her. Anita spoke. "Good morning, Dr. Porter, Constance and I came down to see you off and to let you know that we all appreciate your service here." Anita was smiling and exuding natural warmth that was making me blush like I was too close to the fireplace. It felt almost sexual. Constance smiled, but her eyes were definitely hostile like she had forced to come along.

"Thank you, Anita, I think everything has been taken care of. Will the Ambassador be coming down?"

"He is busy at the moment, dealing with the unfortunate and untimely death of Dick Lawrence." It was Constance who had spoken, and I got the distinct impression that she wished the DCM was still here and I was the one being loaded into the cargo hold in a body bag. Her eyes which had been angry now blossomed into hatred. She must not have been told.

I didn't know what to say, but Anita sensed the void and filled it. "It has been a terrible week for everyone, but the Ambassador and I think that Dr. Porter has done an excellent job. The Ambassador wanted me to stress to you that he expects you to have a long and distinguished career with The State Department and he looks forward to working with you in the future." Anita was smooth, like a well-polished diamond. She would be about as hard to break too. Constance looked like she had developed indigestion and excused herself. Anita shook my hand and followed her. I was feeling tired and closed my eyes for a minute.

"Dr. Porter." I awoke with a start and looked up to see Travis as an adult standing in front of me. My face drained of blood and I felt light headed. "I am sorry I startled you, Doctor. I don't know if you remember me, but my name is Bob Wollinsky, I was...I am Travis's father."

I stood up quickly and the urge to faint was strong but I didn't pass out. Felicity might have come with him and I didn't want to faint in front of her again. "Of course, I remember you. I am so sorry for your loss. Travis was a special child and I wish I could have done more."

His face grew pale and strained. The death of his child had left a permanent scar on him and it showed in his face. "Can we sit down, Doctor? I just got back last night and I am worn out."

290

We sat down and I realized that he was the first person I had seen in days who looked worse than I did.

"Felicity has told me about everything that you did for Travis after we left and I just wanted you to know that my wife and I deeply appreciate all of your efforts." He paused to wipe the tears from his eyes.

"I was just doing my job." I felt uncomfortable and wanted to change the subject.

"How is your wife doing?"

"She is doing OK. She decided to stay in the States since she would have flown back next week anyway. We are going to decide what to do after the baby is born."

"I know this has been a terrible thing for you to go through, and if there is anything I can do for you in the future, let me know."

He nodded his head again and wiped away more tears. "Felicity said you were a good guy. I also wanted to say that if you ever need any help from me, just ask. The things you did have been noticed by me and my wife but also by my organization." He reached into his pocket and took out two business cards. One was a State Department card that had his name, position and cell phone. The other card was blank except for a phone number. "You can always call my cell phone. It is on almost all of the time. If you ever need me and you can't get me on my cell, just call this number and ask to speak with me. They will find me."

"Thanks, Bob, I will stay in touch and call you if I ever need you."

The attendant in the lounge came over and said my flight was ready to board. Bob got up and shook my hand and left. He was very upset and could not speak. I looked around for Felicity but I could only see Rhonda and the attendant. No one else was in the lounge. Stalling for a few more moments, I packed up my computer and sat back down like I was tired.

Billy reentered the lounge and came over to my side. "She isn't going to be coming, Doc."

"Who isn't coming, Billy?"

"Felicity said she was too busy getting everything wrapped up. I told her you would want to see her but she had made up her mind and I couldn't change it." I guess I should have expected it, but it was still a great disappointment. The love we had was simply doomed from the start and I would probably never see her again. In some ways worse than losing my wife but it didn't feel as bad. At least Felicity had loved me once. Billy was holding a small package wrapped in brown paper. "I forgot this in the truck. She was very insistent that I give it to you before you left."

He gave me the package and I debated for a second about opening it in front of him. What if she had sent me a note about her undying love and a plan to meet up later? Coming back to reality I opened the package and looked at the two books it contained. There was no note or writing from her on the books. There was a guide book to Moscow and an English translation of *Onegin* by Pushkin.

"Doc, she gave you a guidebook to Moscow. I'll bet she wants you to visit when you get better. What is *Onegin*, Doc?"

"It is a novel in verse about lost love. It's a classic of Russian literature."

Billy shook his head and smiled. "So kind of a mixed message? She must be more confused about you than I thought. We better go to the plane, Doc."

Rhonda and Billy helped me out of the lounge and down to the boarding ramp. The airport was crowded but everyone was friendly and got out of our way. I must have really looked bad. Before the final security check we stopped. I spoke. "Rhonda, thank you for all of your help. It'll be quiet around here from now on. You'll get bored."

"Isaac, you're one of the worst patients I have ever had, but I will miss you. Take care of yourself."

With that she hugged me tight and it hurt my burned arm but I didn't flinch.

Billy reached out to shake my hand. "It seems like you have been here six months, not a week. I'm really sorry to see you go but I'm sure we'll cross paths again."

His handshake was firm and after he let go, he put his arm around Rhonda and they waited for me to go through the checkpoint before they left. The walk down the jetway took me a while and the flight attendant helped me find my seat. She looked familiar, but I wasn't sure if she had flown out with me. I stowed my computer bag and settled in for the flight to Frankfurt. I would connect there with a flight to D.C. and on to LA in a day or two.

I lost my wife on 9/11 when she left me for another man. I will never get her back. The pain of the loss is gone now, or really it has healed over, replaced by fresher wounds. Closure is such a loaded word. The thing I had waited 10 years for had come that day. It was an email from her. She probably had heard about all the trouble at the Embassy or maybe she wanted to say she made a mistake or maybe she wanted to tell me someone in our medical school class had died or gotten the Nobel Prize. It will remain a mystery. I deleted it unopened in the lounge.